Day of Reckoning

Day of Reckoning

Book 2 of
The Dawn of Rebellion Series

Michelle Lynn

Gram, this one is for you.

The Drylands

St Louis

Cincinnati

Wastelands

Rebel base

REPUBLIC OF TEXAS

Vicksburg

FLORIDALAND

MEXICO

Baton Rouge

Chapter 1

Gabby

So, this is Texas. Vicksburg to be exact. The capitol.

Dawn's hand rests in my, lifeless. I squeeze her fingers, trying to pretend that nothing has changed. She's here with me. A sigh pushes past my lips. In truth, nothing is the same as it was before. They tell me that she'll wake up when she's ready, but what about when I'm ready?

"Dawn," I whisper. "I need you." I want her back.

My stomach twists as I think about what waking up will mean for her. When she comes around, I'm going to have to be the one to tell her that Drew is gone.

Gone. Dead. Never coming back. A tear rolls down my cheek.

They found Drew in the woods with Dawn but there was nothing they could do for him. Sam was there too, a bullet lodged in his skull. Happy, smiling Sam. Dead like so many others. I blink away the tears and rip my hands from Dawn's.

They were going to pay.

I have to get out of this hospital room, with its beeping monitors and suffocating stillness. Walking by the mirror over the sink near the door, I pause, barely recognizing myself anymore. I'm nothing but a grotty wreck. My beautiful hair is no longer sleek and smooth. It's been frayed and damaged by months on the run. I have a scar above my right eye that's still red and painful to touch. My clothes hang off my now thing frame like sacks, clothes I'd never have worn back home; lightweight blue pants and a white shirt; the same as about half the people here. I hate it because I was made to stand out, not to disappear in the crowd. I take the stairs two at a time and slam my hands into the door desperately to open it. It swings open and I gasp in the fresh air.

The Republic of Texas stretches before me. It's a strange place. Everything is so... orderly. The streets are pristine and the buildings, every one of them, are made of red brick to match the wall that encircles the city. I've been told that this is only one of three walled cities that make up the Republic. I don't know whether to feel safe or trapped. I'm going to go with trapped. Then again, I'm not sure I'd know what freedom feels like anymore.

People stare as I walk by. In London, I basked in the attention when I caught someone's eye, but now it's different. Their gazes didn't infuse me with confidence as they once would have. It's no longer my blond hair or long legs catching their eye. It's their suspicions and curiosities. I'm not a freaking side show.

It's close to noon and the streets are full of people. None of them talk to me. Of course.

A bell rings from somewhere on my right and, all at once, the crowd on the street starts moving in the same direction and I'm pulled along. We wind through the streets until we reach a large building, the only one not made of brick. Instead, it's white, with a domed roof and large windows. The group funnels through the front doors and we're in a long room lined with benches. There's a table in the front and a man in a black robe standing behind it.

The entire town must be here. No seat is empty and many people stand at the back. I'm one of them; opting to stand close to the door so that I can easily leg it if I need to. Why are we here?

The man at the front raises his arms and the room falls silent. A chill races up my spine. "My brothers and sisters," he begins, "welcome to the house of the Lord. God invites his chosen people into his prophet's presence."

So, this is church, right out in the open. I've heard about under-ground churches in London, but mostly only the ones that got raided. I've been taught my entire life to fear church; that it's forbidden for a reason. I don't know if I believe that anymore. I'm about to sneak out when a woman appears up front. She too wears a robe but it's white this time.

"Faithful followers," she says, "as mayor of this city and prophet to the people, I must inform you of the heathens that breached our borders. As God willed it, we took care of the enemy soldiers. Just remember, that those who choose the righteous path that we follow will not go without while those who stray will find this world a harsh place." I look around and some people are nodding their heads along with this woman's words while others mumble, "Amen."

Uncomfortable, I move to leave. I barely take a couple steps before two men block my way. They stand with their arms folded across their chests and their feet shoulder width apart.

"The service is not over yet," one of them says, his voice stern. I can feel the eyes of curious worshipers burning into my back.

"You're not going to let me leave?" my voice goes up an octave on the last word. They don't respond. I try to go around them, but they force me back. The woman at the front hasn't stopped her speech and shows no indication that she sees what's going on. Anger rushes through me, but there's no use unleashing it when it would only cause problems for me and Dawn. I take a step back and turn to face the front once again.

When the service ends, the men from before are nowhere in sight so I book it out of there as quickly as humanly possible. I run the entire distance back to the hospital.

What the hell is going on here? I'm not sure I want to stay long enough to find out. If Dawn were better, we'd already be gone, but she's not and I have no choice but to stay put. For now.

Back at Dawn's side, I sit by her bed and only look up when a nurse comes in. She's one of the only people who will tell me anything. She smiles at me as she checks the monitors for my sister's vitals.

"I was here an hour ago and didn't see you," she says as she changes the IV bags around.

"I went for a walk," I respond.

"How nice. Did you attend the service? I'm always sad when I have to miss it, but working at the hospital, you can't just leave."

"Yes," I say coldly. I don't want to talk about it and she doesn't press me further.

"How do you like the city?" she asks.

"I haven't decided yet," I answer, though that's not entirely true.

She must hear the doubt in my voice because she says, "they'll warm up to you. People here have been through a lot." I want to say that I doubt they've been through as much as me. I want to say that none of their sisters are lying in a coma. I want to say so much more, but I don't. The nurse is only trying to help. Instead, I just nod and watch her leave the room.

"Dawn," I whisper. "I love you and I'm so sorry. Don't leave me here alone."

Chapter 2

Miranda

I look up just as the London skies are about to split open and pelt us with a cold rain. "Shite!" It's fittingly gray for a day like this. A day that England will never forget. A day that I will never forget.

This morning I wake just like any other day in London. I live in one of the army barracks and by the time I force myself out of bed and across the cold floor, the lav is jammed with people. I push my way towards the showers and ignore the irritated glances directed my way. I'm not in the mood today and I don't have time to wait in line. None of these women know what the day has in store for me. I shower and let the freezing cold water run the last bits of soap from my hair before wrapping a towel around myself and stepping out. If only the last forty years of my life could be so easily washed away.

I've been part of the rebellion since I was young. I was born into this role, in part, because my father is one of the movement's leaders. I haven't always wanted to play this part, but I've never been able to escape it. I thought I had for a few years, but I was wrong, dead wrong. Wanting to get out and live my life cost me dearly. I was fated to be a soldier and there's no escaping destiny.

Once again, I bull my way through the crowd and hurry to my bunk. I put my uniform on and look in the mirror as I button up my collar, hating what I see. I'm a soldier in the British army. Sworn to keep the peace on London's streets, but I've been betraying this uniform since it was given to me.

I tie my hair into a tight bun and cover it with my cap. There was a time when all I was, all I had to be, was the young and beautiful mother and wife. Now I see an aging widow who abandoned her children. I slip down the back staircase and out onto the street. When I'm sure no one is following me, I head for my father's pub and step in the back door.

I latch the door and find my father waiting for me in the kitchen. He doesn't look up from where he's sweeping the floor. I watch him in fascination. He looks so ordinary performing this simple task. To his customers, he is ordinary; just another barman who was unlucky enough to be assigned to the service industry. It's the perfect cover for a rebel leader. When no one expects much of him, no one will be suspicious of him.

"Were you followed?" he finally asks as he sets aside his broom.

"No," I respond quickly.

"You're sure?"

"I'm not a rook."

My father nods, distracted. He has a lot on his mind today. Today is the biggest day in the history of our movement.

"I have patrol soon, so why am I here?" I ask. "I already know what I have to do."

"There's been a change," he begins. "The drop will take place a block further north. You must make it there in time to obtain your package.

"Okay." I turn towards the door. "I have to go."

"You don't want to eat anything? I've got a morning nosh on the cooker."

I sigh. He'd like me to think he cares about my well-being, and he might, just not as much as he cares about his cause. I'm more like him than I would care to admit.

"No." I couldn't eat if I tried.

"At least take coffee and a biscuit in case anyone asks where you've been."

"Fine," I concede as he hands me a mug and wrapped food. I keep running over the plan in my mind as I step back out into the pouring rain. I look back at the pub one more time before I leave. From the outside, it looks like any other pub. The difference is that there are automatic weapons underneath the bar and a hidden door in the kitchen. Nothing in this world of rebels and cruelty is as it seems.

Twenty minutes later I'm out with my patrol. The morning moves along slowly. I joke around with my fellow soldiers. We harass a few homeless and roust a few young toughs. I check my watch again. It's almost time. When I spot my contact, my breath lodges in my throat.

A young boy in worn clothing with a grotty face is sitting on the street corner with a rucksack at his feet. His name is Caleb. I don't know anything else about him. Only that it's another child risking his life for the rebels. I force myself to avert my eyes and show no interest as my unit passes him.

My unit breaks for lunch and I tell them I'll be back by the time our break is over, even though I doubt I'll see any of them again. When I'm out of their sight I double back to where I saw Caleb. He's still there. Thank God. I release a long breath and walk slowly towards him.

He sees me and gets to his feet before turning and walking in the opposite direction, leaving the pack on the ground. I pick it up without stopping and swing it onto my back. I glance around nervously, but nobody seems to have noticed. My destination is only blocks away so I make it there in no time. I have to remind myself to breathe; in and out. My heart pounds in my chest and sweat dots across my brow as I step onto the escalator that will take me down into the largest tube station in London.

The platform is teeming with people going about their busy Saturday. The children, their parents, their grandparents, I see them at every turn. I want to scream as the tube comes and goes as I stand in the middle of the station, unable to move.

I remind myself that I'm not alone. Rebels have spread across London to follow the same orders I've been given. The best of the best, they'll call us. I've been told we'll be heroes to the cause. Our names will not be forgotten. I grip the strap of the back until my knuckles turn white.

I'm afraid. Fear is a weakness, my father would say. Right up there with empathy or guilt. Useless, destructive emotions. My name is Miranda and I choose not to be afraid. Freedom comes at a cost. We all must do what is necessary. My muscles loosen as I take back control from my emotions, turning them off.

Feeling nothing is better than being weak.

I move one foot forward and then the next until I'm in front of the wall of lockers. I open locker 132 and stuff the pack inside. I jump when I hear three short beeps. It must be time. I only have two minutes now to get away. I run to the nearest escalator.

Coming down the escalator are people who have no idea what's about to happen. Men in business suits. Teenagers chatting away. A woman looking bored. And a child; a little girl with long blonde hair, a yellow dress, and a sunflower hat. I see my girls in her angelic face and sweet smile. I look away.

Our escalators pass each other and as soon as I reach the top, I start to run. Suddenly, the ground shakes beneath my feet and I'm thrown to my knees. Explosions sound in my ears, followed by a loud ringing, and the world moves in slow-motion. People begin to move, groaning as they do. They pick themselves up in a state of stunned disbelief. Cries ring out through the air as a wall of smoke wafts over us.

I choke on the thick air as people in uniform start sprinting past me towards the station. One of them stops to see if I'm okay. When I convince him that I'm fine, he goes to help someone else.

My eyes scanning the destruction in my wake, I tell myself I had to do it. Today is the day when everything changes. Today is the day we become known.

So why am I crying?

Chapter 3

Drew

I'm drowning.

I choke out the water as it's poured down my throat, but it continues to come. Laughter sounds in the background as my body jerks and I flail my arms in an attempt to breathe or break free. I strain against the shackles. I try to scream. I only inhale more water.

Finally, it stops. The water is gone and I'm left gasping for air. I try to catch my breath. Where am I? I look around frantically. Where are Dawn and Gabby?

Two men are standing behind me and a third enters the room. At first, I can only see his dark figure talking to the others. Then he's right in front of me. He bends down and looks at me. He is so close now that I can see the speckles of green in his eyes. I can smell his breath.

I don't know what he's looking for as he stares into my face; maybe a hint of fear? I mean, that's what these kinds of gits live for right? After a few moments, he backs away and straightens up.

"Leave us," he says to the other men. He closes the door behind them, loosens the straps holding me to the board, and motions for me to sit up.

"Drew Crawford," he says. I startle and he continues, "Yes, I know who you are. I also know who your father is."

"Who the hell are you? Where am I?" I sputter.

"Now, Mr. Crawford, no need for nastiness. I only want to talk." I would almost believe him if I wasn't being held hostage and tortured. "We have a simple task for you. If you perform it to our satisfaction, I see no reason why we would need to continue this spectacle." He gestures to the board.

"Who the hell are you?" I repeat, this time through gritted teeth.

"You're in the Republic of Texas. My name is Dr. Cole, but my friends call me Darren. We're going to be friends aren't we Drew? I can call you Drew, can't I?" He smiles at me and all I want to do is slam my fist down his throat. Instead, all I can do is glare. "Well, let's begin, shall we? I have some questions about your father."

"I don't know anything about my father," I say.

"Oh, I believe you. I know how you feel about him, trust me on that."

"You know nothing."

"Well, that isn't true at all Drew." He opens a file that I'd failed to notice before now. "Drew Crawford, fugitive from the English. You hitched a ride on an airplane and landed north of Floridaland. You were not alone. Dawn Nolan accompanied you. She just happens to be General Nolan's youngest daughter. Your mission was to free Dawn's sister from Floridaland. Surprisingly enough, you succeeded with the help of a few Americans. Sam has since died and Lee is MIA as is Jeremy who you also freed."

I'm too stunned to say anything more than "how?"

"Don't be too surprised. We know everything that takes place in the colonies. What we need to know, is if your father is supplying the rebel forces with firearms."

I hold back the laugh that tries to break free. This guy is a nutter. My father, allied with the rebels? He would rather die. I'm sure of it.

"I told you, I don't know anything," I say.

"Let me explain something. We know exactly where the rebel base is. We know who the officers are and we know that there is a high ranking British soldier on her way to join with them." His voice grows louder with every word until he is screaming. "Do not lie to me!"

I suddenly understand what is going on. This man is scared. If the British were to ally themselves with the rebels, the Texans would be facing forces from multiple sides.

"You're right to be scared," I say, my voice low. "They will gut you."

He lunges at me and wraps his large hands around my throat. I gasp for air and try to wriggle free. As if suddenly realizing that he lost his cool, Dr. Cole releases me and backs away, his face still red. He leaves quickly, only to return a minute later with a handheld screen. He forces me to look at it and then turns it on.

It takes me a few moments to realize what I'm seeing. It's a hospital room. Dawn! I suck in a breath. She looks like she's just taking a kip. My heart begins to pound, a panic building in my chest. "Is she-"

"Dead? Not yet. We don't want to kill General Nolan's daughter unless we have to." I quickly realize what he means. They can use her as leverage. "She was injured when we brought her in, but she should be awake by now. We've induced a coma for your benefit."

"My benefit?" I swallow hard.

"Yes. You see, I don't believe that punishment always works. I think you need a reward to strive for if you're going to behave. Although, I'd be happy using both. If you give us what we want, your little girlfriend can wake up." He gives me another toothy grin as if he is doing me some favor by not killing Dawn.

"What do you want me from me?"

"We need to send a message to General Nolan."

"General Nolan doesn't even know me," I protest.

"The name Crawford should be sufficient."

I stare at the screen a little while longer. "Gabby," I say as she enters the room.

"Yes, her sister if I'm not mistaken."

"Fine," I spit, "I'll do it, but you have to promise me you won't hurt Dawn."

"As long as you're cooperating, I have no need to hurt her. As a show of good faith, I'll even wake her up. She won't be allowed to leave the city." He taps a finger against the screen and turns to the door. "I will return, Drew. See, I told you we'd be friends."

As soon as he's out the door, the two men from before come back and deliver a beating. "English scum." They laugh as they're leaving, one of them punches me in the gut and laughs as they shut the door and the darkness surrounds me once again.

"Dawn," I murmur through the pain.

Chapter 4

Gabby

I startle awake when the doctor places a hand on my shoulder. Sleep fades quickly as I look up from my spot next to Dawn's bed into the kind green eyes of the tall man towering over me. His sandy-blonde hair is unkempt in a cute kind of way. He's much younger than most of the stuffy doctors I've seen in London, but it's his gentleness with Dawn that puts me at ease. No other person in Texas has treated us as they would their own people.

"Good morning Dr. Cole," I say.

"I've told you a million times, Gabby, call me Darren." When he smiles, I can't help but smile back.

"How's my sister doing today?"

"Her vitals look good. It shouldn't be long now." He pulls out a large needle.

"What's that?" I ask.

"Something to help," he explains before injecting it.

I guess he is the doctor. There was a time when I would have flirted mercilessly with the hot doctor and he would have responded, but these days I don't feel like myself or at least, I don't feel like the person I used to be. The only thing I can focus on is my sister. The doctor leaves and I scoot closer to the bed. He said I might have my sister back soon.

The minutes pass by and maybe I'm imagining it, but I swear I see her hand move. I look at her monitors. Her breathing is steady and nothing seems to have changed.

I glance at her face and see it again. Her fingers move in my grasp. Finally, her eyelids flutter open and a sob escapes my throat. "Dawn." A grin spreads across my face and Dawn tries one of her own, but smiling is too much for her right now.

"Hi," she croaks.

I jump to my feet and poke my head out the door. "She's awake!"

Stunned, the nurse runs into the room and checks Dawn's monitors. She gets on the phone to call the doctor. Dawn's eyes focus on her.

"Sis, this is your nurse," I say. "She's been taking care of you." Dawn nods and looks around. A few moments later, she opens her mouth.

"Where am I?" she asks softly.

"I'll explain everything as soon as we get you checked out," I say. "Dr. Cole should be here soon." As if on cue, Darren walks in.

"Hello there, Dawn." He brushes her hair to the side. "I'm Dr. Darren Cole. I'm so glad to finally meet you. We've been waiting for you for quite some time." He smiles at her, but she doesn't return it. She looks to me and asks the question that will break her heart.

"Drew?"

I look to Dr. Cole and he gives Dawn a sad look. I squeeze her hand.

"He didn't make it," I whisper.

At first, she looks confused but then understanding registers in her eyes. She starts shaking her head and says "no" in the stubborn way she has. Her hand grips mine tightly as a sob constricts her chest. I can't say anything to make it better. This pain is hers. For once, I can't take it away.

Dr. Cole steps into the hall to give us some space as tears spill from Dawn's eyes.

"What am I going to do, Gabs?" She squeezes her eyes shut.

Cracks spider through my heart and before long, my face is damp with tears. So much pain. So much loss.

This place, these colonies, will just keep hammering us down until we have nothing left to lose. It's like quicksand, pulling us down into the darkness.

What happens when we can no longer see any light?

Chapter 5

Dawn

Has it been days or only hours? I lose track of time as I drift in and out of consciousness. I don't want to be awake. Every time I open my eyes, the pain is new, fresh. I know I should ask Gabby where the others are, but I'm afraid of the answer. I don't know how much I can handle right now. *Drew. I just found you. What am I supposed to do now?*

I'm alive and Drew is gone. I've lost him. The first person who ever made me feel like I was worth something, the first person who ever made me feel beautiful, is dead. Never coming back.

Fresh tears well in my eyes, but I wipe them away.

I've been told that we're in a place called the Republic of Texas. The existence of Texas was kept out of our lessons in London. It's in the Southern part of the colonies; Gabby knows that much. This city, Vicksburg, is apparently the capitol. They say we're safe because the city is walled. Walled from what?

I only remember bits and pieces from the night we were brought here. It usually comes back to me in my dreams. Fire and smoke. Sam. One of the best friends I've ever had. Gunned down right in front of me. In slow motion, I see the bullet. Sam's body hitting the ground. My screaming. Running. It's the same every night.

Gabby is sitting across the room when my eyes snap open, my fists clenched. "Sam! Drew!" It's okay. Gabby is here. She sits on my bed and dabs my forehead with a cool cloth. Once I've calmed down, I truly look at my sister for the first time since I came out of the coma. Something is weighing on her. There's something she isn't telling me.

"Okay," I say. "Tell me."

"Tell you what?" She looks away.

"I'm not daft, sis. I know there is something you're not saying. Is it about that night?"

"I was waiting until you were stronger."

"You were stalling," I state. "Gabs, I need to know where everyone is."

"Let's talk about this when you're feeling better."

"No." My tone makes her visibly start. "It's not fair to me. I need to know."

The silence stretches between us before she begins. "I was with Jeremy and Lee. We were running and being shot at. I got separated from the two of them before I ended up outside the forest with the Texan soldiers. I don't know what happened to them. The Texans only found two bodies in the woods. Drew's and -"

"Sam's."

"You knew?" she asks, sounding a bit relieved.

"I saw it happen," I say bluntly.

"Oh," is all she can manage.

"I hope Lee and Jeremy are okay."

"Yeah, me too." I see the pain dance across her face before she covers it up. I reach out my arms, beckoning her forward. She sits on my bed and hugs me. "I'm so glad you're okay, sis," she whispers.

"You're not getting rid of me that easily."

Chapter 6

Gabby

I'm so happy to have my sister back; to be able to talk to her. She's a part of me and these past months in Floridaland without her have been hell.

Loneliness threatened to overwhelm me in the weeks since arriving in Texas. I've barely talked to anyone. They keep their distance.

Someone knocks on the door and I turn, intending to tell them to be quiet because Dawn is sleeping. I forget about that when Adrian pokes his head around the corner. Adrian was one of the Texan rankers who found me outside of the woods. He brought me back here and then sat with me in the hospital all night as I thought my sister was going to die. He just talked to me and held my hand. I haven't seen him since then.

I rush to the door and throw my arms around his neck.

"Hey," he says, surprised. I release him and step back.

"Hey, yourself. It's been a while." I've asked around about him. All anyone would tell me was that he was probably on assignment some-where.

"Yeah, I was sent to the Mexican front to deliver orders," he says.

"The Mexican front?" I ask.

"The Mexican border. We've been fighting the Mexican warlords since before I was born. I used to be at the front, but my aunt had me brought home and now I just deliver the dispatches."

"Your aunt?"

"My aunt is the prophet which means she's also the mayor and in charge of the city's defenses." I picture the woman speaking at the service that I was forced to see. That crazy woman is Adrian's aunt? "Can I come in and sit? I just got back and I'm exhausted." It's only then that I realize we're still standing in the doorway. I turn and walk farther into the room and gesture for him to have a seat. Dawn stirs and opens her eyes.

"Hey sleepyhead," I say. "This is Adrian." She smiles weakly at him, sleep still clouding her mind.

"I'm glad you're okay Dawn. I was with you when they brought you in," he says.

"Thanks," she mumbles. I look at Adrian as he smiles and take in his crooked nose and the scar near his hairline. He sure looks like someone who's been fighting.

"So," I say, taking a seat on Dawn's bed, "tell me more about this place. I know that you all go to church every day to see the prophet, your aunt. I know that everyone has a job to do. Tell me something I don't know."

He thinks for a moment before saying, "well, the water never stays on for more than a couple minutes every hour."

"Yeah, I found that out the hard way. The first time I took a shower, I had soap in my hair the rest of the day. I felt terribly grotty."

He laughs and it sounds much more carefree than you'd expect from someone with tattoos and battle scars.

"My aunt rules this place with an iron fist. Everything has rules and everyone follows them. If they don't, they have to leave the society and nobody wants that."

This doesn't surprise me. I already know that everything we do is controlled. I've had to wear what they tell me to and eat what they give me since I got here.

"Gab?" Dawn says.

"Yeah?" I respond.

"Can I get some water?"

Before I can get it for her, Adrian says, "how about we get it on the way. It's time to go." He walks into the hall and comes back pushing a wheelchair.

"Where are we going?" I ask.

"The prophet wants to meet you. Up you go." He easily lifts Dawn out of bed and helps her into the wheelchair. I follow them out of the room and down the hall. We wind our way through the hospital until we reach the exit. I hold open the door for Adrian to push Dawn through and it swings shut behind us.

The government headquarters is only two buildings down from the hospital, but we take our time. Dawn is smiling and looks happy to be outside for the first time in weeks. I realize the only part of Texas that she's seen is the inside of that hospital room. We enter through the front door of the government building and the lobby looks surprisingly lush for a society that rations everything. We walk across beautiful wooden floors to the marble front desk. I'm surprised to see a large basket of fruit. This is the first time since getting here that I've seen food outside of the mess or the hospital.

The lady behind the desk is wearing the exact same clothing as me. Blue pants, white shirt - so much for fashion. Her dark hair is tightly braided and her pale skin suggests too much time indoors.

"Hello Adrian," she says, not bothering to look at Dawn and me. "She's ready for you."

Pushing Dawn ahead of him, Adrian leads me down another series of hallways and through security before we stop in front of a set of double doors. He knocks and then enters. A small, dark haired woman is sitting behind a desk that looks like it could just swallow her up. I would laugh if the hard look in her eyes didn't scare the shite out of me. This is a very different woman than the one I saw leading the church service.

"Adrian," she says as she walks around her desk to hug him. "It's so good to have you home." She smiles, but it doesn't reach her eyes. "How was the assignment?"

"I got it done," he says.

"I'm sure you did." Her eyes scan the room until finally landing on Dawn and me as if she's noticing us for the first time. "Hello. I'm Tia Cole. Please, sit."

"Cole?" I ask.

"Yes. Dr. Cole is my husband. I hope he has taken great care of you." The sound of her voice suggests that she doesn't really care about that at all. I'm shocked, to say the least, Darren must be younger than her.

"He has," Dawn pipes in. "I want to thank you for...well...for saving me."

My sister is such a kiss arse. I already don't like this lady.

"It was our pleasure, Dawn." Once again, her smile doesn't go past her lips. "I wanted to make sure you have everything you need."

"We can take care of ourselves," I say. Dawn pinches my leg like she always does when she thinks I'm being rude.

"We're fine, thank you," she says.

"Okay then. Dawn, I think it's time we get you out of the hospital. We've provided Gabby with a room in one of the dormitory buildings. You can stay there. Adrian, help her get settled. Show them around. God has brought you here and as his prophet, I will make sure you're taken care of." She sits back at her desk, dismissing us.

That meeting was strange. I felt like I was being evaluated, read. Once outside again, Dawn decides she doesn't want the wheelchair anymore. She wants to walk. Adrian and I help her to her feet. It's slow going, but she does it. We're all feeling a bit peckish so we head off in the direction of the mess and as we slowly walk with Dawn, I can't help but wonder,

How do two girls like us rate so much attention?

Chapter 7

Dawn

I don't know why Gabby has to be so rude to people; so distrusting. She can be a right prat sometimes. These people saved my life. They got us away from the British soldiers and took us in. The mayor seemed nice; businesslike, but nice. I don't understand what a prophet is, but I'm sure it's nothing bad. My sister just needs to chill.

My legs move frustratingly slow as I walk down the street, regretting my decision to get out of the wheelchair. I grab hold of Gabby's shoulder as a wave of dizziness washes over me.

As soon as we enter the mess, we pass by a throng of people standing in line to get their food. Rank has its privileges. "Sir," they snap to attention as Adrian passes them.

The room is huge and lined with long tables. On one end is the food, buffet style. There must be hundreds of people in here, chatting loudly as they enjoy their meal. Knackered, I slip into my chair and let my sister push me to the front of the line and we slide our trays along the buffet table. The food is similar to what it's been every other day. Bland. The protein is some kind of soy and boiled potatoes and carrots sit beside it on our plates. The ladies serving the food weigh each portion so that we get exactly the amount allotted to us. Everything is rationed.

We sit at an empty table and I turn to Adrian. "Does everyone eat here?"

"Yeah. This is the only mess in this part of the city," he says before digging in. I begin to eat as well. It may be relatively tasteless, but I can't be picky.

"How do you feed the entire city?" I ask when I can no longer contain my curiosity. In England, the wealthy always have food because they can afford the inflated prices, but my plate has never been this full. Why would the Texans give so much valuable food to someone they barely know?

"We control large sections of the rivers," he explains between mouthfuls. "They provide us with the water and fertile land that our farms need. Only certain crops can thrive here anymore. This is pretty standard fare." He looks at his plate distastefully before shrugging and piling food into his mouth once again.

Once we finish, Adrian drops us off at our room and leaves, promising to return in the morning.

I walk to the bed where a pile of clothes sits waiting for me - exactly the same as Gabby's.

Gabby shuts the door loudly and sighs. "I hate it here."

"You hate it everywhere." I turn to her, expecting to see indignation. Resignation clouds her eyes instead.

"But this place is just creepy."

"Creepy is better than a hotbox in Floridaland."

Her body shakes as she walks to the bed and sits on the corner. "At least there I knew I was a prisoner. Here they try to wrap a prison in a cloak of freedom."

I flop next to her on the beds. "You're just paranoid."

"And you're too trusting."

I turned onto my side and closed my eyes. "Good thing we have each other then to balance us out."

She chuckled softly and I didn't catch her last words before drifting off.

Chapter 8

Dawn

Adrian returns in the morning just as he said he would. We're up and have taken our two-minute showers by the time he knocks. I'm starting to feel like myself again. My head isn't so foggy and I've got my legs back, mostly.

"Morning Adrian," I hear Gabby say as she opens the door.

"Hey, guys. Ready to go?" he asks.

"Where are we going?" I ask.

"On a walking tour of the town. You okay to walk, Dawn? If you get tired, we can call for a wheelchair."

"Sure," I say as the three of us head out. I'm kind of excited to see more of this place. Everything is so orderly and clean. It's way different than anything I've ever seen before. Most of the buildings look the same, but a few stand out. The church is beautiful. After my experience with Ma and the group at the caves, I'm mystified by religion. I have so many questions about it, but I don't dare ask them in front of Gabby. She thinks it's better not to know.

As we're walking by, a bell begins to ring and people start to descend on the church.

"Come on," Adrian says. "I can't have people see me walking around out here during church. We're not allowed to skip it and there would be consequences." We duck into a building nearby and they help me climb the stairs. "This is the library."

"Really?" I say. "There are libraries in England but only certain people have access to them. The only books I've ever been able to read are the ones my teachers would give me." We walk through room after room filled with shelves and the books that sit upon them. I glance over at Gabby and she looks bored. I don't know how she could be. I try to think back to London and realize that I don't remember ever seeing her read a book.

I run my hands along dusty spines and feel the grooves of the lettering. Adrian looks back at me and laughs.

"You should see your face right now," he says. "Priceless."

"There are just so many." I don't know why but I feel like I need to whisper. It's so still and quiet in here and I don't want to ruin that. I had less than two years before I would have gone to uni if that was my assignment. In uni, I would have had access to many more books.

Gabby sits at a table in the middle of the room and leans back in a chair, not paying attention to us at all. Adrian plucks a book from a shelf and brings it to me.

"This is my favorite," he says. "I love history." I don't tell him that the only history lessons I've ever liked are the ones about the colonies. I take the book from him. *The Republic of Texas: a history.* I open it and begin to read. I stop after the first paragraph.

"Texas was part of the United States?"

"They didn't teach you that in England?" he asks.

"I don't know anything about this place at all," I admit. Gabby has perked up slightly and is now watching us. She wants to learn as much about these people as possible. Adrian and I sit near her at the table.

"What do you want to know?" Adrian asks.

"Everything," I say. "Start at the beginning."

"Do you know about global warming?"

"Yeah." It's Gabby who responds quickly. She doesn't like to be taught things or told things. It's why she had so many problems in school. As always, I try to smooth over her rudeness.

"What I don't get," I begin, "is that if it's called global warming, why is England so cold."

"I didn't know it was. I've never met anyone that's actually been there. I guess it makes sense though." He pauses.

I lean forward in my chair. "Why does it make sense?" I ask. Adrian gets up to grab another book before sitting down again and flipping through the pages. He stops at a flattened picture of the earth.

"You see here," he says, pointing at an arrow making its way from the United States around to England, "there was once a warm stream of water called the Gulf Stream. It wound its way through the ocean until it got to England where it used to warm the air."

"And that's gone?" I'm confused.

"The ice caps melted and screwed up the ocean currents, including the one that used to warm England."

"Brilliant," I whisper, flipping through the book.

"What's a master race?" Gabby has opened another book and she squints her eyes in concentration.

"You don't need to know about that." Adrian quickly takes the book and puts it on a high shelf.

Gabby just shrugs before saying, "Tell us about the war and such."

"Well, once the currents changed, so did the weather. There were massive storms all along the east coast, but hardly any rain anywhere else. A drought came and never really went away. Wildfires ravaged the west and water became scarce over much of the land because the oceans rose and contaminated the ground water in coastal areas. People were starving, but they were alive. The government was doing research on how to grow food under those conditions and it was working." He stops.

"And then the bomb," I say.

"Yes, but there's more to it than that. The Republic of Texas had already broken away, but the U.S. government was trying to start a war that would bring us back. A prophet had emerged in Texas though and he saved us. The U.S. government had grown corrupt and fascist. It was a Texan that took care of them once and for all. No one foresaw the ripple effects that it would cause. It was a symbol of our strength all those years ago. Our first prophet said that it was God's will that we live on and they fade away." I detect a strange note of pride in his voice.

"But it caused the deaths of so many people," I argue.

"Yes," he pauses, "it touched off a civil war which, of course, we won. It saved the Republic."

"Or what was left of it," Gabby says.

Chapter 9

Gabby

My sister is so gullible.

All of this global warming history is revisionist bullshite. They did something that laid waste to an entire country. A country they once were a part of and they call it patriotic.

If anything, our little library tour a couple days ago made my suspicions about this place and these people worse. They're like sheep. They wear the same clothing. They eat the same foods as each other. They go to church at the same time every single day and think it was noble to kill 100 million people. Even if God does exist, I doubt these so-called prophets actually talk to him.

Back at our room, Adrian is hurrying us along. "Shit, we're running late."

"Why? What are we doing?" I ask.

"We're going to a party." He grins and his white teeth glow in the darkness.

"A party? Here?" I look to Dawn and her face has dropped at the term party. Ever the introvert.

"I'll be back in a few to pick you up," Adrian says and closes the door.

Thirty minutes later we're walking down the dark streets, making a right turn and then a left. Adrian stops us in front of an apartment building. "We're here," he says before pushing through the door. We walk down the hallway until we reach a door. A boy is leaning on the door frame trying to look tough. He can't be much older than ten.

"Password?" he asks, showing his teeth to seem menacing. I stop myself from laughing so I don't embarrass the kid.

"Don't be an idiot," Adrian says and I almost tell him not to be such a git, but the boy steps out of our way and lets us pass.

"What was that about?" I demand.

"This party is not exactly legal," he admits.

"What?" Dawn has found her voice again, but it still cracks with nerves. "Maybe we shouldn't be here."

"No, it's fine." Adrian leads us through the door and down the stairs into the basement of the building. It's cold and only lit by candles, but there are a surprising number of people here. I see Dawn shrink into herself at the sight of so many strangers. She suddenly looks like she did in London, not like the girl who came across the world to rescue me. I link my arm through hers and pull her forward through the crowd.

"Adrian!" someone booms in front of us. The voice turns out to be larger than its owner. A short, round man comes rushing towards us.

"Landon. Hey, man," They clasp hands and then Landon looks at Dawn and me curiously.

"Welcome to my party," he says. "Are you the Brits?"

"The Brits?" I ask. "That's all they're calling us?"

"I'm sorry," he responds, but before he can continue, I stop him.

"I'm joking. I'm Gabby and this is my sister, Dawn."

"Well, Adrian, Gabby, Dawn let me get you guys some drinks." We follow him to a high counter. He goes behind it and returns with three glasses. I take a sip and almost spit it out immediately. Adrian and Landon are cracking up, but one glare from me shuts them up.

"What is this?" I ask as Dawn smells hers.

"Remember I told you this party wasn't exactly legal? Landon here distills his own hooch." Adrian drains his cup and goes for another. I see Dawn take a sip of hers and I grab it from her hands.

"Hey," she shrieks.

"I don't think you need any hooch, little sister."

"Well, maybe I don't think you should be making decisions for me." She snatches it back and takes a long drink as she walks away from me. Adrian shrugs and Landon laughs.

I spend most of the party keeping an eye on my toss pot sister. This is not what I had in mind for fun. In England, people go blind from homemade alcohol. I watch as Dawn dances and talks to people she's never met before. Two things she'd never do if she were sober. At least someone's having a good time.

As the music changes, the little boy who was guarding the stairs comes rushing into the room. "Raid!" he yells at the top of his lungs. Everyone starts running up the stairs frantically, but Adrian comes to me.

"Come on. There is no way we'll make it out of here in time. Where's Dawn?"

"Dawn!" I yell across the room as soon as I spot her. She doesn't answer. She's sitting on a couch looking dazed. I run to her and grab her arm to pull her up.

"No," she slurs, "I want to sleep." She lays her head on the couch as I keep pulling her. I manage to get her off the couch, but she slumps to the floor. I give Adrian a pleading look and he helps me get her standing with one arm across each of our backs. We manage to get through the door to another room and lock it behind us. We set Dawn on the ground and I sit next to her. She leans her head on my shoulder and closes her eyes.

Landon and a few others are already huddled in the room, trying to be as silent as possible. Adrian listens at the door for sounds of the police.

The room is rather small and half of it is taken up by machines. Each one has a screen on the front with a number showing.

"What are those?" I ask, pointing.

Landon is the one to answer. "Each roof in Texas has solar panels on it. We get our energy from the sun. Those machines keep track of it all."

"Cool," I say before whispering, "Why do they send so many police to bust a single party?"

"There is a strict law against gatherings, other than church of course," Landon explains. "The prophet thinks that disease is spread when too many people are in the same place."

"But you say that church is excluded? Couldn't people get sick there?"

"Most people believe that could never happen in God's presence or even in his prophet's presence." Landon's tone tells me he isn't one of those people, but I don't get a chance to ask him.

"Shhh, everyone quiet," Adrian commands. We hear the sound of many footsteps and someone barking orders. This continues for a while before we hear someone speak.

"There's no one here, sir," a voice says.

"Yes, but there was. Check the energy room." My breathing speeds up. If they check the energy room they'll find us. The doorknob turns and someone pulls. It doesn't open.

"It's locked, sir. I don't know how they could have gotten in."

"Check it anyway."

"Yes, sir." We hear scratching and then pounding as they try to bust the lock.

"It's only a matter of time before they get that door open and then we're toast," Landon whispers.

Adrian sighs as he gets to his feet. "I'll take care of it." He unlocks the door and slips out. Everyone stays silent so we can hear what's going on.

"Is there a problem, officer?" Adrian's voice is stern and commanding.

"Sir," the officer sputters, "we didn't know you were here."

"Obviously," Adrian chastises. "What exactly do you think you're doing?"

"Sir, there were reports of an illegal gathering," the officer explains quickly.

"Do you see such a party?"

"No, sir, but…"

"Do you expect me to be at such a party?"

"No, sir."

"Good," Adrian pauses, "then I will not mention this… mistake and neither will you. You may leave now." We hear footsteps on the stairwell before Adrian opens the door. He doesn't look happy as he beckons us out.

I look around at the mess and laugh. Those soldiers had to ignore everything they saw here because Adrian told them to.

Out on the street, I breathe a sigh of relief. Now I just need to get Dawn home and in bed and we can forget all about this night. Dawn is stumbling as she walks so I hold onto her arm to guide her. Adrian bids us good night and leaves us to find our own way back. After a few turns, we're standing in front of our dormitory. I lead Dawn inside and she collapses into bed.

"Gabby?" she says in a slur.

"Yeah, Dawn?" I answer, annoyed, trying to get the shoes off my drunken sister.

"Drew is dead."

"I'm so sorry." I don't know what else to say.

"He's gone and he isn't coming back." She hiccups a sob and shudders.

"I know, sis, I know," I whisper.

"I just didn't want to feel. I wanted to forget, just for a night. I didn't want to be sad anymore." I don't say anything to her as I lean over to stroke her hair and wipe tears from her eyes. "It didn't work, Gabby," she stammers as she speaks. "I miss him so much and I got him killed."

"Of course you didn't," I whisper and my heart breaks for her.

"I…I wasn't fast enough. If I had run faster; if I hadn't tried to get to Sam after he'd been shot, maybe Drew might be alive."

"Don't say that. You didn't kill him. The British soldiers did." I want her to hate them more than she hates herself but I know it won't work. If it did, then maybe I'd be able to forgive myself from getting separated from Jeremy.

Or for getting arrested and taken to the colonies.

Because it isn't Dawn's fault that Drew is dead. It's mine. One day she'll see that and I just hope I don't lose her too.

Chapter 10

Miranda

The "day of reckoning" as they're now calling it, was a brilliant day for the rebels, just not so good for me. I've been stuck in the east end for weeks. The rest of the rebels are out there fighting for our cause and I'm not allowed to leave headquarters. I'm a forty-year-old woman and my father can still tell me what to do. Maybe I need to stop thinking of him as my father since he hasn't really been like one since I was little. He is my rebel commander and he has commanded me to stay put.

Apparently, the cameras in the tube station caught me putting the pack into the locker and the bomb experts have determined that's where the explosion started. I can't ever go back to my military post or walk the streets of London again. To the outside world, I'm a terrorist.

I guess I was luckier than some of the other bombers that day. Two of them died with their targets. The man sent to one of the government buildings was caught by the guards while he was trying to leave. He was still being detained when the building went up in flames. One of the smaller targets was a city bus. There was a soldier on board who caught sight of the bomb and shot the rebel trying to set it off. The bus exploded while he was dying of his wounds.

"Do not mourn our fallen comrades," my father said. "Their deaths were heroic." We're supposed to use their deaths to fuel the fire within ourselves. That's what I would have done if I were allowed to fight.

They'd have had to kill me to make me stop coming at them. But no, I'm stuck here, tending to the wounded.

The military has responded in force and indiscriminately; rebels, civilians, children. No one is safe now, but it has only made our numbers swell. The rebellion is rising across all of England. Last week we gained control of one of the airports. Now we have an entire fleet of planes. Communication with our colonial counterparts has just become easier.

I only recently gained the clearance needed to learn about our colonial base. I was amazed to hear how many people have been sent there. They've allied with some of the Americans. I don't yet know all the details about what they're doing over there, but I know it's big. It could change everything.

Many of my rebel comrades have asked me how it felt to detonate the bomb. I answer by telling them everything that happened that day, step by step. I'm a celebrity now; hunted by one group and revered by another. The rebel leaders tell me to be proud of what I did. "It was a good thing," they say. In truth, it was just another day on the job. No big deal. My conscience is telling me that is wrong, not to feel, but I don't care. It was for my cause. I will do whatever needs to be done and keep my emotions out of it. That's the only way to keep the realization of what I did from grinding me into dust.

My father walks in from the street, his cheeks flush from the cold and his gray hair dotted with snow. He doesn't often come here for fear of being seen. His eyes scan the room as they do every time he enters a place. He's always alert, always on the lookout for something that has gone awry. His eyes land on me. He doesn't smile like a father should when he sees his daughter. He is calculating and weary.

He marches over to where I'm sewing up a gash on a young girl's head and inclines his head to me. That is his way of greeting. No hug. No handshake. No contact at all.

"What do you want?" I ask, not bothering to look up from my final stitch. I should probably be nicer to my commander, but being stuck here makes me feel like a school girl, mad at her father for grounding her.

"Miranda," he begins, "we've made plans for you to leave England."

"What?" I sputter, completely taken by surprise.

"Now that we have one of the airports, we can put you on a plane."

"But I'm not done here. I want to be a part of the rebellion." I only realize I've raised my voice when he grabs me by the elbow and pulls me into an empty room. Now I really feel like a school girl.

"You will still be a part of the rebellion. Trust me." His tone makes me want to do the opposite. "You're going to the colonies." Now he has my attention. "You will be one of the higher-ranking officers there. You will report to a man named Jonathan Clarke tomorrow evening. The plans have been made. An officer will meet you at the landing strip upon your arrival."

"I'll pack my things." I turn to go, then stop. "I guess this is goodbye then." I stand ready to embrace him.

"Goodbye, Miranda." He brushes past me and leaves me standing in the empty room...alone.

Chapter 11

Dawn

"Good morning, party people!" Adrian's voice wakes me from my stupor as Gabby lets him through the door. I open my eyes and the light almost blinds me. My head aches and my stomach is doing flip flops. As soon as I stand up, I start running to the bathroom. I barely make it before all the contents of my stomach come spilling out. I groan and Gabby hands me a towel as she and Adrian stand there laughing. I don't see what's so funny. I use the sink to pull myself to my feet and try to go back to bed.

"Oh no you don't," Gabby says as she pulls me away from the bed and towards the shower. "We have a busy day ahead of us. Go get cleaned up, you're kind of gross this morning." I want to know what our busy day entails, but I'm afraid that if I open my mouth to speak I'll hurl again. I take a very quick shower and get dressed while Gabby and Adrian wait for me.

We leave our building and Adrian tells us that we're going on a job tour. "It's something that every Texan does in school before they're old enough to start working. Jobs here are inherited, but everyone needs to know how the society runs."

"Society…" he says it with such reverence.

"So, if my father cleaned toilets in some dodgy place then I would end up doing that as well?" Gabby asks.

"Essentially, yes," Adrian responds. "The only exception is the military. Every Texan spends two years in the military before they start their given career. But, they can choose to stay in the military if they'd like."

"Even if they end up at the Mexican front?" I ask. I think I'd rather be a janitor than go to war.

"These are dangerous times, Dawn," Adrian says. "Most soldiers help in our fight against the Mexican lords. That's a worthy fight. There are some soldiers, though, who police the town or scout out in the colonies."

"What about you, though? Shouldn't you be out on a patrol or fighting on the Mexican border?" I ask.

"No," he responds sharply. "I have a different assignment." Before I can ask him what it is, he turns away and walks faster.

I don't know what prompted the sudden change in tone, but I let it drop. Gabby doesn't say anything either. She's usually the prying one. I look sideways at her and she's lost in though. Her nose is crinkled like she just smelled something rancid and her lips are puckered.

We've reached the wall and, up close, it's intimidating. It looms over us. There's a lift to take the guards to the top. I can't imagine having to build such a structure, but Adrian tells us that it was built a long time ago so now all they need to do is the maintenance.

"Hey, Adrian." I look around to see who's yelling and a tall, older man is running towards us in full uniform. Adrian shakes his hand and then the man turns to us.

"Clint, this is Gabby and Dawn." Clint's eyes get bigger and he raises his eyebrow in surprise but then catches himself.

"Hello ladies," he says, looking us over a little too long.

Adrian claps Clint on the back and says, "Clint's the commander of the wall. He's a buddy of my uncle's."

"So, what's with this wall of yours?" Gabby asks. "Are you trying to keep people out or do you want to keep them in?" I elbow her in the ribs but that doesn't stop her. She stares expectantly at Clint, waiting for an answer. I don't know what's gotten into her. I'm relieved when Clint starts laughing.

"My oh my, young lady, you have quite the imagination. Well, I need to get back. It was a pleasure to meet you." He tips his hat to us and then walks away, whistling as he goes. Adrian starts talking to a few of the other people standing near the wall so I turn on Gabby.

"What was that?" I whisper urgently.

"What?" she snaps.

"That question. These people have been nothing but nice to us since we got here and you're being an arse." I massage my temples as I feel my headache coming back.

"And why do you think they're being nice?" she asks. "Out of the goodness of their hearts?"

"I don't know." I pause. "Where is this coming from?"

"It's just...nothing. Forget I said anything." She turns away from me and I'm about to ask her more when Adrian walks towards us with an older dark-haired woman in tow. His mood seems even more dour as he introduces her to us.

"Guys, this is my mom," he says. "Mom, this is Gabby and Dawn."

"Oh please, call me Elle." She smiles at us and I instantly feel warm inside. It's a mother's smile. She has crow's feet by her eyes and her skin looks like it's been in the sun way too long, but still, she's beautiful.

"Elle, pretty name," Gabby says. I'm amazed that this woman can lift even Gabby's sour mood.

"Thank you, dear," Elle responds. "Are you enjoying Texas?"

"Yes," I respond, trying to be as polite as possible. "Do you guard the wall?"

"Oh dear no, that sounds awful." A few of the guards nearby glance in our direction and smile. I'm not sure if they heard that slight. Elle continues, "I work in the government building. I'm just doing evaluations of various jobs."

"Oh." I feel pretty daft right about now. Of course, a woman like her wouldn't choose to spend her life in the military. Her family is in government.

"If you will excuse us for just a second, I need to speak with my son." Elle grabs Adrian's arm and pulls him out of earshot like he's still a child. Gabby and I both watch them intently. They're having a row about something. Every few moments they glance in our direction. Elle throws her hands in the air and stalks off. Adrian walks back to us.

"Come on," he says gruffly. We follow closely behind him; both of us keeping quiet for a change. We don't want to upset him further. And besides that, we seem to have picked up a minder.

Everything I see her just reinforces the feeling that something isn't right. I just have to figure out what it is.

Chapter 12

Drew

Pain sears through my stomach as someone kicks me in the gut. He drags me to my feet and pulls me out of my cell. I stumble as I walk and that only makes my captor pull harder. My entire body aches from the beatings that I've suffered day after day. I must have some cracked ribs to go along with the cuts and bruises. At least, that's what it feels like. I wouldn't know if they're actually cracked because the only doctor I've seen is the one overseeing my torture. Every few days they decide to mix it up and use the water like they did when I first got here. I'd rather be beaten.

We reach the stairwell and I'm pushed down. A strangled cry escapes my throat. My shoulder hits first and I let out a cry of pain. I can't break my fall because my hands are tied behind my back. I roll down the last few steps and lay at the bottom, unable to move without feeling like little knives are being stuck in me as my breath wheezes in and out.

Someone opens the door to my left and stands over me, glowering. He reaches down, grabs my shirt, and lifts me to my feet. I yelp as he uses my shoulder to guide me into the room. Today is no different than any other. They're going to ask me questions that I don't know the answers to and then make me wish I'd died in those woods. I've come to the realization that I'm utterly buggered no matter what I do.

I agreed to make the video to get Dawn out of her coma, but we haven't done it yet. I don't know what else they want from me.

I'm thrust unceremoniously into my usual chair. I look up to see Dr. Cole. I still refuse to call him Darren. It's the one act of defiance I have right now and I love how it pisses him off. He probably doesn't give a shite what I call him, but he hates that I won't do as I'm told.

"Hello, Drew," he says. "Sleep well?"

"My night was just brilliant," I say coldly.

"There's no need for sarcasm. I'm just making conversation." His lips curve into a smile. I wish I could wipe it from his face.

"What's on the menu for me today? Beating? Drowning? Beating and drowning? What are you going to do?" I'm hit from behind. Texans have no sense of humor.

"My dear boy, I would never lay a hand on you." He's right, of course. Dr. Cole has never actually hit me himself. He lets his goons do the dirty work while he asks the questions. "Today, I have some pictures I would like you to see."

"Pictures?" I ask. He hands me the first one. It's of Dawn. I haven't seen her since she was unconscious in a hospital bed. They wouldn't even tell me how she was. She looks good. She's smiling and happy. The next picture is of her and Gabby walking down the street. They're free. They're not being kept in a prison like me. Thank God.

"They're okay," I whisper.

"Of course they are. We don't want to hurt them. I'm told, however, that Dawn is quite broken up over your death."

"My death?" I ask, not really looking for an answer because I already know. They've told Dawn that I'm dead. Before I can think on it too much, Dr. Cole hands me one last picture. This one is of Gabby practically carrying Dawn and some guy walking with them.

"What happened to her?" I ask.

"Oh just some harmless, yet illegal fun. She drank quite a bit that night." I don't have time to process this when the door opens and a second man walks through. I look up at him and instantly recognize him as the guy from the picture.

"Ah, Adrian," Dr. Cole says. "So glad you could join us." Adrian crosses the room to stand beside the doctor. "Drew, this is my nephew. He has grown quite close to your little girlfriends." Adrian doesn't say anything as he stares at me. I want to lunge at him and rip his throat out. I kick my leg out, hoping to hurt him. He steps back, out of my reach. I search his face for any sign of emotion. He's hiding it well. I find no hatred, no anger, and no joy.

"Drew, that's not very nice. Adrian was just coming here to report on your friends. You see, he's a soldier. His assignment is to become friends with the girls and report back on their behavior and their conversations." He looks at Adrian. "Nephew, why don't you start?"

"Gabby and Dawn seem to be happy here. There's no sign that they suspect anything. I took them to the wall like you wanted. They met Clint, but then we ran into my mother." Adrian pauses.

"Who's Clint?" I ask, needing to know everything.

"It's not polite to interrupt," Dr. Cole snaps. "Adrian, I hope your mother didn't cause any problems. How was my dear sister?"

"She's angry with me for taking this assignment." His eyes shift down, as if embarrassed.

"Of course she is. She should understand more than most, though, that a soldier doesn't choose his tasks. Soldiers do as they're told."

"She should," he agrees.

"Tell me, nephew, are you willing to do what needs to be done?" Dr. Cole asks.

"I am."

"Good." He turns to me. "You see Drew, you need to cooperate or my nephew here may have orders that you don't like."

"What do you want from me?" I ask in desperation.

The doctor smiles. "You may go, Adrian." As Adrian leaves the room, two more men come in. I recognize them instantly. I probably still have their footprints on my chest or their hand prints on my arms. They come closer and one of them punches me in the face. Blood trickles over my lips, warm and metallic.

"We need the bruises to look fresh," Dr. Cole explains as a woman walks in with a small camera in her hand. "Now, Drew, we've prepared cards for you to read. Do not deviate from them unless you want me to call Adrian back for his new orders."

I nod as the cards are set up in front of me. I'm given the cue to begin and I start to read out loud without thinking. I tell myself that I can't stop. I can't mess this up.

"Hello, I'm Drew Crawford, son of Commander Crawford." My voice cracks as I speak. "I'm being held by the Texans for questioning. This message is for General Nolan.

You do not know me, but I came here with Gabby and Dawn Nolan. They too are being held in Texas. Our captors won't release us until you agree to a peace meeting. Tensions with the rebels are heating up and the Texans need guaranteed aid. If you do not agree to this, your daughters will not live long past your refusal." I stop as I choke on the last sentence. This is a ransom note. I'm hit from behind and told to keep going even as a single tear falls from my eye.

"I plead with you, sir," I read. "Don't let Gabby and Dawn suffer the same fate as me." As soon as the last word passes my lips, the camera is shifted away and a single gunshot pierces the silence.

Chapter 13

The General

"Keep moving!" I bark as I walk the perimeter of the training field. The new batch of rankers that Commander Crawford sent over is even weaker than the last. I put them through drill after drill as the intense sun hangs above us. I wipe the sweat from my brow and turn towards the exhausted group of men and women. I look on in disgust as a few soldiers fall to their knees and retch. Others have collapsed to the ground and are breathing heavily.

"Pathetic!" I scream. "Pitiful. Deplorable. Useless." I turn to leave and yell back over my shoulder, "Dismissed!"

I could care less if these incompetent soldiers can eventually help the British military. The problem is that the state of the armed forces has a direct impact on my reputation. Reputation is key.

"Sir." A squaddie runs down the steps of the plantation house and sprints towards me, waving something in the air. He's panting when he reaches me.

"Calm down soldier." I wait until he catches his breath. "What is it?"

"There's a dispatch waiting for you in your office sir." He pauses. "It's from Texas."

I speed up and by the time I reach my office, I'm running. I push open the door and step inside. A small man in a crumpled uniform greets me with a salute. I don't return the gesture.

"Sit," I command. I don't like having a Texan fanatic on British grounds. We've grown used to these messengers showing up as the Texans realize they can't fight the Mexicans, the British, and the Rebels. They want an alliance. Each time, we send their messenger back with our denial. Last year, Darren Cole, husband to their supposed prophet, even paid us a visit.

I move around my desk and straighten the papers on it before sitting down. Neither of us speak as we evaluate each other. Finally, I ask, "What do the Texans have for me today?" When he hesitates, I raise my voice. "Hand it over." The nervous man opens his bag and produces a small screen. He hands it to me as he presses play.

It begins with a view of the hospital building before heading into a sterile room. The video zooms in on a sleeping girl. She shifts and my eyes widen. Dawn. I bring my hand to my mouth as the image becomes dark. I now see a boy tied to a chair in a concrete room. His head hangs on his chest. Someone comes into view and lifts the boy's head. His eyes open and he stares at the camera. His voice quivers as he begins to speak.

"Hello, I'm Drew Crawford."

Shite, a Crawford. The commander will not be happy.

"I'm being held by the Texans," the message goes on. "Texans need guaranteed aid. If you do not agree to this, your daughters will not live long past your refusal. I plead with you, sir, don't let Gabby and Dawn suffer the same fate as me." His voice grows quiet and the screen turns to black. Before I turn it off, the unmistakable sound of a gunshot rings in my ears.

"Dammit!" I scream as I slam my hands on my desk and shoot to my feet. The Messenger jumps back to stay out of range of my fury. "You can go and tell your 'prophet' that they are on their own. You can't threaten me and get what you want. Go!" I yell. He scurries from the room.

I immediately try to come up with a plan, needing to get Dawn and Gabby out of the Republic. They're not safe there.

Allison... one of the rebel spies in Texas.

She must still be there. I haven't received any notices to the contrary. I step into the hall and inform one of the guards to find me Locke. He's one of the few people I can trust with this. He knows of my connection with the rebels because he's a part of the movement as well.

He arrives twenty minutes later and I press the letter into his hand. I tell him who it's for and he nods. He'll be able to find a way to get it to her. He sets off to prepare for his journey. I sink onto my couch and close my eyes in prayer. Please God, let them be okay.

Chapter 14

Gabby

Dawn won't listen to me. She thinks we should stay here, that we're safe. I want to shake her until she opens her eyes to what's around us. She's so desperate to have a place to call home that she can't see it. Jeremy would believe me. I miss him more than I can admit to my sister. I feel it in my bones that he's alive. He has to be. I know we'll see him and Lee again.

I needed some space to clear my head so I left Dawn back at the flat and decided to go for a walk. I'm nearing the center of town when a kid bumps into me.

"I'm sorry, lady," she says sweetly. To my surprise, she shoves something into my hand before running off. It's a crumpled ball of paper. Confused, I unroll it to see the message.

Be at the chapel in 10 minutes... 23rd pew

I don't know who could be sending me a note. It's probably a daft move, but I turn around and head in the chapel's direction. I've been here long enough now that I can find my way around pretty easily. It only takes me about five minutes to reach the beautiful building and climb the front steps. I step inside and immediately feel that I don't belong here. There are only a few people milling about; some lighting candles near the front and others kneeling. I count the pews until I find the 23rd and take a seat. Whoever sent me the note isn't here yet.

It's so quiet that I almost can't take it. I've decided to leave when a woman slips into the pew beside me.

I look at her, my eyes widening.

"You're Adrian's mother," I state.

"I told you I prefer Elle. We don't have time for this. Act like you're praying," she commands.

"How do I do that?" I ask. She sighs and gets to her knees on the bar in front of our seats. I imitate her. She lowers her head. I lower mine.

"I'm here to help you," she whispers.

"What do you mean?" I ask.

"You're not safe here. This society is a cult. It's dangerous and you need to get out and follow the river north."

"Why?" I ask. "How do I get out?"

"I can't explain right now, but just know you need to go there."

"Why isn't Texas safe?"

"Go to the labs. They're on the northern edge of the city. Here, this will get you in." She hands me a plastic key card.

"Why are you helping me?" I ask.

"Because there are limits to what a person should do for their country. Many Texans are way past those limits. After you see the labs, we'll meet again."

"How can I contact you?" I ask.

"You can't." And just like that, she is gone.

Chapter 15

Gabby

I leave the chapel and immediately start moving north. It's not just curiosity; I have a need inside of me. I need to see the labs, whatever they are. I need to know what's going on in this city. At first, I consider that this might be a trick; some kind of loyalty test. That thought doesn't last for long. I've always been someone that listened to her gut more than anything. My gut is telling me that whatever is in the labs, it isn't good.

It takes me the better part of an hour to reach the edge of the city. I'm not sure which of these identical buildings holds the labs so I choose the only one that has a key card entry. I examine the card that Elle gave me. There's an arrow on one end to show me how to put it in. She has also written a four-digit code on the back; 1142. Underneath that, in smaller writing, is the code 1167. I decide to try the first code.

I push the card into the slot and enter the code on the keypad above it, hoping I'm doing it right. There's a series of clicks and a green light appears on the lock as it gives me back the card. I push open the door, preparing myself for what lies on the other side. To my relief, there's not a single person in sight. I walk through the doorway into a long hallway lined with doors. Each of them has a plaque to its right, telling me where it leads.

I'm halfway down the hall when I hear footsteps. I duck through the nearest door to my right; the one that says cell block. It also says authorized personnel only, but I choose to ignore that. There's no going back now.

The room I enter is dim, lit only by a single fluorescent overhead. I don't take the time to look at my surroundings as I sprint across the open space. I'm confronted with another locked door and another keypad. I take Elle's card from my back pocket and flip it over. I don't know what will happen if I punch in the wrong code, but I don't give it a second thought. Pushing the card in, I type 1167 and, once again, the light turns green and the door clicks open.

As soon as I step through, the sounds of pain reach my ears. From every direction, I'm confronted with groans and screams. The room is white, sterile. It's almost like the hospital, except for the cells stretching as far as I can see. Of course, the door said cell block, like in a prison. The only thing that separates these prisoners from me is a wall of Plexiglas. Every cell has a sign that says Warning: Contagious. I can see each and every one of them as I slowly creep down the hall; their gaunt faces and hollow stares; their ragged clothing and matted down hair.

I recognize the look in their eyes. It's a look that I saw constantly when I was being held prisoner by the British. I feel their eyes on me as I pass by. Goosebumps prickle their way down my arms causing the hair to stand on end.

What have these people done to deserve this fate? I lose count of how many there are when I'm only part of the way down the hall. My head is spinning as I see children and adults alike being kept like animals. This must be what Elle wanted me to see.

"Gabby?" The sound is barely audible, but I whip around, trying to find where it came from. It's hard to hear anything over the coughs and moans.

"Gab?" It's louder this time.

I see a wretched man lying on the ground in one of the cells. I crouch down to get a better look, but it's hard to make out any recognizable features through the cuts and bruises that disfigure his face. The man shifts a little more and pushes the mop of dark hair out of his face.

My heart stops as recognition takes hold.

I choke out one word. "Drew."

I fall to my knees in front of his cell to get a better look. "Drew, is that really you?" I hold back a sob. It's him. His hair is longer and red with blood and a beard covers his bruised face. He looks like he hasn't eaten in days and can barely move without a flash of pain crossing his face. What have they done to him? I put my hands to the glass. I thought he died in the woods. Looking at him now, he probably wishes he had.

"Dawn?" Once again, Drew's voice is no more than a whisper but I know what he's asking.

"She's fine." I shake my head, still not quite believing what I'm seeing. "She's going to be so happy to see you." This time I can't stop the sob that hiccups out of my chest. Before I can say anything else, however, an alarm sounds overhead. I cover my ears to drown out the deafening sound, but I see Drew mouth the word *Go.*

"I'm coming back for you. I promise," I yell as I scramble to my feet and sprint towards the end of the hall. Prisoners bang on their walls as I go past, but I don't stop. I keep my feet moving until I reach another door and barrel my way through. I crash into a railing and realize I have nowhere left to run. I'm standing on a balcony overlooking a massive room. Like the one before, it's white and sterile. People move around in large medical suits that cover every inch of skin. They even wear helmets. There are metal tables spread throughout the room. A few of them have people strapped to them.

I look around frantically trying to find an escape. To my left, there are lifts that would take me to the lab floor. I push the button and try to drown out the alarm that's still screeching. There's now a mechanical sounding voice saying, "Intruder," over and over again. Many of the men and women in the lab are looking towards the balcony and pointing.

Panic surges through my veins as the door I came through is shoved open and men in uniform start piling through. I kick and scream as they grab my arms and drag me back into the cell block. They take me all the way down the hall and into a separate area. "Let go of me, you stupid gits!" I'm then shoved into a chair and my hands are cuffed behind my back. The alarm has finally stopped, but the sound is still ringing in my ears.

Chapter 16

Gabby

My pulse has calmed and the sweat across my brow has dried, leaving behind a greasy shine by the time Tia Cole walks into the room. I think I've been sitting here for hours, but I have no way to be sure. She sits across from me and rests her hands on the table as the men in the room mutter "your Reverence" and back out through the door.

"I was wondering when I would have to see you again," Tia begins.

"Waiting for me to find out how messed up this place is?" I ask in a voice that suddenly doesn't sound like my own. It sounds harsher, angrier.

"We were hoping you wouldn't be a problem, but I see that isn't going to be the case, is it?" She looks towards the door. She's waiting for something. I just don't know what. I don't answer her question because I don't see the point. Instead, I ask her a few of my own,

"What are you doing to those people? Who are they? What did you do to Drew?"

She checks her watch and sighs before responding. "Too many questions. You do what you have to do to survive."

"That's not an answer," I growl.

"You Brits always think the worst, don't you? Those people have been diagnosed with deadly diseases. They're kept away from the rest of the population while we find cures and vaccines."

"By holding them against their will and using them as lab rats? What would the rest of your people think if they knew?"

"I wouldn't expect a silly girl like you to understand. I'm the prophet to these people. I'm the law. I'm the only truth that exists here. They follow me because it's the only way to salvation. There's a reason Texas has survived this long. We were chosen. I was chosen." I don't have a chance to process what she says because as she checks her watch again, the door opens. I look up as Adrian enters followed by a contingent of guards. I narrow my eyes as our gazes connect.

"Adrian, finally," Tia says as she stands. "We have a little test for you, nephew. It seems that your mother is causing trouble again and I need to know that you can do what is necessary." Adrian breaks his eyes from mine to look at his aunt.

"Of course. My mother is a traitor. She has gone against you, our prophet and, in doing so, against God himself," he says without flinching.

"I'm glad you see it that way." Tia motions to the guards to leave the room. They return a few minutes later dragging a semi-conscious Elle between them. They drop her to the ground and her eyes open completely as she lands with a thud.

"Adrian," she whispers.

"What have you done, mom?" Adrian's voice is cold. It's not the voice of a son speaking to his mother. Instead of responding to him, she looks at me.

"Be brave, Gabby," she croaks. One of the guards kicks her in the ribs and grabs her by the hair, pulling her head up to look at Tia.

"Elle, my dear sister in-law. Don't worry, you won't be sent to the labs that you so detest." Tia reaches towards one of the guards and he places a gun in the palm of her hand. She doesn't close her fist around it. I watch in horror as she spins and offers the gun to Adrian. His eyes go wide as he catches her meaning.

"I told you, Adrian, you have to be willing to do whatever it takes. Now is your chance to distinguish yourself from your traitorous side of the family." She places her hand over her mouth. "Oh I forgot, I promised your mother I would never tell you the truth about your father's death. Although, his fate was worse than this one. A clean death is more than we do for most traitors. Your mother is lucky that we need you to do this." Her arm is still outstretched towards Adrian. He grabs the gun, holding it as if it's a ticking bomb, ready to go off.

"Adrian," I plead, "this is your mother. There's no coming back from this." As he looks at me, there are tears in his eyes. He looks down at the gun.

"Nephew, it's the only way. If you don't do it, she will suffer something much worse. Prove you're one of us. Prove that you're a Cole. Prove that you're a pure Texan." Tia places a hand on Adrian's shoulder. She makes it seem like a sign of support, but she uses it to turn him towards Elle.

Elle looks surprisingly serene. A small smile plays on her lips as she looks at her son. She loves him very much; I can see it in her eyes.

Adrian points the gun at his mother, the woman who raised him. He holds it out from his chest, closes his eyes, and pulls the trigger. I scream as she falls sideways, blood pouring from the hole in her chest, near the heart. I look frantically from Adrian to Tia, thinking I'm next. This is the end.

Adrian drops the gun to the floor and stalks out of the room. Tia grins and nods to the guards. They move forward and grab me underneath my arms, lifting me from the chair. I don't even bother to kick as they carry me down the hall. It wouldn't do any good. Instead, I hurl obscenities at them until they dump me in a cell and shut the door. I lean my head back against the wall and tears begin to flow.

Chapter 17

Gabby

Will I ever be free of these prisons? This cell. The Floridaland hotbox. Adrian's eyes find mine as he closes the door and looks at me through the glass. I could be wrong, but I think he even mouths the words *I'm sorry*. His eyes are full of pain. I must be imagining things. He just killed his mother in cold blood and then locked me up. I stand and spit on the glass. It streaks down the glass, blurring my view of him. He just shakes his head and walks away, leaving me to the awful sounds of this place.

Occasional shrieks come from the direction of the labs. Tia Cole told me they're experimenting on people down there. They're using the sick to create vaccines. She was trying to terrify me. All Texan medications come out of these labs and most of the people they use never make it back out. By the time the meds are ready for use, the test subjects are already too far gone.

I watch men and women in lab coats hurry along the corridor without so much as a sideways glance at the people in cages. We're their lab rats. Nothing more.

After a while, the lights go out. Why waste precious energy on people you're going to kill? I lay on the cold floor, hoping that sleep can be my escape. As soon as I begin to doze off, I'm startled awake by some-one tapping on the glass door to my prison. She doesn't say anything as she points at the biometric scanner that opens my cell.

"What's going on?" I ask suspiciously. "Who are you?"

"There's no time for explanations," she says. "You're Gabby Nolan, right?" I nod. "Good." She looks nervously down the hall. I follow her gaze and a man comes into view, dragging an unconscious guard be-hind him. Up and down the hall prisoners are cheering as they see the fallen guard. They bang on the glass and plead to be released.

The man and woman lift the guard together and place his palm on the scanner. After a few seconds, my door swings open.

"We have to hurry," the man says as he drops the guard to the floor. They move towards the exit, but I stop.

"Come on," the woman urges me.

"We need to get Drew," I whisper to myself as I run towards his cell.

"We were only sent here for you," the woman protests. Her com-panion, however, has already started dragging the guard after me.

"Come on, Jess," he strains. "We won't get her out of here without him."

"Is he sick?" She hesitates.

"Of course not," I interject.

"Fine." Jess moves to help him.

Drew's door swings open and I rush in towards him. He tries to get up but falls backward. I catch him and he looks at me, defeated. I recognize that look. Jess helps me get him to his feet and we leave the labs behind us.

"Jack, have your gun ready," Jess says. "The police would have been notified as soon as the power was cut."

"That was you guys?" I ask as we move through the building. The doors in our path stand open and the keypads have been pried off.

"It was the only way to get past the cameras, alarms, and keypads. We had to disable the backup power as well. The only equipment that was still working was the biometric locks. They're on batteries so that the cells stay closed during an energy crisis."

We leave through a back door and hurry down the street as my arm turns numb from holding Drew up. But we can't stop now. I don't know who these people are, but they're our new allies and our best chance of getting out.

Chapter 18

Dawn

I woke up this morning and Gabby was gone. I don't know where she would go without me, but I'm worried. She's probably doing something stupid and reckless like the prat she is at times. I went looking for Adrian but couldn't find him anywhere. I ended up back here at our flat, alone. I pace back and forth across the room, unable to control my nervous energy. What has she done now?

I almost jump out of my skin when there's a knock at the door. I rush to open it and find a man and a woman standing in the hall, looking around anxiously. They shove me aside and bull their way into my room. I shut the door and the man comes up behind me and locks it. The woman has gone to the window and lowered my blinds.

"What's going on?" I ask, irritated. "Who are you?" I try to channel Gabby in my voice so that it sounds bigger, less me, because I'm scared of these strangers.

"Don't worry, we're here to help," the woman says.

"Help with what?" I ask. They look at each other before the man speaks.

"Elle sent us," he says as if that should answer all my questions.

"Who's Elle?" I still don't understand.

"You met her at the wall," he answers.

"Adrian's mother?"

"Yes," the woman says hurriedly, "look, we don't have time for this. Yes, Adrian's mother sent us. No Adrian is not to be trusted. My name is Allison."

"And I'm Clay," the man says as he peers through the blinds. "We need to get you out of here now."

"Why? I still don't understand."

"Your sister was caught in the labs today. We think Elle is dead. You need to get out of Texas. You need to escape."

"What? Why should I –" They cut me off and steer me towards the door. I look from Clay to Allison, trying to comprehend what they're telling me. Gabby was caught in the labs. What labs? What are they going to do to her? Who are these people? Hoping they can help me find my sister, I step through the door and they follow me out. We get out onto the street and Allison's arm shoots out to keep me from going further.

"Stay close to the buildings so we can use their shadows," she says. I do as she tells me and we hurry down the street. We can't run because we have to be careful not to draw attention to ourselves. We pass the chapel and the government building. I hold my breath when a friend of Clay's stops him to say hi. They exchange pleasantries before we keep moving. The tension is driving me nuts.

They still haven't told me what exactly is going on or who they are. I wouldn't have come with them, but I've had a feeling in my gut that something wasn't right ever since I woke up and my sister was gone. I can't explain it, but I know she needs my help. My mind is taken over by the fear that something has happened to her.

I follow Allison up the steps to a building and Clay brings up the rear. Allison enters a code and the door swings open. She ushers us in before clicking it shut behind us. I breathe deeply, trying to calm my nerves now that we're no longer out in the open.

At this late hour, there's no one in any of the offices we pass. We reach a stairwell that takes us down into an underground car park.

"Where are we?" I ask, taking in the rows of government vehicles.

"We're at a government facility," Clay responds, clearly not interested in giving me any answers. He scans the garage, looking for something.

"I don't see him yet," Allison says before we hear the screech of tires as a truck pulls into view. The car stops in front of us and a heavy-set man steps out from behind the wheel.

"Landon," Clay says as they clasp hands, "good to see you're still breathing."

"Yeah, you too," he chuckles. "These are dark days, my friend." Then to me, Landon says, "it's good to see you again, Dawn, even under the circumstances."

"Do I know you?" I ask.

"I guess you wouldn't remember. You were pretty wasted that night." He laughs again, but it's not the laugh of a carefree man. He's trying to hold himself together. I can tell by the way his hands tremble. I only remember parts of that night, but I do recognize his face. I just hadn't realized from what.

"Did they get the other girl?" Allison asks impatiently.

"They should be here soon," Landon answers.

"Someone went to get Gabby?" I ask.

"Yes," Clay answers. "Now, here's the plan. Landon and Allison are scheduled to make a supply trip to St. Louis. You and your sister will be hidden in the truck."

"But we'll still be in Texas," I state.

"Yes," he responds, "St. Louis lies on a lightly guarded section of river. There's absolutely no way we could get you out of the Vicksburg port."

"So you all are rebels." I look around at this group and am once again amazed at the reach of my own people, whether it be the rebels or the government.

"Yes. But we prefer to call ourselves 'True Patriots'. Are we done with the questions now?" Clay says harshly. I'm suddenly glad that he isn't coming with us. I begin pacing. It helps me to keep moving. Every minute we wait is another chance that something has gone wrong.

"Why are you helping us?" I break the silence.

"This isn't for you," Clay answers irritably. "We have Intel that needs to get to the rebel base. You're only coming along because of who your father is." Of course, my father. I'm about to ask another question when we hear footsteps on the stairs and Allison pulls me down behind the truck.

"Allison," the whisper comes from near the stairwell, "you down here?" Allison peers over the hood for a moment before standing. She motions for the rest of us to follow.

"You made it," she says as she makes her way towards him. She embraces him for a second longer than is comfortable for the rest of us. Clay clears his throat and they sheepishly break apart.

"Jack," Landon says, "where's the girl?"

"Jess is helping them down the stairs. The boy is in pretty bad shape," Jack answers, looking behind him anxiously.

"What boy?" Allison asks. Before Jack has the chance to respond, the door to the stairwell opens and two people step through supporting a third.

Gabby shrugs the arm from her shoulder and runs towards me. I go to hug her but she stops me. "Sis, it's Drew." I don't ask her what she means because, suddenly, I know.

My heart feels like it's beating for the first time in weeks. I breathe heavily as a veil of darkness lifts and all I see is him.

He's here. He's alive.

My face fights between smiling and crying as his barely conscious eyes find mine. Gabby is trying to speak but all I hear is white noise. All I see is him.

"I thought you were dead," I say, stopping in front of him. When had I started walking?

"I was, Dawn. I was." His legs give out and he falls forward into my waiting arms.

Chapter 19

Dawn

What have they done to him? If he's been alive this whole time, that means the Texans were holding him prisoner.

"Well, isn't this romantic," Clay says. "It's not something we have time for, however." As soon as Clay breaks the silence it's as if a spell has been lifted. Everyone starts moving.

"Looks like we'll have three of you to hide," Landon states as he opens the back of the truck. "Get in," he says gently. Gabby and I climb in and then help Drew. I grab his arm but he doesn't look me in the eye as I lay my hands on him. He's spent.

The truck is loaded with boxes of clothing. We've been told that all the clothing in Texas is made here so they have to make regular deliveries to the other cities. It's a good thing too because that's the only reason we're getting out. They use these supply runs to transport people all the time right under their government's nose. They also use these runs to pass messages. They're part of the network the rebels have put in place throughout the colonies and even Mexico.

We crowd into a false compartment up front. There's a clatter and a scattering of metal and wood.

"Don't sit on the rifles," I'm scolded.

Landon tells us we must be silent until we're out of the city and Jack wishes us luck before closing the door, leaving us to the darkness. I'm wedged in the corner, arms wrapped around my legs, shrinking into myself.

I can feel Drew near me, but I can't even begin to process him being here. It was only minutes ago that I thought that he was dead and I would never see him again. Heck, it was only hours ago that I thought I could make my home in Texas. Now I know the truth. I should have trusted my sister. I should have listened to her. Drew. I reach out in the darkness, but he flinches away from the touch.

After what feels like an eternity, Allison opens the small door that leads from the back of the truck to the cabin. "We're clear," she says. "You guys good?"

"Yeah," Gabby answers, breathless. She must have been holding her breath too.

"Okay, well, it'll only take us a couple hours to get there. You might want to close your eyes for a bit because who knows when you'll be able to sleep next." She shuts the door and I lean my head back against the wall. Tears prick my eyes, but I wipe them away quickly. We're on the run again. It feels like I've been running my whole life. I just want to find a place where I can stay put for a while.

"You okay, Dawn?" Even in the dark, Gabby knows something is wrong. Maybe it's just common sense that I should be upset. My boyfriend did come back from the dead. I don't answer Gabby, but I reach out and pat her arm.

Then, I whisper, "Drew?"

He doesn't respond right away so I assume he's just knackered. But in a moment, he answers, "I'm okay, Dawn." The weariness in his voice frightens me. He doesn't sound like himself.

"Good." I'm not sure what else I can say and the uncomfortable silence stretches between us before I say again, "I thought you were dead." I hiccup back a sob.

"I know," he says. His voice has lost its fire; its passion. His usual confidence is gone. "I didn't think I'd see you again."

Words fail me. I had dreamed about being reunited with Drew, but it was nothing like this. I never imagined that it would be so uncomfortable. I never imagined I would feel this lost around him. He was going through hell while I was spending time with his captors.

Chapter 20

Gabby

The ride in the truck was almost unbearable. The air was claustrophobic with things unsaid. Dawn doesn't know how to talk to Drew after everything he's been through. She is afraid of what she saw and what is happening. I'm not the same person that went into the hot box in Floridaland and Drew is not the same person she thought had died in the woods.

Relief floods through me as Allison opens the door and lets us out. Drew seems to be a little more stable on his feet, so I don't need to help him walk. Allison leads us through an underground car park identical to the one we left from. We said our thank yous and goodbyes to Landon at the truck before he drove off to make his delivery.

We still have the cover of darkness to hide us as we step outside. At night, this town looks eerily similar to the one we left. We wind through the streets and I feel like we're in a maze. We have to stop a few times for Drew to rest, but never for long. We need to be gone by sunrise.

I'm surprised when Allison tells us that she's coming with us. She says that her mission in Texas is complete, whatever that means. I doubt she was there just to help us escape. I ask her about Jack and her face falls. She loves him, but she doesn't have the option of staying. "I have been ordered to return to the rebel base," she explains.

After walking for about an hour, Allison takes us into a building that looks no different from any other. We end up in an empty warehouse near the docks.

"St. Louis is a farming area," Allison says. "Most of the Texan farms are along the rivers. This port is mainly used by the ships transferring food. To our benefit, this is also where most of the smugglers bring their boats. The dock workers are paid to look the other way. You see, almost everything and everyone can be bought in St. Louis. To the people here, the Prophet is some far away person who they only talk about in church. St. Louis is much less of a cult than Vicksburg."

A gruff looking man steps into the empty room and Allison walks towards him. She hands him a small pouch and then turns to follow him. We do the same.

"I have an order of seed that needs to get pretty far up the Mississippi," the burly man says to Allison.

"That's perfect," she responds. He hands her some paperwork and they shake hands.

"I'll have it delivered to the docks." He leaves and Allison turns to us.

"Let's go find us a boat." She smiles in satisfaction.

"What was that all about?" I ask.

"You won't get very far on the rivers without a legitimate reason for doing so. These papers give us that. We're delivering seed to the northernmost Texan village."

We walk silently to the docks. Curfew must apply differently here because the boats are teeming with people. They're cleaning fish, scrubbing docks, and fixing sails.

"How do we get someone to take us on?" Dawn asks. Allison doesn't answer as she scans the boats.

"Found him," she states.

"Who?" I ask, but Allison is already on the move. "You guys stay here, and don't talk to anyone."

We find a place for Drew to sit down, but I don't take my eyes off of Allison. She's boarded a boat and I see something change hands between her and a man. He says something to his men on deck and they hurry along. After a few minutes, Allison calls us to her.

"This is Captain Collins," she says.

"Ah," the captain says. "General Nolan's daughters." He gives us a toothy grin.

"Are you a rebel?" Dawn asks.

"No. I'm just an honest smuggler."

"An honest smuggler?" Allison raises her eyebrows.

"Yes," he responds. "I'm honest about the fact that I'm a smuggler." I like this man. "Now," he continues, "let's get you below deck before my men return."

We follow him down a narrow staircase and into the ship's storeroom. The captain moves some boxes out of the way to reveal a hidden door. He pulls it open and a burst of stale air escapes.

"In you go," Allison says.

"You first," I say. She shakes her head.

"I have that seed, remember? I'm on this boat legally. I'd rather be on deck."

We reluctantly climb in. It's tight with the three of us and the only light is a dim lamp overhead. The captain shuts the door and there is a scuffle above as he drags boxes to conceal it once again.

Dawn curls up in the corner as her breathing becomes labored. Until the truck ride from the capitol, I'd forgotten about her claustrophobia. The dank air certainly doesn't help. Drew leans his head back against the wall and closes his eyes. He gasps in pain.

Suddenly, I start to laugh. Quietly at first, and then I can't hold back any longer. Drew glares at me and Dawn tries to kick me.

"What the hell is so funny?" she demands.

"You two are quite the pair," I manage in between fits.

I don't try to stop because, right now, laughing is the only thing keeping the tears at bay.

Chapter 21

Miranda

"We're here," my driver says as the car pulls to a stop. Along with the other men and women on my plane, I was picked up in a black SUV from the landing strip. We've been driving for over an hour, so I quickly step out of the car to stretch my legs. For years, I've wondered what the rebel base in the colonies would be like. This isn't right. We seem to be in the middle of nowhere. There is a single building that looks like it hasn't been used in decades. The only other structures that I can see are a series of large windmills spinning rapidly.

"This can't be right," someone says from behind me. I'm thinking the same thing, but I don't say it. Our driver smiles at me and begins walking towards the dilapidated building. I follow him through the door. It's as I expected, the inside looks no better than out. I watch as he lifts a plank from the floor, revealing a keypad. I expect him to punch in a code but instead, he yanks the keypad free, revealing a single button underneath. He hits the button and replaces the keypad. I wait for something to happen, but nothing does. After a few moments, we hear a voice. I look around but can't find the source.

"Code," the voice says dryly.

"This is Officer Dale Turner, ID Chi 3 Alpha 8 Nu 1 returning from mission 34293." Dale stops, waiting for an answer.

"You and those you accompany are authorized to enter."

I follow Dale outside to the others and look around. To me, it still seems that we're in the middle of nowhere. The ground beneath us begins to shake. Everyone else from my plane starts to panic, but I look to our driver and he looks calm, expectant. I mirror his stance with my arms crossed over my chest and face the same direction. A door opens in the ground right in front of us and a ramp leads down into the darkness. I can fully comprehend what is happening, a man walks up through the door, followed by three others. He heads straight for us.

"Thank you, Turner. That is all," he says to Dale.

"Yes, sir," Dales nods his head as he walks down the ramp and disappears.

"Officer Edwards." He extends his hand towards me. "I'm Jonathan Clarke."

"Hello." I grip his hand. "I'm excited to get started."

"I imagine you are. This way." He turns and I follow him. My fellow rebels are escorted down the ramp and into a separate area by other officers. The door slides shut as soon as we're through and a light overhead switches on.

The ramp takes us far underground into a cavernous room filled with cars and other vehicles. Lights flicker on as we pass and I take in my surroundings.

"We're glad to have you here," Officer Clarke starts. "You will be second only to me in your rank."

"This is quite the operation. Very impressive, Officer Clarke." Men and women in sharp blue uniforms salute as we pass by.

"Please, call me Jonathan." He smiles, a gesture that I do not return. I don't find the need to be friendly with co-workers. "This base has been operational for 112 years. Of course, it was quite small back then. It was an old shale mine if you can believe it. We continually improve and expand." I detect pride in his voice and rightly so. "Would you like a tour now or would you prefer to get settled first? I've had your things brought to the officer's quarters."

"Now is good," I respond. I'm knackered from my flight, but my curiosity gets the better of me.

"Alright then, this is the carport. We've commandeered many trucks and all-terrain vehicles from those we fight."

"You were able to nick them?"

"If that's what you want to call it."

We push through a door that takes us into a room with weapons hanging along the walls. "Here we have the armory. We're working on increasing our supply of weapons. With the rebels in London gaining more footholds, they should be able to help in this department."

"Do you have enough to arm all your soldiers?"

"Yes, guns aren't the problem. We have been very successful in raiding the Texan gun factories. We're looking to acquire more advanced weaponry; bombs and the like," he answers.

I only nod, taking in the information. The next room we enter is a large gymnasium. There are ropes hanging from the ceiling and mats scattered across the floor. People are spread across the space boxing, climbing, and working out. "We may not have all of the equipment that other groups have," Jonathan begins. "But you won't find a better trained force. Everyone here takes their workouts and training very seriously."

We pass into another space with targets on one wall and divided stalls in which soldiers are standing and firing their guns.

"So, what exactly are you doing in the colonies?" I ask the question that has been on my mind since I was told I was leaving London.

"We're here to help in the fight against the corrupt fascists that control large parts of the world. Unfortunately, our own government falls under that as does the Republic of Texas. We want our proper share of the power."

"I know that, but what are you actually doing?"

He eyes me shrewdly. "It is not many who can distinguish between purpose and action. We have a wide network of people throughout the colonies that are working to free people from the slave camps in Floridaland and the Prisons in the Republic of Texas. We're building a guerrilla force. We're also gathering Intel about their operations. You'd be surprised how much we know. You'd also be surprised who we're working with. Enough about that for now, though. It's all in the dossier I've left in your quarters. You can get settled and then someone will come to escort you to command for a meeting this evening."

We've stopped in front of a small room. I look inside at the single bed and small table. It's not much, but in London, I lived in the army barracks, so this is much better. As soon as I enter the room, Jonathan is gone. The few things that I brought with me are sitting on the end of the bed next to two perfectly folded uniforms. I remember all those days in London when I would put on my uniform and betray it time after time. I was never a true British soldier; not in my mind. I finger the buttons and run my hands over the smooth fabric. Here is a uniform that will truly be mine. A uniform I will finally be loyal to.

I grab a folder with my name on it and begin my education. *2096: In the wake of the American collapse and the food riots that took place across the world, the new Tory party suspends Parliament. The rebellion begins.*

Chapter 22

Dawn

I hate this. I hate the room they've put us in. I hate the way the boat rocks. Back and forth, back and forth until I feel like I need to puke. I hate the creepy captain who lets us out whenever his men have gone to shore. It's all shite. We stop often to make deliveries at the tiny farming villages along the river. They're nothing more than ramshackle huts grouped together on the edge of a field.

Allison tells us we're on the Mississippi river and only have one more Texan checkpoint between us and the rebels.

We're tied up on the river bank when they come.

The captain's men are on shore picking up merchandise so Gabby, Drew, and I are on deck. I see it first. A truck is driving straight towards us and they'll be here in no time. I immediately duck down behind the railing and drag the other two with me.

"Ouch, Dawn," Gabby protests.

"Shit," the captain says as he walks up behind us. "Get below deck." We don't hesitate. We pull the hidden door shut behind us and the captain conceals it.

I grab onto Gabby's hand as we hear them board. The sounds move closer. Heavy footsteps sound on the stairs.

"What's in these boxes?" someone asks.

"Oh, a little of this and a little of that," the captain responds evasively.

More footsteps on the stairs.

"Captain," someone says, "we are looking for three escaped prisoners. You wouldn't happen to know anything about that, would you?"

I tense up.

"No, I'm afraid not, soldier," he answers, much to my relief. "I like to stay on the right side of the law and stay in the Prophet's good graces."

"We'll see about that." There's more noise as boxes are moved around and opened. I wait for them to find the hidden door but they don't.

I grip Gabby tighter and reach out for Drew, but he doesn't take my hand.

"Like I said," Captain Collins states angrily. "I know nothing."

"Well, that's too bad because you're carrying stolen merchandise. My second in command will escort you to the capitol."

Just like that. It's over. We're headed back to the capitol. I lean my head back and squeeze my eyes shut. This can't be happening.

A little while later, our door creaks open. Here it comes. They're giving us up. I look towards the door and Allison is beckoning us out. She leads us up onto the deck and I look around, panicked. Surely we'll be seen. Towards the back of the boat, there's a small wooden dinghy.

"You expect us to get away in that?" Gabby snaps.

"I'm getting away in that," Allison says. "You can come if you want. I don't really care. It's your choice." She gets in and waits for us to follow. Having no other option, that's what we do.

The tiny boat sways, suspended in midair. Allison works a hand crank that lowers us slowly. We hit the water with a loud slap, but no one seems to have heard us. Allison hands Gabby an oar and together they row us away from the larger boat.

I look back and the captain is standing at the rail, watching us row away. We've gotten away without being seen by the soldiers.

"Don't worry," Allison assures us. "Even if they knew we got away, they won't be able to come after us tonight."

"Why not?" Gabby asks. "We're barely moving."

"Captain Collin's men won't be back for a while yet and it takes time to get a boat that size moving."

"Why didn't the captain just give us up?" I ask.

"He's a smuggler," Allison shrugs. "I chose him to take us because of his reputation. He's loyal to the money and if he were to give up his client's illegal business, no one would trust him." She pauses. "It's ironic how the most trustworthy people are the ones dealing outside the law." Allison grows quiet and hands me her oar before leaning back. Drew tries to take Gabby's but she won't let him. He's still too weak.

"Are you okay?" I ask him for the millionth time as I dip my oar back into the water.

"I'm fine," Drew mumbles. In the darkness, I can't see his face but I can hear the pain in his voice. I want to be there for him, but he's retreated further into his own mind since we left Vicksburg.

I look away to stare into the dark water. When I speak again, my voice is no more than a whisper on the breeze. "I don't believe you."

Chapter 23

Gabby

I don't know how far we've come by the time the sun rises. We can't be seen on the river so we pull the small boat up the riverbank near a thick patch of trees. Allison tells us we can only spare an hour or so to rest. It's not nearly enough.

My stomach gurgles and growls. I don't know how we're going to find something to eat out here. We have nothing to hunt with and even if we did, we can't risk the fire to cook it on and the smoke that would come with it.

We leave the boat hidden after about an hour and get moving. According to Allison, there's a farming village nearby.

"A Texan village?" I ask.

"In name only," she explains. "These people don't like the Texan soldiers any more than we do. They're forced to give a majority of their crops to the cities while they live in squalor. They feel abandoned by their prophet, but her soldiers rule them with an iron fist. They have no choice but to do as she says."

We pass field after field with busy people doing back-breaking work before we reach the village. Village might be too big of a word for what we find. The light is fading in the distance as we take in the small cluster of homes. The east end of London looks a lot less dodgy than this place.

Allison knocks on a door just as three Texan soldiers come into view. A woman answers and ushers us inside. She sticks her head out the door to make sure we weren't seen and then promptly closes it.

"Allison, what are you doing here?" she asks. I guess I shouldn't be surprised that they know each other.

"We had no other choice," Allison says.

"Do you even know what's been going on here?" the woman asks, but she doesn't give Allison the chance to answer. "We've been flooded with soldiers. They say they're here to check on the crops, but I know there is something else going on. You being here proves it."

"Bria," Allison pleads, "I'm so sorry to involve you in this, but we have to reach the rebel compound."

"There are troops stationed from here to the final checkpoint." She looks at the three of us behind Allison. "You're never going to make it in your condition. Sit. I'll get you something to eat." We do as we're told. She didn't ask who we are and I get the impression that she doesn't want to know. It's safer that way.

She brings out small plates of salted fish and potatoes. "I'm sorry it's not much," she says quietly. We dig in, too hungry to really care what it is. We finish eating and give our plates to Bria just as two tall men barge into the room. They each give us a nasty look before turning their attention to Bria.

"Hey, Mom," the younger of the two says as he kisses her cheek.

"I told you never to come back here, Allison," the other man says dangerously. "Bria is done passing along your messages."

"She doesn't have to do anything this time, Tom," Allison says calmly. "I'm going myself."

"Good," he responds. "Then you can be on your way." He points towards the door.

"Tom," Bria chides.

"Don't. They're not welcome in my home. Allison only brings trouble."

"Corey, dear, there's a plate for you by the stove," Bria says. "I need to speak with your father alone."

They step outside and their raised voices drift into us. In the end, Bria comes back in alone. "Now," she begins, "I'm sure you're all tired. You may rest here, but you must be gone by sunrise."

Chapter 24

Gabby

It's still dark when Bria's son Corey shakes me awake. "Is it morning already?" I ask sleepily.

"No," he answers, "but my dad gave you up." That jolts me awake. Corey hands me a bag filled with food. I look inside and it dawns on me that this is probably all they have.

"I'm sending Corey with you," Bria informs us. Allison tries to protest, but it doesn't do any good. "He knows the land in these parts and can get you through unseen."

"Mom," Corey says, "I need to stay here to protect you."

"No, you don't." She stands on her tip toes to kiss his cheek and hug him before pushing him towards the door. He gives her one last look before bowing his head in obedience and stepping outside. We follow him just in time. As soon as we round the corner of the hut, a group of squaddies barge through the door without knocking. Bria screams as they drag her out.

"Where'd they go?" a soldier barks at her.

"I don't know!"

"Let her go," Tom yells, "you promised you wouldn't hurt my family if I gave you the fugitives!"

"But you didn't give us anything and your wife has even aided them. You have gone against the Prophet and that can't go unpunished," the soldier pauses, "I wonder, where is that lad of yours?"

Corey pulls out a knife and starts to make a move to help his parents, but Allison stops him. "They'll only kill you too," she whispers. "There's nothing you can do."

He leans his head back against the wall and squeezes his eyes shut as silent tears spill down his face.

"They're not here, sir, what should we do?"

"Take care of those two and then check the river. To get here this fast they must have come by boat."

Bria and Tom's screams are cut off abruptly by two quick pops. The soldiers leave the bodies where they lay and head off to the river.

Chapter 25

Dawn

Corey is silent as he leads us into the tree cover. Allison says he has to come to rebel base with us now because, if he goes back, he's a dead man. Talk about a wounded group. Gabby and Drew with their mental scars that will never heal completely. Corey still reeling from losing both his parents only hours ago. I don't know Allison's story yet.

"Someone's been on this trail recently," Corey says.

"Texan soldiers?" Allison asks, suddenly alert.

"No." He bends down to examine something in the dirt. He pinches his lips into a worried expression.

"What's wrong?" Gabby asks.

Corey straightens up. "Let's keep moving," he responds, completely ignoring Gabby's question. "Stay alert."

"Not until you tell us why." Gabby stands her ground. Corey glares at her.

"Gabby..." I try to diffuse the situation, but she cuts me off.

"Shut it, Dawn," she snaps, "We deserve to know who's after us this time." Corey lunges for Gabby and grabs her by the throat. He holds her still with one arm. Drew and I try to pull him away, but he's too strong.

"You don't deserve a damn thing," Corey yells. "People like you go around doing whatever the hell you want without a thought about who you hurt in the process. I'll bet most people tend to die after helping you."

I stop trying to pull Corey away as Sam's face shows up in my head. Corey isn't finished. Gabby kicks at him, trying to break free.

"Before you all showed up, I had a life. It was a hard life, but it was a life all the same. My parents..." He takes a long pause. "My parents were good people." He releases Gabby and backs away. Gabby rubs her throat and glares at him.

"The only people who would use these trails are freedom fighters," Corey says, regaining his composure.

"This close to the rebel compound?" Allison gasps.

"They've been coming down here for the past few years to pillage our farms. They don't care about the rebels in the area because they can move pretty well unseen. We need to keep moving."

Eventually, Corey finds us a spot to rest for the night near a stream that feeds into the river.

Gabby, Allison, and I immediately head for the stream to wash up. We don't have soap or clean clothes, but I still can't remember the last time water felt this good against my skin. The boys wash after us and Allison starts a fire. She says we should be fine this far from the river as long as we contain the smoke.

"Dawn, would you get me some water?" Allison hands me a small pan. It was one of the few possessions Bria had and she sent it with us. I pass Corey on the way, but Drew is still getting dressed when I reach the stream. His linen pants no longer look white and he has yet to put his shirt on. I freeze when I see the bruises that stretch across his chest. He looks at me and I see the pain in his eyes and in his every movement. He reaches down to grab his shirt and noticeably winces.

"Here, let me help you." I rush towards him, but he steps back.

"I can do it," he protests.

"Obviously not. Let me help you." I take the shirt from him and reach towards his chest. I wish I could make everything better.

"Don't." He grabs my hand in midair and then recoils from the contact. It takes time, but I finally get his shirt on him. As I pull it down,

I catch his eyes before he quickly looks away. Taking the hint, I turn away from him.

"I have to get some water," I say, hurrying away.

Chapter 26

Gabby

We exit the woods after what seemed like an eternity and an empty plane stretches before us. The hills roll in the distance. "We're close to the final Texan checkpoint," Corey informs us. "We should be fine as long as we stay far enough from the river, but keep an eye out." We've been lucky enough so far to not run into the type of trouble Corey thought we'd have.

About midday we see a truck crest over a hill on the horizon. It's coming straight for us and there's nowhere to hide. I look around, but we're right in the open. We can't run. I curse the fact that I only have my knife to protect me. I take it out and hold it behind my back. The truck is closing in. I step closer to Dawn to protect her. She doesn't even draw her knife.

The truck stops and a man in a Texan uniform steps out; his rifle resting lightly in his hands. He steps closer. He's so close I could slit his throat right here. I hold back for now. The soldier pulls out a piece of paper from his pocket. Silently, he unfolds it and holds it next to my face.

"It's them," he yells back to the truck. To our group, he says, "You are hereby arrested as fugitives trying to flee the republic. On orders from the Prophet, we're returning you to the capitol." More soldiers pile out of the truck, as do men in grotty street clothes.

Before I can make a move, Corey pushes me out of the way and grabs the soldier by his collar. There's a quick flash of steel and then Corey has his knife pressed against the soldier's throat.

"Back up," Corey yells at the rest of the Texans. Half of them now have their guns raised and the other half don't know what to do.

"Do it," the soldier being threatened by Corey demands.

"Take his gun," Corey orders. I yank it out of the man's grasp, feeling the heavy weight of the firearm in my hands. Adrenaline pumps through me.

The standoff ends abruptly when a Texan soldier fires at Corey. The bullet hits the soldier Corey is restraining instead. Corey's arm shoots out and his knife flips end over end before plunging into the chest of the man who took the shot.

What happens next is a blur. Dawn retrieves the dead soldier's gun as the rest of the Texans duck behind their truck. After tearing his knife free, Corey runs after them. Alison cuts down two men in civilian clothes who don't seem to know what to do with their guns.

A large man runs at me so I duck sideways and spin around. He's moving fast and my first shot misses. I fire again and hit his leg. He screams and clutches at his thigh as he tumbles to the ground. I jump back to keep him from pulling me down. The look on his face is one of complete horror when I pull my trigger once more. Point blank. His head jerks back from the impact and then the still mask of death covers his face.

Dawn is on the ground nearby so I run to her to make sure she's okay. She's only had the wind knocked out of her. I breathe out in relief. She's alright. Drew is sitting nearby with his head in his hands, breathing hard. Allison's arm has been grazed by a bullet and she holds it close to her chest. Corey took out a majority of our attackers and doesn't even look like he's broken a sweat. I watch him pull his knife free and clean it on the grass.

"You all take a lot more effort to protect than you're worth," Corey says as he pulls a man out from behind the truck.

"What now?" I ask.

Chapter 27

Dawn

That's not a man. He's only a boy. Dirt streaks down his face as his sobs become audible. His shorts are fraying and his shirt is torn. He wears no shoes and he looks like he hasn't had anything to eat in days. Corey drops him in front of us before dragging an old gaffer into the open.

"Dad," the boy screams.

"Please," the father urges. "Don't hurt my boy. He's only twelve years old."

Corey pulls Allison aside to talk, leaving Drew, Gabby, and I to watch this man and his son.

"Why should we spare anyone?" Gabby snaps. "You tried to kill us."

"They made us do it," the man says fervently. "We're just farm workers, see?" He holds up his hands to show us his callouses. I crouch next to him and speak softly.

"They forced you into the army?" He nods. "Your twelve-year-old son too?"

"They needed men on the ground searching for fugitives in the area," he explains.

I straighten up. "We have to get them back to their village," I tell my sister.

"No way," Gabby argues. "They tried to kill us."

"They didn't have a choice."

"Something has to be done about them. We can't trust them enough to leave them behind us." Her grip tightens on her rifle.

"Gabby's right," Drew chimes in. I turn on him.

"They deserve our help, not our hatred. Why can't you prats understand that?"

"Rubbish. Did I deserve the hatred in Texas?" he yells. "Did Gabby?"

"There is a major difference here."

"I don't see it," Gabby says. "They're Texans; their only purpose is to obey their prophet."

"How many Texans have helped in our escape?"

Gabby and Drew share a look that I'm not privy to. The boy is still sobbing on the ground and his father's eyes are asking for our help. They widen in shock as his body goes rigid and he falls to the side.

"Dad," the boy screams, crawling over to the dead farmer. I look to Gabby who still has her gun drawn. Her face is unreadable. I tear my eyes away from her and run to the boy who is hugging his father's lifeless body with all his strength. I kneel down and pull him to me. He's stiff at first, but then he buries his face in my neck. His tears dampen my shirt as I rub his back to calm him down. I look up at my sister.

"Who are you?" I say to her.

"What the hell?" Corey screams as his eyes fixate on the dead man and his sobbing son.

"It needed to be done," Gabby shrugs.

"The hell it did." His voice quiets into a low, menacing drawl, "That man was practically a slave. They used to take men from my village. They take them from the fields for a specific job and return them when they're finished. When I was a kid, I was taken to fight a group of Americans." His face is dangerous as he regards Gabby and Drew. "You really don't care how many people have to die because of you, do you?" He turns. "Get in the truck. The boy comes with us."

Chapter 28

Gabby

I'm wearing a Texan uniform that stinks of the dead man I took it from. This is how we're going to get through the Texan checkpoint. The boy is hidden in a crate in the back because they would never send someone so young on a trading expedition. We're supposed to be heading north for negotiations with the Americans.

With that story, we get through the checkpoint without any problems. The soldiers believe us right away because they don't believe anyone would willingly leave the protected lands of Texas. They believe that their God only protects people in close proximity to their prophet. Their mistake.

We let the boy out once we're sufficiently clear. Dawn immediately starts to dote on him. His name is Matthew, but Dawn has already started calling him Matty. The kid is scared to come near me. I don't blame him. I hear him crying at night and it reminds me of when Dawn and I were first on our own. At least he has Dawn to look after him. When I was his age, I had to take care of both myself and my little sister.

There's nothing out here, well nothing big enough to be rebel headquarters anyway. Allison and Corey say we're close but the empty hills stretch far into the distance. It'll take us days to cross the expanse. The only structures I see are a small shack and the windmills that surround it. Something around here is using energy. What is it?

"Shit," Corey says as three trucks seem to come from nowhere. Corey turns us around and floors it. Allison grabs for the wheel.

"Chill out," she yells. "Stop the car." Corey ignores her. "Now," she commands. She yanks the wheel and Corey slams on the brakes. The vehicles that were chasing us only seconds ago surround us. We're circled by a group of people with their guns drawn. They're not Texans. I notice that with one glance. I grip my gun tightly and step out. I'm no match for them. As soon as I'm out, they disarm me and cuff my hands behind my back. I try to jerk free as they push me to the ground.

"Sir, we've got the intruders," the soldier says as he digs his knee into my back. It takes a couple of guys to subdue Corey. Eventually, they jam the butt of a gun into his head and his strength drains immediately.

I only see the commander's feet as he circles us silently. "What are Texan soldiers doing this far North?" he demands.

"Screw Texas," Drew spits.

"Get him to his feet," the officer barks. Drew winces as they pull him up by the shoulders but then he stares straight ahead defiantly.

"Let's see..." The commander stops mid-sentence, "Drew?" Drew's eyes widen in recognition but he does not speak. "Don't pay attention to the uniforms." The commander turns away from us. "They're not Texan. They're British scum."

Chapter 29

Dawn

A cold, stone floor greets me when I wake.

"I need to see Jonathan," Allison is saying to the guard.

"He'll be here shortly," the guard responds. Allison isn't satisfied. We wait all morning until he comes, trying to suss out what to say to him. The door opens and in he walks.

"Jonathan," Allison says, relieved.

"Sorry for the rough treatment, but we had to check out your story that you've been operating as a rebel spy. It's not often my men see a bunch of Texans drive right up to our front door.

"No problem, sir," she says.

From a dark corner, Drew emerges and walks towards the commander. "James?" he utters in disbelief. "James?"

"Hello, Drew," the commander says as their eyes meet.

"Wait a second," I say, "Jonathan Clarke is-"

"James," Drew finishes my sentence.

"Your brother? The brother your dad sent to Floridaland?" I look from Drew to Jonathan and neither can take their eyes off the other.

"I thought you were dead," Drew says.

"That was the point," Jonathan says. "Heard you were dead too. Regardless, you aren't supposed to be here. You nearly got yourself killed again." He effectively ends the welcome speech. He turns to Allison.

"We found valuable Intel among your possessions," he accuses.

"For the rebels," she explains curtly.

"So you say."

"Sir, with all due respect. You have only been in charge here for a short time. I have been a rebel asset in Texas for years."

"What about them?" he gestures towards us.

"A couple farmers and…" she pauses, "General Nolan's daughters."

Jonathan coughs suddenly. "What? Our Intel told us they were killed."

"Your Intel was wrong." Allison stares him down. I watch him consider us. There's something not quite right in his eyes. They look wild while his demeanor remains calm.

Jonathan turns abruptly and leaves. No one speaks. I try to talk to Drew, but he won't say anything about James or Jonathan or whoever he is. The hours roll by. I stare at the door, willing it to open. It finally does and a familiar man steps through.

"Lee." A grin breaks out on my face.

His face is serious, as per usual. Forgetting everything, I jump up and run the short distance to him. He catches me and hugs me tight before setting me down.

"It's so good to see you," I say. "I didn't know if you were alive or…" I stop, unable to complete the sentence.

"If I'd known you were okay, I never would have left those woods," he says as a flash of guilt crosses his face.

"I know."

"Sam didn't make it, did he?"

I shake my head and his shoulders hunch forward.

"I'm sorry," I say, feeling like a proper prat for not coming up with something better.

"He was a good brother," Lee says. "He deserved better."

"What's with the uniform? You a ranker now?" Gabby asks, ruining the moment. Lee straightens up.

"I'm a rebel soldier," he says proudly. "I've been sent to take you to your room."

"Finally." Gabby pushes past him. "I'm so sick of being a prisoner everywhere I go."

Lee shows us to our assigned bunks. The room is tiny, with just enough beds for the six of us. "There are some clothes in the closet so you can stop looking like traitors. I suggest you make use of the shower as well." Lee leaves us, saying he has a meeting to get to and that he'll be back when he can. Something has changed in him. There's an edge to him, a professionalism in every move he makes. It's probably the uniform. His posture is straighter. His eyes are sharper. His presence is larger.

As I watch him walk from the room wondering what's gotten into him, I realize I've missed Lee. Having him around provides a sense of comfort and safety. He's my protector. After washing up and changing, I lay back on my cot and only close my eyes for a second before I feel the end of my bed move. Matty has curled up near my feet.

"You okay, buddy?" I ask him.

"I don't like it here," he whispers.

"Why not? We don't know anything about this place yet."

"I want to go home."

I lean towards him and kiss the top of his head. "Me too, kid."

Chapter 30

Miranda

I walk through the underground labyrinth, making my way to command for yet another meeting. It seems like the only thing they do here is hold meetings. I'm getting really tired of it. I haven't seen the sky since the day I arrived. Everyone here is so pale from living underground. The only people that get to venture outside are those on the patrols. Shite, I would love to be on one of those right about now.

I open the door to the meeting room and Jonathan immediately comes to shake my hand. He's started to call me Miranda. I prefer Officer Edwards to keep it professional, but he's hell bent on becoming friends. I want to keep my distance. Something isn't quite right about him. His eyes are shifty and his smile is just...off. To be a rebel, you have to be a little crazy, but sometimes I think he might be the biggest nutter of us all.

"I have a couple of soldiers I'd like you to meet," he says as he leads me across the room. Two men in uniforms are standing along the wall. They salute as I walk up.

"At ease," Jonathan orders. "Miranda, this is Lee and Jeremy." Once again, I'm struck by his informal nature.

"Soldiers." I nod in greeting.

"These two are our shining stars," Jonathan yells suddenly. "They have only been here a few months and have already mastered their training."

"Is that so?" I ask distractedly, trying to figure Jonathan out.

"Yes, sir," they snap in unison.

"Well, congratulations."

"Jeremy here was actually in one of those Floridaland camps until Lee went and pinched him from right under the slaver's noses," Jon explains. "We're going to get those fascist bastards eventually."

"That's quite the accomplishment." I ignore his last comment as I turn to Jon. "How many escaped prisoners have you enlisted?"

"Here? Oh, I don't know. Probably about ten or so. But, beyond here, hundreds. They're a very resourceful people. I was in one of those camps myself for about a year or so before General Nolan was able to fake my death to help me escape." To Lee and Jeremy, he says, "that will be all soldiers. Our meeting is about to start so you should be on your way." They salute and hurry off.

I don't even understand why this meeting has been called until it's half way through. The first part is all nonsense. We talk about which soldiers are ready for active duty and which are struggling. Then awards and commendations are discussed until finally, Jonathan says, "For those of you who haven't heard, we've released the intruders we captured." This sets the room abuzz.

"Mind telling us why?" I ask the obvious.

"Allison has brought us some valuable information," he says.

"Who's Allison?" I interrupt.

"She's a rebel spy that has been living in Texas," he explains irritably. "Her final mission was to get herself out and get here. My predecessor put her final orders into play over a year ago. She was able to get here, but not alone." His eyes scan the officers around the table and then land on me. I do not like the look he gives me. "She brought General Nolan's daughters." Everyone starts talking at once, but I don't hear any of it. All I can hear is a rushing in my ears.

I steady my breathing so that I don't draw attention to myself. I don't know how Jonathan seems to know I'm the girls' mother.

"I thought only one of them was in the colonies," a woman to my right says.

"That was Gabby," Jonathan says. "Dawn is her younger sister. She got Gabby out and then they ended up in Texas."

Hearing their names sends a shock wave through my body as a panic starts to build.

They were supposed to be out of my life forever. I was the mother that abandoned her children, but I had a reason. I had a really good reason. Tears well up, but I wipe them away quickly.

"Are you okay, Miranda?"

"I'm fine."

"We all owe General Nolan a lot," Jonathan is saying. "Let's make sure his daughters are taken care of. They had a tough journey to get here. The boy, Drew, is already being treated in Medical. He was held prisoner in Texas and we all know what that means." The sympathetic murmurs around the table are almost too much for me. "The rest of them need quite a bit of rest." Jonathan stands. "That is all for now." I move to follow the others out the door, but Jonathan calls me back.

"Yes, sir?"

"I respect your choice," he says.

"What choice?" I ask.

"You've made some tough decisions in your life. We all have. The rebels are better for it. I thank you for your sacrifice."

As I walk down the command hallway, I think about what he said. Somehow, I don't think I want that man agreeing with anything I've done.

Gabby. Dawn. Oh my God, they're here.

Chapter 31

Gabby

I follow Dawn out into the hallway, trying to get her alone to talk. I'm so sick of her being mad at me. She doesn't give me the chance to say anything. She keeps walking in front of me. I leg it to catch up with her and am surprised to find her calm and even smiling. We wander past rankers at their posts. Their eyes follow us as we go. It's late and most of the doors are locked, but some of the training rooms have been left open.

In London, I already had my military assignment. That's the life I saw for myself and after everything I've been through, it's finally possible. I look sideways as Dawn and her eyes are wide in amazement. I can almost see the wheels turning in her head. She'll want to know how this place is possible; how it was built, pretty much everything about it.

After a while, we're stopped by two soldiers on their night shift rounds.

"Curfew was twenty minutes ago," the first one says gruffly. "Do you need to be escorted to your bunks?"

"No," I snap as Dawn stands silently beside me. We quickly run back to our rooms and are laughing by the time we step through the door. It feels good to laugh with my sister again. It's been a while. She looks at me as if to say something, but reconsiders it and crawls into bed. I don't have time to dwell on that before I hear someone knock on the door.

"Pssst, Gabby." I look around, but I'm the only one still up. "Gabby." I hear again. I get to my feet and tip toe to the door so as not to wake anyone. I push it open and have to contain a scream.

Jeremy.

I jump towards him and he catches me in a fierce hug. He buries his face in my hair and whispers, "I've missed you." I lean back to look at his face and run my fingertips down his cheek. I smile and he leans in and kisses me softly. He sets me back on my feet.

"You have no idea how happy I am to see you," I say.

"I think I do," he responds. He hears something behind him and turns to look but there is nothing there. "I have to go back to my dorm," he says. When my face falls, he explains, "If I break curfew, I'll have to pull extra duties tomorrow." He leans his forehead against mine. "I just had to see you though." He sighs, before kissing my head and leaving in the direction he came.

Chapter 32

Dawn

I don't know what we're supposed to be doing here. I feel like rubbish just sitting around. I've explored a bit, but I don't like walking around here on my own. Corey decided to leave yesterday to go look for a settlement up north. He decided that this wasn't his fight and he wanted nothing to do with these people. I asked him to take Matty with him because this compound is no place for a kid. I don't want the rebels pressing him into service. It was a tearful goodbye. I promised him I would see him again. I just hope my last words to him weren't a lie. His absence has left me gutted because kids have the ability to make everything just a little better.

I haven't been able to see much of Lee. He's stopped by a few times just to say hi, but he can never stay for long. Other than that, we sit around our dorm, doing absolutely nothing. Allison comes and goes as she attends all sorts of meetings but the rest of us have been left to our own devices.

Drew hasn't seen Jonathan since we were his prisoners and he's doing his best to avoid dealing with it. I wish I could talk to him about it; be there for him. I know how much his brother means to him. We've made some progress, Drew and I, but nothing substantial.

Done exploring for the day, I walk into the room to find Lee waiting for me.

"Hey, little lady," he says. I cringe as he tries to imitate Sam.

"Please don't call me that," I say as I sit next to him.

"Still too painful?"

"It isn't for you?"

"I guess thinking about him and the way he was is less painful than forgetting." He looks away from me and I put my arm around him.

"You're right. Sam was the best friend I ever had. I won't soon forget that."

"Ma is going to be devastated when she gets here," he says.

"Ma is coming here?" I ask.

"Yeah. There are American refugees here from all over. Shay got here ahead of the group, but she says they're on their way. Even the caves weren't safe anymore and it isn't easy to reach the Americans in the North."

The mention of Ma makes me happy, but the fact that Shay is here does not. She had a thing for Drew and she hated me. She acted like such a slag last time I saw her. She's going to make it that much harder to get things with him back to the way they were. Wanting to change the subject, I ask, "So, how did you and Jeremy make it here?"

"Well," he begins, "after we were separated from Gabby, we ended up in a different part of the woods, away from the fighting. Jeremy was injured. A bullet had clipped his leg. He wanted to go back when we heard the bomb, but I wouldn't let him because he wouldn't have made it. I bandaged him up with my shirt and we stumbled off towards the river. We walked for three days until it was too much for Jeremy. His leg was infected badly. I lay him down, expecting him to be dead in the morning, but we were awakened by rebel soldiers pointing their guns at us. They saved our lives."

"Wow, and now you're soldiers."

"Yes we are," he says with a sense of pride.

"Soldier," a command rings out from the door. Lee shoots to his feet and raises his arm in salute as Jonathan Clarke stands in the open doorway.

"Yes, sir?" Lee responds.

"I believe you have a training session scheduled right about now," Jonathan says sternly. "Off you go." Lee gives one final salute to Jonathan and a smile to me before he leaves. Jonathan doesn't follow him. Instead, he steps further into the room and studies me.

"Why did my father tell me to find you," I blurt after a few moments of uncomfortable silence.

Jonathan smiles. "General Nolan has been a great friend to the rebels and an even greater friend to me. He helped me escape the Floridaland camps." There is something sinister in the smile he gives me.

"I forgot, Drew told me you were sent to be a slave," I respond. My father seems to be a popular man in the colonies.

"Ah yes," he says, "my little brother, Drew. Never thought I'd see him again. I suppose I should thank you for saving his life. But then, he's not the same Drew, is he? Something seems a bit off with him." I want to tell him that he's one to talk, but I don't.

"That's because he was detained and tortured in Texas," I snap, suddenly defensive of a boy who has barely spoken to me in weeks. "All because of who your father is."

"My father," he says under his breath, but it's loud enough for me to hear. There's something about the way he says it though that I don't understand. He straightens up and flattens the creases in his uniform before saying, "well, Dawn, it's been a pleasure talking to you, but I must be on my way." He leaves before I can even say goodbye.

Chapter 33

Drew

I can't help but watch Dawn from across the room as she talks to Lee. I missed her smile. Her eyes wander over to me and she looks away quickly. I don't blame her. I've been a right git lately, but I can't help it. I have so much anger right now. Dawn wants to comfort me, but I can't let her.

I'm not myself.

As she tucks a strand of hair behind her ear, I can't take my eyes away.

Please, Dawn, don't give up on me yet. Give me time to come back to you.

Chapter 34

Drew

I've been walking through these halls for hours. I think I've seen pretty much every inch of this place, but I don't stop. Walking keeps my mind occupied. I focus on one step and then the next. I stop in and watch some of the training. Some of these soldiers are amazing at what they do.

Jeremy can hit the center of a target nine times out of ten when you put a rifle in his hands. Lee can beat almost anyone in hand to hand combat. These soldiers climb the ropes hanging from the ceiling like they're nothing. They throw knives and never miss. I've seen some of the training for the rankers in London and it's nowhere near as intense as this. I guess it doesn't need to be when they're only used as a police force. This army of rebels is meant for something so much more.

I don't know where I am now. I got turned around a few minutes ago and never sussed it out. I walk past what seems to be a row of offices. As I pass, I hear my name.

"Drew," Jonathan yells from a nearby office. I decide to ignore it because I don't know if I can handle him wittering on about duty and whatever else excuse he tries to give me for not reaching out since I got here. I wouldn't know if I was talking to my brother or the leader of the rebels. Which one was it that was unhappy to see me?

"Drew." He's right behind me this time so I turn.

"What?" I snap.

"You're not supposed to be in this area." Oh, it's the rebel leader, not my brother.

"Sorry, I'll just go." I try to get away as quickly as possible, but he grabs my arm.

"We need to talk," he says as he pulls me into his office and shuts the door.

"Well," I say, "first answer me this, do I call you Jonathan or James?"

"That's what we need to talk about. My name isn't James. I was born as Jonathan Clarke."

"Then who is James?" I ask, irritated.

"My assignment," he says.

"What?" =

"I'm not explaining this well," he says. "I'm not your brother. I never was."

"I don't understand," I say.

"My mother had an affair with your father, yes, but my mother was also a rebel. She had me a year after the affair and my real father had died. The rebels saw the perfect opportunity."

"Opportunity for what?" I ask harshly, beginning to understand how daft I've been.

"To place me in the Crawford household," he admits. "While I was spending summers with you, I was reporting back on your father."

"But you were just a kid," I snap, the anger boiling up inside of me, trying to break free.

"The rebels use kids for a lot of things." He's quiet for a moment before he continues. "That's not all."

"What more could there be. I already know that the brother I thought I had was a lie. I know what a fool I've been to miss you and try to find you. My father was right about you all along." It's harsh, but I can't help it. James was the one member of my family that I thought I could count on before he was sent away. My father never trusted him. He thought James was dangerous. I always defended him. In one short moment, the life I thought I had has been reduced to shambles.

"As we got older my orders changed," he says. "I still had to report on your father, but I had previously reported that you and your father did not see eye to eye. I was told to drive that wedge in further- to make sure you remained distanced from him. That's when I started teaching you about the Bible. I knew that would cause irreparable harm to the relationship. I was following orders."

In an instant, I lunge across the desk and punch him in the face. He tries to block me, but my anger is too strong. "It was all a lie. You. My father. Lies." I scream, but he doesn't look scared. He actually has the audacity to look sad for hurting me. I punch him again and, this time, soldiers come rushing into the room. They grab my arms to restrain me but Jonathan puts up his hands.

"Let him go," he says. I yank my arms free of their loosening grips and stalk from the room.

Chapter 35

Drew

My fists clench and unclench repeatedly as I walk down the hall. I don't know where I'm heading, but I know I need to get as far away from that office as I can. As I'm wandering aimlessly, I feel someone fall in step beside me. It's Shay, from the caves.

"Hey stranger," she says.

"Hi, Shay." I don't look up.

"Geez, what's wrong with you?" she asks.

"Nothing," I snap.

"I don't believe you," she says. Why won't this girl just leave me alone?

"I don't want to talk to you about it." I regret the harshness in my voice as soon as I let it out.

"Ouch," she says, placing a hand over her heart, feigning hurt. "Well, Dawn is in training room A if you need to talk to someone." She speeds up to walk past me, but not before turning one last time. "Oh, and I know what a dick you've been to her lately. Lee told me. She'll forgive you if you let her." With that, she practically skips away. I'm sure if my pretend brother saw her do that in uniform he'd be narked. I smile. Anything to upset that arse.

I don't realize where I'm going until I find myself standing outside training room A. I reach for the door handle and then pull my hand back. How can I talk to Dawn? I haven't been able to control the way I've been treating her. I have this anger inside of me that makes things come out of my mouth that I instantly regret. I can't help it. My bruises are finally healing and it's no longer painful to move, but I still can't stand to be touched. The entire time I was in Texas, every touch came with pain. Every word had a motive.

I tell myself to grow some balls and I reach for the door again. I pull it open and search the room for Dawn. I find her near the back wall with Lee. He's teaching her to fight as I walk up.

"Okay, Dawn, now I want you to do the sequence we worked on before. Punch, punch, punch, kick. Aim for the pads each time. Use all your strength," Lee instructs.

I watch as she follows his lead. I didn't even know she'd started training, let alone that she isn't half bad. It shows how out of touch I've been. Lee spots me first and waves me over. Dawn turns and her face drops when she sees me. I don't blame her.

"Drew," Lee says. "Are you finally starting your training?" This Lee is much different than the one that helped us get to Floridaland. For one, he talks a lot more.

"Not today," I say. "Dawn, can I talk to you?" I wait for her answer anxiously. She has no reason to say yes. She looks to Lee, unsure of what to do.

"We'll pick this up later," he tells her, "go."

She turns to me and nods slowly. I lead the way through the maze of soldiers honing their skills. Once we get to the dorm and shut the door behind us, we're alone. There's no commotion to distract us now and I don't know what I should say. How do I start?

The shyness in her demeanor is killing me. I did that. I know I did. She is no longer comfortable around me and the air is charged with things unsaid. I take a seat on my bed and Dawn sits on Gabby's, which is right next to me. She scoots to the opposite end so we're not right across from each other. We sit in silence for what seems like an eternity before I begin.

"I didn't know who else to talk to," I say. "I wasn't sure if I could still come to you." She nods and I continue, "I talked to James or I guess his name is Jonathan."

"James as in your brother?" she asks patiently.

"As in my fake brother," I say. I tell her the entire story of finding myself in his office and learning the truth about my supposed brother and his mother. I even tell her about my reaction to him without glossing over the violent parts. As I talk, she listens, but not like most people listen as they think of other things. She truly listens. I can see it in her eyes. It's the same look I saw when I told her about James in the first place. We were sitting on the ground leaning on the cabin wall at the caves. That's when I fell for her, only I didn't know it yet.

I finish my story and she moves from Gabby's bed to mine and grabs my hand. For the first time since Texas, I don't flinch away. She doesn't say she's sorry as most people would. She knows how empty that word is. Instead, she reaches up to touch my face. I lean my cheek into her palm and she wraps her arms around me in a hug.

"It's going to be okay," she whispers.

Chapter 36

Miranda

One of the benefits of my high rank is access to the security cameras. I lean back in my office chair and watch the two images side by side. On the right, Gabby is in the shooting range. She has remarkable aim. On the left, Dawn is doing strength training. Strength conditioning and hand to hand fighting are the only two training exercises that Dawn will attempt. She refuses to pick up a gun and won't touch the knives. Her superiors tell me that she can't be a soldier without these skills. I don't know if she even wants to be a soldier. For one, she asks too many questions about everything.

Gabby is a gem. She seems to excel at whatever she tries. She was already assigned to the military in England. She will make a great rebel soldier even if she is a little cheeky at times.

They still don't know I'm here. I keep to the officer's wing and the command rooms. Jonathan keeps telling me that I need to face them if only to get it over with. He seems to think that I'm just scared of how they will make me look in front of the other soldiers; that it will undermine my authority. Only someone with a mindset like his would think that. He abhors family connections that get in the way. It's almost as if he is missing a part of his humanity. What I'm scared of is that I will meet them and instantly feel a motherly connection. I don't want to start questioning all of my past decisions. I don't want to start questioning my cause.

There's a knock at my door and I quickly switch off the screens.

"Come in," I call. Kira walks in. She's the soldier who has been assigned to assist me in whatever I need. She stops abruptly and salutes. I still haven't gotten used to that. The rebels in England seem so unorganized compared to these people. In London, they're not all soldiers. Some of them are in the English military but when they're about rebel business, they're just people.

"Sir," Kira says.

"Yes, soldier. What is it?" She doesn't flinch away from my abruptness as she did when I first got here.

"Officer Clarke would like to see you," she says. I wave her off and gather the papers on my desk. I need to see him as well. I walk the short distance to his office and enter without knocking. His assistant tries to stop me but I pay no attention.

Allison and Jonathan are hunched over the table in the middle of the room, looking at something. "Miranda come here," Jonathan beckons.

"What's going on?" I ask.

"Sir," Allison begins, "these are the maps that I brought back with me from Texas."

"Why wasn't I told about this sooner?" I demand.

"That doesn't matter now," Jonathan says excitedly. "This is why Allison was there for so many years. We now have almost everything we need to launch an attack." I walk to the table and look down. The maps are incredibly detailed. There are maps of the government buildings, the labs, and even the church. The street map alone is invaluable. I quickly get over my irritation of being out of the loop.

"Brilliant," I say softly.

"Yes," Jonathan begins, "now we just have to wait for our shipment from London."

"The one scheduled for two weeks from tomorrow?" I ask.

"The very one," he responds. "It will contain everything we need to take care of the Republic of Texas. We need to start our planning sessions right away."

"Sir, with all due respect, we don't have the numbers to launch a full-scale attack." Sometimes I think he doesn't live in reality.

"You are my second in command, Miranda. That doesn't mean you question my decisions. You're here to carry out my directives."

"Yes, sir." If there was one thing I learned in London, it was to follow orders. "I'll schedule the first meeting."

"Miranda," Jonathan calls as I'm leaving the room.

"Yes?" I ask.

"It's time." I don't need to ask him what he means because I already know. Before I can protest, he continues. "You will be leading the attacks with me. You will no longer be able to hide in your office watching them on screen. This is not a suggestion. It's an order. If you want to be the one to do it, you must tell them soon." I can't even be upset with him for forcing this on me. I know he's right. I need to get this in the past so I can focus on the battle to come.

Chapter 37

Gabby

This is where I belong. This is where I fit. I'm a soldier. I have not been given my uniform yet because I haven't officially been put in a unit, but I know I will be. This is what I was meant to do.

I pull the headphones down over my ears and square myself to the target. The simple round targets have been replaced by silhouettes of actual people. I've been told that this usually means that this isn't just target practice anymore. We're training for a mission. I raise my arm and tilt it sideways. This is my favorite stance. I squint my eyes and pull the trigger once; the bullet pierces the heart. Twice, it hits the head. The third bullet hits the eye. I never miss my targets. I feel good with a gun in my hand; powerful. Both Floridaland and Texas made me feel weak, unable to protect myself. I will never feel that way again.

I remove the head gear and set down the gun. I make my way to training room A. Jeremy has promised to teach me some combat moves so I can pass the test in a few weeks to make it into the military. Every waking moment is spent training for it.

Jeremy is waiting for me when I get there. "You're late Gabs," he says. "Were you at the shooting range again?"

"What's the big deal?" My exasperation gets the better of me.

"The big deal is that you spend way more time there than you should. You're a perfect shot so why waste training time there?"

"Let's just get started, okay?" He lets it go and we start sparring. I master every move he teaches me in only a couple of tries. My favorite is when takes me to a punching bag and I can hit it as hard as I want. I punch and kick until I'm too exhausted to do it anymore. Jeremy puts a towel around my shoulders when I'm finished.

"Are you alright?" he asks. For a reason that I don't quite understand, that question leaves me narked.

"I'm fine," I say before shoving him away from me and running from the room. I don't get far before I collide with someone out in the hall. I fall to the ground, panting.

"I'm so sorry, Gabby." I look up at the mention of my name and see a woman standing over me. She looks vaguely familiar, but I don't know from what. She grabs my arm to pull me to my feet.

"How do you know my name?" I ask.

"Everyone here does," she responds. "I was looking for you anyway. Will you come with me?"

"Who are you?" I demand.

"I'm Officer Edwards," she says. "I'm the second in command here." So, she's Jonathan's lackey. I follow her out of curiosity more than anything else. We end up in a part of the compound that I have never seen before. I hear the waterfall before I see it. At the far end of the room, there's a large pool and water splashes down the rocks in back. "Careful, the floor can be wet in here," she warns.

"What is this place?" I ask.

"We have to get our water from some place, right?" she asks. "This is an underground spring. The river isn't far from here so we always have water."

"I never knew this was here."

"You'd be amazed at the secrets this place holds." She smiles but there's a sadness behind it. "That's what we need to talk about." Before she can explain a radio in her pocket sputters on.

"Does anyone know the whereabouts of Officer Edwards? We need Miranda's signature." As soon as the voice cuts off and others respond to it, I look up and study her face more closely. Miranda.

"Mom?" I whisper, narrowing my eyes. She gives me that same sad smile and nods. I have no words as the thoughts and emotions swirl around in my head. Should I be hurt? Angry? Happy that she's alive? "Mom," I test out the word again.

"Gabby," she says, "let me explain." I nod, unable to speak. I don't know if her explanation will make a difference, but I want to know why. "I've been a rebel my whole life," she begins. "I tried to get out when I had you girls, but that wasn't so easy when my father was the leader of the rebellion. When we got the phone call that your father was dead, I knew it wasn't true. I knew that he was sent to a post in the colonies. I thought it meant they suspected me. I thought it would be safer for you girls if I left."

"Wait a second," I interrupt, finding my voice. "You thought it would be safer for us to live on the streets? We were kids and all of a sudden we were on our own, living in dodgy places."

"You were supposed to be taken in by the neighbor. I made arrangements. You're the ones who ran away," she snaps. "I had to choose between giving up my life with you girls or giving up my life as a rebel."

"You chose being a rebel," I say tiredly.

"You don't understand. I'm part of a cause that I would give my own life for. I will do whatever it takes for the rebels to succeed."

"You're wrong," I say.

"Gabby –" she begins, but I cut her off.

"You're wrong to say that I wouldn't understand. I do. I'm a rebel now too, Mom, and I will do what needs to be done to defeat those bastards. So, yeah, I forgive you because I get it. I wouldn't count on Dawn though. She won't understand and she won't forgive you."

"I know," she responds.

The radio crackles again. "Officer Edwards to the Commandant's office." One more look. A moment of sadness. One of hardness. And then she leaves.

When I get back to the dorms Dawn is in there talking to Drew. They've taken steps towards normalcy, but they still have a long way to go. I wouldn't know much about it though because Dawn barely says two words to me. I train with Drew a lot of days and he has regained his chattiness, but he won't talk to me about Dawn. They look up as I walk in and we exchange hellos before I collapse onto the bed. I love training because it usually makes me so knackered at night that I fall right asleep. It doesn't work like that tonight. My mind won't let me sleep as it sifts through everything that just happened. I should probably tell Dawn, but I don't. Not right now. I've spent most of my life thinking my parents were dead and it was all a lie. A thousand questions become one. I'm not happy about the life our mother subjected us to, but I understand it. I may be a prat for thinking like this, but I might have done the same thing.

Chapter 38

Dawn

"No, no, please. No more. I'll tell you. Please." I wake to Drew talking in his sleep. His head jerks from side to side and he's breathing heavily. I push back my blanket and climb out of bed. I walk around Gabby's bed and start shaking Drew, trying to wake him.

"Drew, wake up." His eyes pop open wildly.

"Dawn," he sighs.

"Were you having a nightmare?" I whisper.

"I was back in Texas." He pushes himself up. I cringe as I realize what that means. In his dream, he was being tortured. I push the damp hair out of his face and he shrinks away from my touch, but then catches himself. "Shite, sorry, I didn't mean to do that." He has really been trying to get better, but dreaming about the past doesn't help.

"It's okay Drew. Just try to go back to sleep," I say.

"Would you sit with me and talk?" he asks. As zonked as I am, there's no way I can say no to this boy. The room is pitch black so we walk into the hall. Here, there are fluorescent lights on all night long. We sit on the ground, leaning our backs on the wall.

"Are you okay Drew? I mean, after everything that happened to you?" I ask.

"I think I will be," he answers softly. "I have to hope it gets better." He smiles and it's reminiscent of the old Drew.

"Did you talk to Lee yesterday?" He changes the subject.

"No, I looked for him, but couldn't find him," I respond.

"Ma didn't make it here." He looks down at his shaking hands. I reach over to still them.

"What do you mean?" I ask.

"The rest of the group from the caves arrived yesterday, but the trip was too much for Ma," he says sadly. As the tears begin to spill from my eyes, Drew shocks me by wrapping his arm around my shoulders and pulling me to him. I bury my face in his chest. How can she be gone? The only person I've ever known who can be tough without an ounce of cruelty; compassionate without pity. I wipe the tears from my eyes because I know Ma would not want me crying over her.

"How's Lee?" I ask quietly.

"I only saw him for a few minutes, but he seemed okay. I think he knew there was a chance she couldn't make the trip."

I bring my knees to my chest and hug them with one arm as Drew rests his head on top of mine. I feel his hot breath as it blows through my hair. This feels good. This feels right. His breathing becomes softer as he dozes off.

"Ahem." I wake and realize we're still out in the hall as people walk by us. Jeremy is standing over us with a smirk on his face. I look up sheepishly and shake Drew awake.

"Morning Jeremy," I say before looking away.

"Hey man," Drew says, still half asleep.

"Sleep well?" Jeremy asks. When I don't respond, he says, "Can I borrow Dawn for a bit?"

"Have at it," Drew says, getting to his feet. I stretch out my arm towards him and he pulls me up before heading back into the dorm.

"Can I go grab a nosh first, or at least a shower?" I plead. He tosses me an apple.

"I grabbed this for you and you can shower later. We need to talk and then I've got something to show you." He leads me away.

"What do we need to talk about?" I ask, confused. I barely know Jeremy. We haven't ever really talked much.

"Gabby," he states. As soon as I hear her name I turn around. He grabs my arm to stop me.

"Oh no. She is not my problem anymore," I say stubbornly.

"She's still your sister," he responds simply.

"Try telling her that. She hasn't acted like a sister in quite some time," I snap.

"I'm worried about her," he says in a more serious tone. I turn back towards him and search his face. He really is worried. I sigh because I know that I'm the person that cares no matter what. I will help Gabby even when she doesn't help herself.

"What did she do now?" I ask as we start walking again.

"It's not any one thing. She's angry all the time. She spends most of her time at the shooting range and the intensity in her hand to hand practice scares me. I can't seem to get through to her."

"Gabby has always had that anger inside of her. Being in Floridaland and then in Texas probably only made it stronger. I always thought she was her own worst enemy. I've never been able to suss out how to help her with the darker part of her personality." Maybe I should be more emotional when I'm talking about all of this, but I'm just so tired of Gabby's shite.

"I'm afraid she's going to get herself killed when we launch our attack on Texas," he says.

"Wait a second; we're launching an attack on Texas?" I ask hurriedly.

"Yeah. A buddy of mine who's a technician here told me they're having him build a bomb that can wipe out an entire block. They're just waiting on one last part to get here from London."

My mind starts racing. An entire block full of people? I know Texas needs to be stopped, but most of the people have no idea what their government is up to. They're brainwashed; sheep. "Jeremy," I grab his arm to make him look at me, "most Texans are completely innocent. How can we just kill them?"

"How are they innocent?" he asks. "From what I've heard, they have people locked up and experimented on."

"The average person has no idea that's going on. If we kill innocents, how are we any different from them?" I ask. He doesn't respond. Instead, he starts walking again.

"Come on," he says. "You need to see our version of labs. They're way cool." He completely ignored what I said. Does anyone else care about anything other than this damn cause?

We step through a door marked authorized personnel only, much like the one Gabby told me about in the Texas labs. Here, though, there are no people being experimented upon. There are rows and rows of computers. Men and women in light blue lab coats are sitting at evenly spaced desks, manipulating the screens in front of them. As they speak, the words show up and they use their fingertips to move from screen to screen. Others fiddle with gadgets that I have never seen before on metal tables in the back. Jeremy looks at me and says, "See, way cool, right?" I nod as we head further into the room.

No one looks up as we pass by. They're all too engrossed in what they're doing. "This is where they keep track of all the energy produced by the wind mills and solar panels. This is also where they built them. Pretty much everything we use was built here. They even figure out how to keep everyone fed. See, certain crops need to be modified to grow around here," Jeremy explains.

"How did you first come here?" I ask as we stop in front of a desk. A frazzled looking man sits behind it. He looks like he just got out of bed. His hair is mussed and his lab coat is wrinkled. Even his glasses aren't sitting straight on the bridge of his nose.

"I met Conner at meal time and we got to talking. He eventually brought me here." Conner doesn't look up as Jeremy says his name. He's squinting at something on the screen and talking to it furiously. Jeremy moves closer and claps him on the back in greeting. He startles and looks confused until he recognizes who it is.

"Oh, Jeremy, hello," he stammers.

"Conner, this is Dawn," Jeremy says. Conner looks at me like a scared boy seeing a girl for the first time.

"It's nice to meet you," I say, trying to ease his nerves. "This place is brilliant."

"Yes, it serves its purpose well," he says, starting to navigate from screen to screen again. I look at Jeremy, unsure of what to do next.

"Conner," Jeremy says slowly as he places his hand on the boy's shoulder to stop him from working. "I was hoping we could see what you were working on. You said it was important." Conner runs his hands through his hair.

"Important. Very, very important. Yes," he says, then he leans towards us and whispers, "I don't think I'm supposed to show you."

"Why not?" I ask. I'm tired of secrets and don't have the patience for them.

"Well, I don't know," Conner responds, confusion once again clouding his face. I know why they told him to keep it to himself. They don't want anyone to know how many people they're planning on killing.

"I'm sure it would be fine if you showed us," Jeremy says.

"Well, okay," Conner responds. He stands and starts walking towards the back of the room. He doesn't beckon for us to follow him, but we do anyway. At the very last table, there are parts scattered about and cylindrical objects with wires attached. It doesn't look like much has been done here, but I've never seen a bomb so I wouldn't know.

"This is the bomb?" Jeremy asks.

"Almost. It's missing something," Conner answers. "They're sending me the detonators from London. This is old tech though. It isn't supposed to have these wires." He genuinely looks worried about that.

"So, this will take out an entire block full of people," I say, almost to myself as I look over the explosives. I don't touch them. It's the same as a gun; I don't want something that deadly in my hands.

"No, of course not," Conner says.

"Oh, that's good," I say in relief.

"This will affect three blocks at least," he says regretfully. "We're just lucky that there are only a few like this. Most of the explosives will level a building, but that's about it." I cover my mouth with my hand and glance at Jeremy who has gone pale.

"I need to go." I back away from the thing that will be the death of hundreds of people. I don't want to spend another second in its vicinity. Jeremy and I leave Conner to his work and leg it out of there. I let out the breath I had been holding as soon as we are alone on the other side of the door. "How can they do this?" I gasp. Jeremy grabs me by the shoulders and looks me in the eye.

"Dawn, get a grip. Someone will hear you." He lets me go and turns away. "We can't tell anybody about that," he says before facing me once again.

"Bugger that! Why the hell not?" I demand.

"Because there's a right time for everything." He covers his eyes and sighs. "I'm not even sure there's anything we can do about it."

"There's always something we can do," I say stubbornly.

"Okay, well, first you need to make sure you're there when the rebels take down Texas. It's the only way to save anyone. That means you have to pass the soldier entrance exam," he says.

"Yeah, I can do that," I say even though I'm not sure that's true. Before I even think it, Jeremy says the one thing that could get in my way.

"You're going to need to learn to shoot a gun."

Chapter 39

Gabby

I race Jeremy up the ropes again and again. I win every time which is strange because he always beats me. He's just not into it this morning.

"What's wrong with you?" I ask.

"Nothing," he responds. I don't believe him.

"Stop lying to me," I snap. "You're slow and weak this morning."

"Well, thanks." He grabs his towel and wipes his face.

"I'm not trying to be a bitch, I just won't coddle you," I say. I won't lie to make someone feel better.

"I just don't feel like training today." He grabs his water bottle and is about to leave when Dawn joins us.

"Hey guys," she says. I narrow my eyes because she still isn't talking to me.

"What do you want?" I ask, my mood turning from bad to worse. She doesn't flinch at my barb but looks at Jeremy instead.

"You up for teaching me how to shoot?" she asks.

"Sure." They walk away without a backward glance. Shite, what a pair of gits. I don't know what's going on with the two of them, but I don't care right now. I have my own secrets from Dawn. I leave the training room and grab a couple lunches from the cafeteria. Balancing a tray on each hand, I find my way to my mother's office. She looks up as I walk in.

"I thought you might want some lunch," I say, putting the trays on her desk.

"I'm not hungry." She looks back at the papers she's working on. When I don't leave, she says, "Would you like to have a seat?" I sit across from her and study her face. When she finally looks up again I have picked out three features of hers that I have.

"What?" she asks obviously annoyed.

"I have your ears," I say. She sighs.

"If you're looking for a mother, look somewhere else," she states.

"I don't need a mother. I've done just fine taking care of myself and Dawn, no thanks to you."

"If you're trying to hurt me, don't bother. I hurt myself when I gave you up, but I'm over it now. This cause is the only thing that matters to me now," she says.

"Point taken." I get why she wouldn't want to be my mother, but Dawn is like the perfect child. Any mother would love to claim her. I lean back in my chair. "So, when are you going to tell Dawn?" I ask.

"In time," she answers. "I've got to say, I'm surprised that you haven't told her already."

"Dawn doesn't want me to tell her anything right now." I say it and instantly know it's true. It's not me keeping us apart, it's her. I wish I had my sister to talk through all of these emotions with. Our mother is back from the dead and I can't even tell her. She's too focused on the damaged part of me. The part of me that changed because of what was done to me in Floridaland and Texas. The part of me that is angry.

"You might want to make up with her before we head for Texas," she says. "I have a feeling that you're going to pass your test and she is not; just a tip. Now, I have lots of work to do. Please shut the door on your way out." I get up to leave and almost dare to say something kind, to reach out, but I don't. Apparently, the apple didn't fall far from the tree.

Chapter 40

Dawn

"Your feet need to be shoulder width apart and point your toes at the target. Square your shoulders and stagger one foot behind the other," Jeremy instructs as he positions me.

"The target looks like a real person," I hesitate.

"But it's not. In the shooting section of the tests you'll need to hit the heart at least once and each of the other five bullets needs to at least be on the body. Here." He hands me a rifle. I hold it away from myself as though it will bite. Jeremy uses his to show me how to hold it. "Put the butt high on your chest and grab the pistol grip in the V of your hand." I do as he tells me. "Now, take your other hand and grip the hand guard, about midway down the rifle."

"I don't like this," I say. I didn't mean for him to hear me, but he says,

"I know you don't, but it needs to be done. Press your cheek firmly here." He reaches over and taps a part of the gun that he calls the stock. "Okay, now aim at the target and align it with this here." He points to a piece on the top of the gun. "Now, squeeze the trigger." I do, but nothing happens.

"It didn't shoot," I say.

"You need to squeeze it harder. Don't stop until it fires," he explains patiently. I feel the gun press hard into my chest as a bullet explodes free. "Shite!" It misses the target completely. I lower the gun and rub my chest. I'll probably have a bruise there tomorrow.

"I missed," I state.

"That's okay," Jeremy says. "It'll take practice." It takes me over an hour before I even hit the border of the target. Jeremy, of course, hits it every time. He already passed the test so he must be pretty good. We give up around dinner time. My arms are aching and I still can't believe I've been shooting a gun all day. I hope I never have to actually use one for real.

Gabby sees us walk into the cafeteria together and goes off in a huff. Jeremy goes after her so I find Drew and Lee to eat my stew with. They're sweaty and knackered from training, but they smile as I sit down.

"Where have you been all day?" Lee asks. "I was looking for you at lunch."

"Around," I say, taking a bite of food. "This is good." I deliberately avoid Lee's question because I don't want them to know I've been in the shooting range all day. Only Jeremy will understand why I'm doing it. For some reason, I don't think Lee and Drew would be against the bombing of Texas. Lee is practical and getting rid of an enemy will make sense to him. They messed Drew up pretty bad and I'm sure he would like nothing more than to turn the cities to shambles. They don't seem put off by my avoidance. Instead, the conversation turns to some meeting that has been called for tonight.

"Do you have any idea what it's about?" Drew asks Lee.

"They haven't told us, but everyone who lives in the rebel compound is expected to attend. That means you two as well," Lee responds.

"I didn't hear about this," I say. "When is it?"

"In just a few minutes," he answers. As if on cue, Jonathan Clarke walks into the cafeteria. He is wearing a headset so that we can all hear him.

"Hello everyone," he says. Every soldier in the room stands and salutes before he continues. "At ease soldiers. We have lots to talk about." Gabby and Jeremy slide into chairs at our tables and I look around to make sure no one saw them come in late.

"First, we must discuss Texas. Their soldiers have been coming as close to our base as they can without trespassing and alerting our patrols. It's been going on for months and continues to be more of a problem. They're acting on orders from the woman they call a prophet. The power she holds over her people is incredible." His eyes gleam with envy as he continues. "Most of you are religious people. Well, their "prophet" has them believing us to be heathens. She is an abomination to the faith and something needs to be done. For God and for the cause!" The quiet erupts into applause and cheers. People here are hungry for a fight. It's what they've been training for. Their enthusiasm scares me.

"Since this is the first all rebel meeting since her arrival, I would like to introduce you all to my new second in command, Officer Miranda Edwards." A stern looking woman comes into the room. "Officer Edwards was sent here from London to aid us. Some of you may have met her in the month since she arrived, but she has been very busy in the command rooms." He pauses and a cruel grin spreads across his face. "She is also the mother of two of our newcomers." Officer Edwards gives Jonathan a sharp look and he just keeps on smiling. "It's past time," he says. "Gabby and Dawn will soon be taking the military test, but don't worry, they will not get preferential treatment." I look around and see eyes everywhere, staring in my direction. I feel the heat rise up my neck and spread across my face and my palms sweat as I look at Gabby. As soon as I take in her calm demeanor, I realize that she already knew. She knew the secret that could change everything and she didn't tell me.

My head is spinning. My mother is alive. My mother is here. My mother is watching me. Where has she been all this time while Gabby and I were eating scraps and living in squalor? Where was she? Do she and Gabby distrust me that much that they would keep this from me?

"That brings us to the next topic." Jonathan has moved on, but I can't. I vaguely hear him tell us that the next test is in two weeks. I feel Drew's arm around my shoulders and Lee reaches across the table to grab my hand. I glare at my sister. How could she? No matter how strained our relationship is right now, she is still my big sister. I'm supposed to be able to trust her. This is bollocks.

When I can't sit still any longer, I shoot to my feet and dart around tables and out of the room.

Once I reach the quiet hallway, I put a hand on the wall to steady myself and squeeze my eyes shut. Tears force themselves through and soon my chest is heaving with sobs. I hear footsteps behind me and whip around.

"Dawn," Gabby says quietly. At least she has the good sense to sound contrite.

"Get away from me," I snarl, pushing past her. She grabs my arm to stop me, but I yank it free.

"Are you okay?" she asks. What a daft question.

"No, I'm not okay." I turn to face her. "My mother is alive and my sister didn't care enough to tell me."

"I'm sorry, alright?" There's venom in her words. "I knew you wouldn't understand."

"Understand what?" I demand.

"She's not the bad guy, Dawn," she whispers.

"So you're defending her now?" I accuse. "That's just great, Gabby. Go ahead and forgive her for leaving us, but I will never understand and I'm glad for that." I try to walk away without any more confrontation, but Gabby stops me again.

"She did it for the rebels; for something she believes in." Gabby's voice scares me. She is starting to sound like so many of the people here. I don't trust them and I don't know if I can trust her anymore.

"Anything for a cause, right?" I snap. "That's not how life should work."

"Then tell me, since you seem to know everything, how does it work?" she asks. I don't respond at first, we just stare at each other in a standoff. I move closer to her so that I'm right in her face.

"Do you want me to tell you about these people that you follow so blindly?" I ask, not expecting an answer before I continue. "They are building bombs to use on innocent people in Texas."

"Innocent," she scoffs. "How are any of them innocent?"

"Wow." I step back and massage my temples to stave off the oncoming headache. "You actually believe all this bullshite, don't you?"

"And you actually think you're above it all, right?" she responds.

"Gabby, most of those people have done nothing wrong. Why should they pay for their governments' crimes?"

"You don't get it!" she screams. "They all deserve what's coming. They choose to follow their prophet."

"You really think they choose it?" I'm yelling now too. "They're brainwashed; sheep. There is no choice involved."

"You really are daft. You know that? You didn't have to experience their cruelty first hand. You've never been held prisoner. You've never been beaten and starved. You don't know what it's like to live with that."

"So, that's what this is about? Payback?" I ask. "If we act like this, how are we any different from them?"

"We have a just cause," she answers.

"I'll bet they think they do too." The meeting must be over because we've attracted an audience. Gabby sees the crowd and leans in to whisper,

"I'm going to do this, Dawn. Nothing will stop me." She backs away.

"There is no coming back from this," I yell after her.

"Maybe that's the point." She throws her arms in the air. "Maybe the Gabby you knew died when they put her in that hot box in Floridaland."

Chapter 41

Miranda

"How could you do that?" I demand as Jonathan and I walk back to command.

"It was time," he states simply.

"I was handling it," I say.

"Actually, you weren't," he responds. "If we're to move forward with our plans, everything needs to be out on the table. Let's be frank," he pauses, "Dawn is not exactly the type of soldier that we want representing us in Texas."

"If she passes the test, you have to make her a soldier. There is no way around that," I state plainly.

"Yes, but there are ways to keep her from being able to perform her duties." I look at him as if he has just sprouted a second head. This man scares me.

"Jonathan," I say, "do you even know what you're saying?"

"She does not believe in our purpose. I'm sorry; I know she is your daughter." He looks away.

"Correction, she was my daughter a long time ago. Now she is just a girl who shares my DNA; a girl that could make things difficult for us," I say without emotion. I don't see myself in that girl at all. She is weak. She lets her feelings get in the way and she will never be able

129

to do what is necessary. If anything, she is a hindrance to the cause. But I still don't want anything to happen to her. I feel… protective.

"If she passes the test, I will take steps."

"Please don't do anything rash," I beg. I know he will do what he wants. I haven't been here long, but I already know how Jonathan tends to deal with "problem" soldiers. I need to do something.

As soon as I'm alone once again in my office, I power on my computer and begin to speak. The words show up on the screen as I say them. When I feel confident in the letter, I tell it to print. Now I just need a messenger that I can trust. If this letter falls into the wrong hands, I'm completely buggered. If it doesn't reach the right person, the rebels might be screwed as well.

Chapter 42

Gabby

The sound of bullets bursting through the air fills the room. I find that the shooting range calms me. It puts my mind at ease. I'm able to release the anger that is constantly boiling inside of me. I hit the heart once again and go to get some more ammo. I have been in here for hours, hiding out from the rest of the world.

Our assault on Texas can't come soon enough. There are three walled cities. We are going to hit all of them simultaneously. I didn't think we'd have the manpower for that, but Miranda says that we don't need the numbers when we have the bombs. She seemed like she was trying to convince herself of that as much as me. The plan is set, but we're waiting until after the tests are administered. Like me, there are a number of people chomping at the bit to be a part of the assaults who have yet to gain soldier status.

There is no doubt in my mind that I will pass. I don't know about Dawn though. I don't even know why she's trying. She obviously doesn't want to be a part of this. I wish I could make her see that I have to do this; that it's the right thing to do. Those people deserve what's coming to them.

Miranda explained to me how the Texans have too much consolidated power and they're growing restless. The fear is that they will come for us and we have no chance against their army. That's why the plan has been moved up. Currently, the majority of the Texan forces are concentrated on keeping the Mexicans at bay. If we hit them before they can bring enough troops home, we can crush them.

"Gabby," Drew is yelling to me. I hadn't seen him and Lee walk in. I remove my head gear to hear them better.

"Hey guys," I say.

"How long have you been in here?" Lee asks, eying my target and all of its holes.

"A while."

"We came to find you," Drew says. "The test has been moved up."

"To when?" I ask.

"Tomorrow," he responds.

Excitement stirs inside me. "Does this mean the assault is happening sooner?"

"I think so," Lee answers. "Are you two ready for the test?"

"More ready than ever," I say.

"Definitely," Drew grins. I knew he would feel the same way as me. Lee is eager for the fight as well. I told him all about the labs and he's passionate about destroying them. Jeremy is another story. I thought he would want to take down Texas and then the British army. He suffered in that slave camp more than anyone. He was born there. His sister died there. He almost died there.

I think about his sister Claire all the time. She would still be with us if she had any medical care. Sweet Claire. Jeremy won't talk about her. I don't get it. She was his only family; it hurts him too much to think about her. Whenever I think about her, it only fuels my fire. One day, I will get revenge for her.

I follow Drew and Lee to training room A for some last-minute combat practice. The test will consist of three parts. The first section is the easiest for me; weapons. That's where we put together our weapons and then shoot them. The second part is hand to hand. Third is the psych test. We have to prove that we can handle everything that comes with being a soldier. I'm not worried. I was born for this.

I don't see Dawn all day until we finally stop training for dinner. She looks up briefly as I sit down at the table and then focuses on her stew. She doesn't say a word until Drew and Jeremy sit down.

"You ready?" I overhear Jeremy ask her. Shouldn't he be asking me that?

"I think so," she says, sounding unsure.

"We're all going to pass, don't worry," Drew says, seemingly unaware of the tension around the table. He's distracted when a group of girls wave to him from across the room. He waves back in that friendly way that he has. He probably doesn't even know what that smile and charm does to girls. It hasn't been that long since I experienced it myself. He can turn perfectly nice girls into complete slags.

"I'm knackered," Dawn says with a fake yawn. "I'm going to get some sleep." She walks off without another word.

"Yeah right," I say under my breath once she's gone.

"Cool it, Gabby," Jeremy snaps. I glare at him and shut my mouth.

"I should go talk to her," Drew says reluctantly. "She's probably going nuts thinking about the test tomorrow." He follows her out. As soon as he's gone, I turn on Jeremy.

"Why do you insist on defending her?" I demand.

"Because, she's right," he responds.

"How can you think that?" I plant my hands on my hips. "These people might not be the British slavers, but they're similar enough. They imprison people and torture them. They believe that they're right in everything they do. I thought you of all people would feel the same way I do."

"Having horrible things done to me does not give me the right to do horrible things to other people." His eyes don't leave my face.

"Claire," I whisper.

"What?"

"What about Claire?" I ask loudly. "What about what was done to her. She didn't have to die."

"Don't you dare use her to justify this," he says harshly. "She was my sweet sister who would never be okay with any of this. Your memory of her has been corrupted by your own need for revenge. In Florida-land, she saw something good in you. I did too." He narrows his eyes. "I don't think I see it anymore. All I see is anger and hate."

Chapter 43

Dawn

I wake to Drew sitting on the end of my bed and instantly think of those beautiful girls that flirt with him everywhere he goes. Why does he want me? Scratch that. I don't know if he even wants me anymore.

"Time to wake up," he says excitedly. I wish I could feel his excitement. Today I become something that I never wanted to be, that is if I pass. If I make it through, I will be a soldier. If there was any other option, I would take it. Jeremy and I decided that we both need to be there. We can only be at one of the three cities, but we'll save as many people as we can. I don't know how much of a difference I can really make, but that doesn't mean I shouldn't try. I stretch my arms towards Drew and he pulls me up.

"You ready for today?" I ask.

"You bet," he responds. "You?"

"I think so."

"You'll do great." He smiles.

"Thanks," I mumble, not really believing him. He hands me some kind of fruit bread.

"I didn't think you'd want to be around all those people in the cafeteria today," he explains. My answering smile tells him that he was right. How does this boy know me so well in so short a time? He's always able to calm my nerves and insecurities.

I get out of bed and head for the showers. I let the cold water run down my back for as long as I can before I step out and get dressed. I twist my scraggly, too long hair into a messy bun. Drew walks up behind me. He doesn't touch me, but I can feel his closeness. I turn towards him and without even thinking, I wrap my arms around him in a hug. Our relationship is still strained, but in the absence of romance, we've become friends. He still keeps me at arm's length, though, and that hurts because I still love him.

He hesitates before hugging me back and resting his chin on my shoulder. I pull back reluctantly because I know it's time. My test is scheduled for the morning. Drew and Gabby are both in the afternoon. We won't find out the results until later tonight, after the psych evaluation is analyzed. I give Drew a small smile.

"Good luck," he says.

"You too," I respond as I walk out the door. I join the group of potential soldiers making their way to the waiting room. We're the lucky ones that were scheduled for the morning trials. I don't think I could handle waiting around all day. My nerves would eat me up.

The waiting room is small and cramped. The rebels have never had this many people set to become soldiers before. Most of them are Americans who've found their way here, I know that much. I've met a few of them in the training rooms, but the rest are strangers to me. I'm not comfortable around strangers.

By the time I cram into the room, all the chairs are taken, so I sit on the ground. I pick at the carpet to busy my shaking hands and keep my eyes focused on the ground.

Back in London, my lessons came easily to me, but exams were still terrifying. I would be so nervous my stomach would cramp up. Compared to this, those tests were cake. I seriously consider giving up my bid to become a soldier. It's not like I actually want to be one. Every time I think about it though, I know that it would be wrong. I'm not doing this for myself.

"Welcome to the soldier trials," a voice brings me back to the present. I look to the front of the room and Jonathan Clarke is addressing the group. "A panel of officers will be assessing each section of the test. Target shooting is first, then the combat section, and last is the psych evaluation. Our forces are highly trained and we only want those who fit into that mold. Good luck and I hope to see each and every one of you in uniform when we march on Texas." A woman walks into the room and hands Jonathan a clipboard. He looks down and reads the first name. "Sarah Thurman," he calls. A blonde girl about my size stands and follows him out.

I wait as a few others are called. Some are young, but some are surprisingly older. Everyone is chomping at the bit to become a part of this revolution; everyone except me. The room is dead silent when I finally hear my name. "Dawn Nolan," a woman calls. I stand and slowly walk towards the open door. My brain is screaming at me to go back; to forget about all of this. My legs keep moving forward. The woman leads me down the hall and into the shooting range. Four officers with headphones on stand along the wall. The one with the clipboard will be taking note of everything I do. I'm handed a rifle and ear coverings. After assembling the rifle, I'm directed to face the target. It's only the outline of a person, but it still gets to me. I squeeze my eyes shut and breathe deeply. I exhale as I open my eyes and square my feet to the target.

I hear Jeremy's voice in the back of my mind telling me what to do. I forget about the officers standing behind me. It's just me and the target. I raise the rifle and press the butt to my chest. I still have a slight bruise from all of my time spent practicing. I position the gun as Jeremy taught me and line it up with the heart on my target. I breathe in and exhale as I squeeze the trigger. The gun digs into my chest as the bullet pierces my targets arm. I do it again and a hole appears in the face area. My third and fourth bullets hit the stomach area. It's on my fifth try that I finally pierce the heart. Relief floods through me as I realize that my last bullet just needs to hit somewhere on the body. I once again press my cheek to the gun and take aim. As if in slow motion, the bullet flies through the air until it hits the foot. I just narrowly made it. I don't smile as I walk towards the judging officers and hand them the gun. They barely look at me as I leave the room. Shite, that was close.

My feet feel lighter as I'm led down the hall. "You have to wait here," I'm told. "They will come for you when they're ready." And then I'm alone. This part of the compound has been blocked off for the tests so there are no squaddies rushing by as I lean against the wall. The silence is deafening until, finally, after what feels like an eternity, a man in a soldier's uniform comes to me. I don't think he's an officer because I've gotten pretty good at spotting them. He is tall and lean, but muscular at the same time. His black hair is shining with sweat and his every movement is precise.

"Are you ready?" he asks.

"Yes," I respond. We head into training room A and it has been transformed. The obstacle course that usually occupies the back wall is gone, as is the strength training equipment. The center of the floor has been covered in bright blue mats. Nearby, a table has been set up for a group of officers to sit at. I don't look at them as I walk by, but I feel their eyes on me. We stop when we reach the mats and the man turns to me.

"This is a hand to hand combat test. You'll be fighting me." I gulp air as I look him up and down. He is twice my size. I'm so buggered. I'm not even good at fighting someone who is my size. He steps into the center of the mat. I stand across from him. He raises his arms into a fighting position and I follow suit. "You ready?" he asks. I swallow hard and nod. We begin moving in a circle, neither wanting to make the first move. He tries a punch combination that stings as I block it with my arms. I try a kick to the side, but he grabs my foot and I tumble to the ground. I roll and pop back up, only to be punched in the gut. I double over in pain and then force myself back into a fighting position.

I punch right. When he blocks the jab, I connect my left fist to his jaw. He doesn't even flinch. I take a knee to the ribs and the pain spreads throughout my body. I double over. I can't give up now. I throw jabs towards his face and his stomach as we circle each other. None of it seems to do any damage. I try to spin and kick, but he knocks me to the ground with a quick elbow to the head. Stars float in front of my eyes as I stumble to my feet. He hits me to the ground again and it's all I can do to stay conscious. I push myself from my knees to my feet and throw my body into his. I jam my shoulder into his stomach, but he barely moves. He pushes me away from him and then sweeps his leg behind mine. I tumble backward and he kicks me on the way down. I try to stand again, but my head is spinning and I can't get my legs under me. I try to trip him, but he doesn't even stumble. Instead, I see his fist coming towards me and then a spark of pain as I fall sideways. The last thing I remember is my head hitting the mat.

Chapter 44

Dawn

I come to after a few minutes. My cheek is pressed into the mat beneath me as I open my eyes. The training room appears around me. The pain is intense and when I raise my eyelids, the first thing I see is the cause of that pain. The large man I fought, if you can call it a fight, is leaning over me.

"You alright?" he asks.

"No," I state. There's no use denying it. I'm definitely not alright.

"Well, you did great!" He grins. I let out a groan and the smile fades from his face. "Let me help you up." He reaches down and pulls me to my feet. My whole body screams at me to lay back down, but I know I can't. I shoot a hand out to steady myself as a wave of dizziness comes over me. The big man grabs me before I fall.

"Thanks," I say. I look at the officers' table and they're whispering to one another and sneaking glances at me. I must have just ruined my chances of becoming a soldier. That's just brilliant.

"Soldier Dillon," one of the officers says. That must be this man's name.

"Yes, sir?" he responds crisply.

"Escort Miss Nolan to psyche while we discuss her scores," the officer orders. The soldier salutes and then takes my arm to lead me from the room. I wince at his touch, but there is no way I can walk on my own right now. He steadies me as I move slowly down the hall.

"You're going to be fine," he tells me. "I made sure I didn't break anything. You'll probably just have a lot of bruising."

"You think?" Sarcasm tinges my words.

"I'm Lucas, by the way, and I wasn't lying when I said you did great," he says. "Your scores should be pretty high."

"How is that possible?" I ask. "You kicked my arse."

"Do you really think they expected you to do well against me?"

I stop walking and look up at him. "What do you mean?" I lean against the wall for support.

"They weren't judging you on how well you can fight a man twice your size," he begins, "they were evaluating how hard you tried to fight a man twice your size. I guess you could say they wanted to see how resilient you were."

"So they wanted me to get pummeled?" Every time I find out something new about these rebels I like them even less. Why can't anyone else see how ridiculous all of this is?

"I wouldn't go that far." He hesitates. I start moving down the hall again, not really sure where I'm going. I keep one hand on the wall to keep from falling. Lucas doesn't touch me again as he leads the way. He can probably sense my irritation and knows it's best not to make me angrier. The longer I'm on my feet, the blurrier my vision gets. The hall feels like it's closing in on me. Every part looks exactly the same as the last, making this walk seem endless as it stretches out before us.

We stop outside of a door marked Psychology. "This is where I leave you," Lucas says. "Good luck." He's gone before I even knock. A thin woman with a high blonde ponytail opens the door. She'ss beautiful, with high cheekbones and a pointed chin. She pushes her glasses up the bridge of her nose before saying,

"Miss Nolan, welcome. I'm Doctor Eberly. You can call me Amelia." She steps out of the way and waves me in. "Have a seat and we can begin." She sits across from me and folds her hands on her desk. "This is the final part of your trials, but it's also the most difficult and most important. Shooting a gun and fighting are good skills for a soldier to have, but they can be taught. The mentality of a soldier cannot. Loyalty, courage, and the willingness to follow orders no questions asked are much more difficult to teach. Some are born with these traits; others develop them over time."

"How can you determine that I have what it takes?" I ask, suddenly very nervous. I already know that I'm not soldier material and I've never been very good at lying. I'm loyal, but not to the rebels. I was brave enough to save my sister, but I'm not stupidly brave, which I suspect they would like. I won't face danger if no good can come of it. I'm definitely not willing to follow their orders. Questioning things is in my nature.

"I have some questions that I need you to answer," she states.

"Okay," I say, trying to sound confident.

"Why are you here?" she asks.

"I had to save my sister."

"No," she says, "not in the colonies. Why are you here with the rebels?"

"I have no other choice," I answer honestly. "At least, if I want to stay alive." She looks surprised at my admission for a moment and then looks at her notebook and jots down some notes.

"I see," she says. "I see here that you spent some time in Texas and even came face to face with their Prophet. What's your opinion of her?"

"She's a proper nutter." I don't even hesitate.

"Would it surprise you that Texas is gearing up for more expansion?"

"Nothing would surprise me about those people. Can I ask what these questions have to do with being a soldier?"

"In order for you to answer the important questions, you need to have all the facts."

"Okay," I say.

"Cults are dangerous, Miss Nolan." I nod and she continues, "There are many people in Texas who follow Tia Cole blindly. They will do whatever she tells them. The battle to come will be less about our cause and more about our survival. That is something that everyone needs to understand. If we can't beat them back, the Texans will come for us in full force and they will win. Even those who do not believe in the rebels' ultimate goal of beating our oppressors in England and Florida-land must fight for our very existence in the colonies." She looks at me as if she knows my true feelings about the upcoming fight. Everything she says makes sense, but I still have to believe there is a different way to protect ourselves than to kill hundreds of people. Why should we survive at the expense of someone else?

"Why are you explaining all of this to me?" I ask. I doubt she tells this to every recruit.

"I just…" she pauses, thinking, "It was the request of someone in command who doesn't want anything to happen to you."

Someone in command? "Miranda?" I ask, suddenly understanding.

"Your interview is over," Amelia cuts me off abruptly and stands to open the door. I'm confused because she didn't really interview me. I take her cue and leave without another word.

Why do we have to go to war? Isn't there plenty enough land to coexist with these people. Will those in power ever stop yearning for more? I saw it in England, in Texas, and now here. Power is like an addictive drug. Once you taste it, the cravings overcome everything else, leaving death and destruction in its wake.

As I hobble down the hall I use the wall once again to steady myself. I'm almost to my dorm when I run into Drew.

"Oh my God," he says. "Dawn, are you okay." Unable to stand any longer, my knees buckle and I start to fall. Drew catches me under the arms. "Let's get you to medical."

"No," I say, not in the mood for any more doctors after that shrink. "I just need to lay down."

"Okay." He lifts me easily and carries me into the room. I hear Gabby gasp as Drew lowers me to the bed, but she doesn't come closer. My head spins as I sink further and further away from Gabby and Drew until finally, I welcome the sleep.

Chapter 45

Gabby

It takes all of my strength to knock on the door. This is the final step to becoming the soldier I always wanted to be. I aced the shooting trials of course. I was brilliant. The hand to hand was brutal, but Lucas told me that I was one of the only people who didn't pass out. Now is the Psych test. I'm confident it will go well because I know I have what it takes. A woman opens the door and ushers me in. She cuts straight to the chase.

"I'm told that you shot someone on your way here. An unarmed Texan farmer," she says. "When you think about that now, what do you feel?"

"I had to. He'd tried to kill us," I say honestly. "They attacked us and they got what they deserved."

"Good," she says. "I hear that you've talked to your mother a few times. What emotions does she evoke?"

"I understand her," I admit. "I'm like her." When I don't say more she nods and looks at her papers.

"You say you understand her. Does that mean that you would do the same thing to protect the rebels?"

"It does," I respond.

"Good. Command has told me that you will make the perfect rebel soldier. Do you agree?" I give her a wide smile as my response and she takes more notes. She asks me only a few more questions before releasing me.

Chapter 46

Gabby

I'm pretty sure I aced the trials. By tonight I'll finally be a soldier. I hope Dawn did well, but the rebels might be better served if she failed. No matter how far apart we've grown, I love my sister; I really do. But this is bigger than the two of us. That's the reason I can't hate my mother. Because I'm not so sure I would make a different choice than she did. I finally have a reason to live. That's what everyone that comes here is searching for. Americans and British alike, we all want to fight for something we believe in.

I believe in freedom; freedom from slavery and laboratory experiments; freedom from poverty and hunger. The rebels want to better the lives of the people that deserve it. There are going to be a lot of people dead by the end of this, but there are always casualties in war. Jonathan tells us that we need to accept that fact in order to achieve our goals.

We've been getting an influx of British rebels lately. The compound has become a bit crowded and these rebels are different than the ones that have been here for years. They're not soldiers. They're loud and grotty. They have trouble following orders and most of the time their assigned duties are not done. Jonathan is at his wits end with these people. Even Miranda, who was once one of them, is losing it. I don't know how we're supposed to accomplish our mission in Texas if half the soldiers don't do as they're told. The worst of it is that they don't even have to go through the test because they're already considered rebel soldiers. Thankfully, I don't consider myself a British rebel even though I'm from London. I'm a colonial rebel.

I'm in a lot of pain as I walk slowly to the cafeteria. It's not always easy finding a seat in here these days, but I spot Jeremy and Drew saving an empty table. Every step makes me wince. Lucas really did a number on me. I'm almost to the table when a girl runs into me, knocking me over. I bite my lip to keep from crying out as I hit the floor. I look around, but the girl is gone. Damn British rebels. Jeremy and Drew run over and help me to my feet.

"Thanks," I say through the pain. Drew looks about as bad as I feel. His left eye is swollen shut and a large bruise peeks up over the collar of his shirt. By the time they lead me back to the table, Dawn and Lee are there.

"So," Lee starts, "how'd everybody do?"

"I guess we'll find out soon," Drew says as he points to the front of the room where Jonathan Clarke is standing behind a microphone.

"We don't get to eat first?" I say. "I'm really peckish." The words die on my lips as I watch as two soldiers walk in carrying stacks of uniforms. They set them down behind Jonathan and stand at his sides.

"Hello soldiers," he says. Every man and woman in uniform stands and salutes. Jonathan smiles before giving them permission to sit. "Hello everyone else." His voice is sweet yet authoritative. "Today is a great day," he continues. "We welcome new soldiers into our ranks. It's always a pleasure to watch you all train and gain the skills that are needed. Now that the trials are over, I can tell you the truths of them. Part one, the shooting range, is supposed to show us how well you can shoot a gun, yes, but that's not all. We wanted to see your concentration and also your preparation. You can't pass that section without a lot of practice. Practice proves one's dedication and drive."

"Part two was the hand to hand combat. Did anyone really think we expected you to beat Lucas Dillon, the best fighter in this compound? We did not. We expected you to get the stuffing beaten out of you. But, we also expected you to keep going. We wanted to see your resilience. In the coming months, there will be times when you're at a disadvantage. How are you going to react? Are you going to run? Or are you going to fight? As rebels, we fight to the very last. We wanted to see you fight through the pain."

"The last part was a bit more straightforward. The Psych evaluation is about mental stability. Will you be able to do the things that may need to be done? We wanted to see courage and loyalty. Many of you showed us everything we were looking for. You're an impressive group." He looks to the man beside him. "Officer Clifton will now read the names of those who passed. You will then come and retrieve your uniform and your orders." Jonathan steps back and Officer Clifton steps to the microphone.

"Grant Harding," he says. The man that walks forward is much older than me. He is handed a uniform and an envelope before sitting back down. "Tess Smith," he continues. Everyone that steps up is badly bruised. There are a few more names before the officer calls, "Dawn Nolan." There's a look of surprise on her face. Frankly, I'm surprised too. I didn't think she could do it. She hobbles forward and by the time she sits back down, five more names have been called. Drew and I were the last two tests so it takes a little while to get to us. When I finally hear "Gabriela Nolan" I almost jump out of my chair. I take my uniform and envelope with pride. Drew is called after me. By the time we're back at the table, everyone has gone to get in line for food.

I'm so excited that I forget all about my hunger and I go straight to the dorm. I'm not alone in here because some of the British rebels have been placed in our room, but right now I couldn't care less. I throw the envelope on my bed and immediately put on my uniform. It fits perfectly, almost as if it was made for me, or I was made for it. I run my hands down my sides to flatten out the creases. The uniform is navy blue with brass buttons. I tie my hair into a ponytail and place the hat on my head before running to the lav to look in the mirror. As soon as I see myself, I stand up straighter and raise my hand in salute. This is me now. This is Gabby Nolan, rebel soldier.

Chapter 47

Dawn

My uniform is uncomfortable and itchy. It's baggy in some places and then it's tight across the shoulders. Today is my first day as a soldier. I don't know what I'll be doing yet because I haven't had the nerve to open my envelope. Drew and Gabby were so excited and yakking on about nothing this morning and I couldn't stand it. I escaped to the lav and haven't gone back. When I look in the mirror, I see a stranger. My hair is tied up neatly under my hat and I still have bruises on my face. I look like I've already been in battle. I try a salute, but I look so silly that I start to laugh.

"What's so funny, soldier?" someone barks behind me. I turn and am relieved it's only Jeremy.

"What are you doing in here?" I say. "This is the girl's lav."

"No one else is in here, don't worry about it. You're looking mighty spiffy," he remarks.

"Thanks," I groan.

"It'll be fine, Dawn. Just go about your duties normally. What'd you get assigned to?"

"I don't know." I look down at my hands. "I haven't looked."

"Really?" He raises his eyebrow before taking the envelope that had been poking out of my pocket.

"Jeremy," I start to protest, but then I just sigh and let him have it. "Fine, it's better if you look at it." He opens the envelope and unfolds the paper. I tap my hands on the sink as he's reading, unable to contain my nervous energy. "Well?" I ask.

His brow furrows in confusion. "This can't be right."

"What can't be right?" I demand. He looks up at me with worry etched into his face.

"You've been assigned to the patrols," he says quietly.

"What does that mean?"

"The patrols go far out from the compound looking for Americans to bring back but also looking for any trouble. It's dangerous and sometimes they're gone for days," he pauses before continuing quietly. "Lee tried to get assigned to a patrol, but he was told that they only take soldiers with years' worth of experience." I swallow hard as I try to keep my breathing steady. Why would they assign a small girl who's never won a fight in her life to a patrol? I start pacing back and forth across the tile floor. Jeremy looks lost.

"Shite, I don't understand this," I say. "What can we do?"

"Assignments are usually final. They're not just handed out randomly. There's a process. A committee makes preliminary assignments and then high command approves or changes them. This had to have come from them." He grabs me by the shoulders so I stop moving. "You're going to be fine." I know he's just saying it to make me feel better, but I appreciate it. I tell myself that I will not cry. I need to be tough if I'm going to survive. Jeremy must not be buying my tough girl act because he pulls me into a hug.

I back out of his arms and grip the sink to lean over it, ready to hurl. I splash cold water on my face. My chest heaves as I fail to stop the sobs from escaping me this time. Jeremy stays silent until I pull myself together. I wipe the tears from my face and straighten my cap.

"It's time to go," I say, reaching for the door. "I have to be at the car park in ten minutes so I'll see you later."

"Okay, good luck," he says. I turn back when I open the door.

"Hey Jeremy," I say, "thanks."

Chapter 48

Dawn

I'm the last one to arrive at the garage and I'm the only person who's new to this squad. I start to say something, but my nerves get the better of me and I shut my mouth. There are ten soldiers standing around a truck. I look at each face, hoping to see someone I know. I don't recognize anyone until I reach the very last person and he smiles at me. It's Lucas, the guy who beat the shite out of me during my trials. I give him a tight smile and then turn to listen to the woman who has started to speak.

"Hello soldiers," she says. "We have an addition to our team today." She walks towards me and speaks lowly, "Dawn Nolan, I don't know why you've been assigned to our patrol, but I don't trust you, not yet." She turns to everyone else. "And patrol is all about trust. Am I right?" Shouts of agreement ring in my ears as she turns to me once again. "I'm Officer Mills. Soldier Nolan, I've got my eye on you." She walks back to the front of the group. "Our mission for the next few days is an important one. We're going north." She doesn't give us more explanation than that and everyone else seems to accept it, so I don't ask as we all accept our firearms from her and pile into the truck.

The truck lurches forward and before I know it, we're outside. I pull aside the canvas flap at the back to look around. It's only been months since I've seen the sky, but it feels like years. The sun is out in full force today and only a few puffs of clouds block the brilliant blue. The land out here is as empty as I remembered. The trees are naked and sit in harsh contrast to the open space around them and the hills loom large. The road we are on is broken. It must have been paved and smooth once, but now the concrete is cracked and twisted, allowing the wild landscape to overrun it. The truck lurches and bumps, jostling my still sore body.

We reach the river in good time and leave the truck hidden. The river is wide and the dark water has been kicked up by the wind.

"What are we waiting for?" I ask Officer Mills.

"Our ride," she responds. I start to ask her what she means, but her face tells me to stop. She turns to the rest of the group, "who has the flag?"

"I do, sir." A soldier hurries forward and plants a small blue flag on the bank.

"Thank you, soldier King." She focuses her attention on the trees behind us. "Let's pitch the tents back in those woods."

I've never set up a tent before and don't even know where to start. "Rubbish," I yell in frustration as Officer Mills walks up behind me.

"I don't know why they would ever think to assign you to my patrol. You're way too green for this." She shakes her head as she takes the poles from me. The words hurt, but I know she's right. The camp is set up quickly. I mostly just watch.

"Rookie," Soldier King yells. "I think you'd be of better use looking for firewood. We all pull our own weight around here." I follow King and two other guys in search of timber. As soon as we're out of sight of the camp, the three men stop and circle me.

"So," King begins, "some of us were wondering how you got this gig."

"What gig?" I ask, confused.

"How'd you get assigned to a patrol?" King asks harshly. "There's a waiting list, you know." Warning bells are going off in my head, and I look around for an escape.

"I don't know," I say quietly, staring at my feet.

"Oh, come on," one of the other men says. "What'd you do? Did you beg mommy?" All three of them laugh. I look away, unable to hide my embarrassment. So, that's what they all think? That my mom pulled some strings. If these guys knew me at all, they would know how much I don't want to be on a patrol. I don't want the danger or the adventure. This should have been Gabby's job. When I fail to respond, they only laugh harder.

"Or maybe," King starts, "maybe she's a present from Jonathan? Honestly, he could have gotten us a prettier one." Tears pour down my face as the men grab at me from every direction. I try to get away, but King wraps an arm around my waist and pulls me to him. I slam my fists into his chest repeatedly, but his grip never loosens and his smile never wavers.

"King!" Officer Mill's voice stops them in their tracks. "What the hell do you think you're doing? Is that how you treat a fellow soldier?" King smirks at her, but the smile fades from his face as Lucas appears.

"No sir," King finally answers. The soldiers around me scatter until I'm left alone with Officer Mills and Lucas.

"You okay?" Lucas asks.

"I'm fine," I mumble as I hurry past them. I need to find some space. I need to be alone.

I avoid the camp as I leave the tree cover and soak in the quiet. I take a seat by the river. A silver light reflects off the water as the full moon overhead illuminates the darkness. Occasionally, a jumping fish startles me. I barely notice Officer Mills sitting beside me.

"What are you doing, soldier?" she asks softly.

"Nothing, sir," I respond as I pick at the grassy bank. A cold wind blows through and I pull my jacket tighter around myself.

"My name is Grace," Officer Mills blurts.

"Okay."

"I just thought you should know."

"Why?" I ask, finally looking at her.

"I don't really know." She laughs softly. "I'm sorry they treated you so horribly. I wish I could say I was surprised."

"They don't seem to have much respect for you."

"No," she agrees quietly. "It's the woman thing."

"But Miranda is one of the rebel leaders and people respect her."

"Your mom-"

"Don't call her that," I interrupt.

"Miranda," she continues, "is not seen as the real leader. She doesn't interact much with the troops and many see her as Jonathan's lackey."

"Sexist pigs," I say under my breath.

"That's why Lucas is my second in command. He scares them into following my orders."

"Doesn't surprise me." I show her the most painful bruise from my trials.

"He's a good guy, though," she says. "I just hope he can keep everyone in line if we have to stay here a few days."

"Can I ask what we're waiting for?"

"A boat," she explains. "A smuggler to be exact. They're the only ones that travel this part of the river this time of year. The flag is a signal to them that we're here and we can pay." She sighs.

"Where exactly are we going?"

"There's an American village in the North," she whispers. "We're delivering a message."

"I didn't think there were any American villages."

"Just the one. It serves as the connection point between the Texan smugglers and the Chinese timber trade in Canada."

"When I first came here," I say, "I thought the colonies were a desolate, empty country."

"It used to be." She stands. "Come on; let's go see if those boys left us any food.

Chapter 49

Gabby

I salute as officers walk by my post, trying to hide my annoyance. I shouldn't be here, guarding the door to command. I should be outside on patrol like my sister. I don't understand how she got a job like that. Lee told me they wouldn't even take him. I'm so sick of little miss perfect Dawn. She's out exploring while I'm stuck here. Every morning I'm at my post outside of command. Every afternoon I'm training.

Jeremy and I have barely been speaking, Drew just walks around and mopes, all worried that something will happen to Dawn, and Lee is jealous of her for getting assigned to a patrol. Does everything have to be about her? I'm relieved of my post at lunch time, but I don't want to eat. I head straight for the training room.

Miranda stops me on my way there. "Gabby!" she says cheerfully. "I was just looking for you."

"Why?" I ask suspiciously. My mother has proven time and again that she wants nothing to do with me.

"I was wondering if we might have a word."

"Okay," I say, unsure of where this is going. She leads me down the hall and into an empty room.

"So," she begins, "I hear that you're one of our most promising shots."

"I can hit a target," I shrug.

"Good," she responds. "You're being reassigned."

"What? Already?" I want to jump for joy, but not in front of her.

"Would you rather continue at your current post?" she asks.

"No," I say quickly. "What's my new assignment?"

"You are to be trained as a sniper."

"Really?" I grin.

"Yes, we will have need of many snipers in Texas." She stands suddenly and walks to the door. As she passes me, she hands me an envelope with my new orders and then she is gone. I'm so excited that I can't even be upset about my mother's coldness towards me. I have long since written her off. I run down the hall, wanting to share my excitement. I stop completely when I realize that I have no one to tell right now; no one that would care anyway.

Chapter 50

Gabby

The beauty of being a sniper is that we train outside. There isn't a training room that can provide us with the long-distance shooting that we need. Today is the first day that there even is a squad of snipers because they never wanted to risk having soldiers train outside, in the open. They put us together specifically for the assault on Texas. Some of the people here have been a part of the rebels for years. I'm the newest. We keep our eyes open and our guns at the ready as we walk towards the nearby tree line for some cover. When anyone is outside the compound, they have to be careful to look for ambushes or just groups of Texans out on patrol. We stop as soon as we reach the patch of woods and turn towards the sergeant.

"Soldiers, I'm Sergeant Lincoln," he says as we salute. I'm surprised at the accent in his voice. He isn't British. He's the first American officer that I've met. "You have been selected for a specialized task. Snipers will play a very important role. We don't have the numbers to overwhelm the Texans, but we will have the training." He drops the duffel bag he was carrying on the ground. He unzips one and pulls out a rifle. "This is a sniper rifle," he explains. "Come and take one."

As soon as the gun is in my grasp, I run my hand down the length of it. It's much longer and heavier than anything I've shot before. The grip is almost too big for my hand. I peer through the scope and my heart begins to race as the excitement builds. I'll bet this thing is so much more accurate than the rifles in the shooting range.

We practice taking apart the gun and putting it together for the next hour before the sergeant instructs us in how to rest the gun on the ground and take aim. I feel weird shooting from so low.

"This is going to be great!" the girl next to me says. I smile at her in agreement and she continues, "You're Dawn's sister, right?"

"I prefer to say that she's my sister, on days I actually admit it," I respond.

"I like you," she says, laughing. "I'm Shay."

"Gabby." I point to myself. "How do you know Dawn?"

"I used to live in the same caves as Lee. Your sister is a piece of work, isn't she?"

"You have no idea," I say softly.

"I don't get what Drew sees in her," Shay whispers.

"He loves her, although you wouldn't guess that these days. They're not even together."

"I noticed that," she says. "He still walks around like a lovesick puppy, though."

"Soldiers!" Sergeant Lincoln barks. "Can anyone tell me why we're not using guided ammunition?"

"Sir yes, sir," a man in the back responds. "The Texans have developed jamming technology."

"Good, soldier Harmon," the sergeant says. "You're correct. They're now able to block our guided missiles. This means that we will have to rely on our aim to hit the targets. This is a much more difficult and old fashioned way to fight and we only have a limited amount of time to train. This is why you were chosen. Each of you has excelled in the shooting range. Let's see how well that translates to an open battlefield."

"Sir?" a man beside me says.

"There is no need for all this sir business," Sergeant Lincoln says. "Out here, I'm a rebel just like all of you. Call me Linc."

"Okay, can I ask a question?" the man says.

"Of course Greene, ask away."

"If the Texans have the jammer, wouldn't they also have guided ammunition?" Greene asks. "How are we supposed to compete with that if we can't use it ourselves?"

"Good question." Linc scratches his head. "We've recently had a rebel agent bring us the specs of the jammer from Texas. Our technicians are working on it now. We will begin this fight on even footing, I assure you."

He must mean Allison. I know she was bringing back some blueprints to some of the buildings in the capitol, but this is so much bigger than that.

Linc orders us to grab our guns and follow him. He takes us to where he has painted targets on trees in the distance. "We will practice until you can hit the center of the target with every shot," he explains. "Let's get to work."

Chapter 51

Dawn

We've been in the same place for two days now and the boys are getting restless. They're bored of their cards and we found snakes in our camp last night. It's time to go. It doesn't help that it's been raining for the past twenty-four hours. The ground has turned to mud and my boots are like suction cups as I pull them free every few steps.

The rebel uniform only provides minimal protection against the cold that finds its way into my bones. Each night, the fire thaws my limbs, but it doesn't warm me. I'm staring into the flames when Officer Mills takes a seat beside me. Everyone calls her Mills except for me. Leaving the respectful title of officer from her name is only one of the things they pull to try to show her who's in charge. Nothing seems to bother her, or at least, she's very good at hiding it. I try to stay away from most of the group because they do the same shite to me. It's a good ole boys club for sure.

During the day, I hang out in my tent to stay out of the rain and away from the others and at night I don't join in the conversation. Tonight is no different. Finding dry firewood was difficult so we had to make do. The flames are little more than glowing ashes on the ground; not large enough to cook on. We ate a cold dinner and then most people went straight to sleep. I try to escape this place and shut my eyes, but as zonked as I am, no sleep will come.

It's a strange feeling, to have my body ache with exhaustion and at the same time, not be able to quiet my mind.

"You should get some sleep," Officer Mills says quietly.

"You should too, Officer Mills," I respond. Neither of us moves as we soak in the stillness. The silence is punctuated by the occasional popping of sparks from the dying fire.

"These parts used to be full of animals." She sighs. "Have you noticed that we haven't seen many around?"

"Yeah." My voice is a whisper so as not to wake the others. "What happened to them?"

"They were hunted almost to extinction when the rebels and the Americans moved into the area. Before people found a way to alter the crops, the animals were a main source of food. There are rumors that if you were to go out west, you'd see tons of them. Bears, lions, wolves, all of them."

"It's kind of sad," I say as an image of the bear that almost killed me comes to mind. That seems like a lifetime ago. Sam with his crossbow. Me with my twisted ankle.

"It is." Officer Mills brings me back to the present. "I just hope we don't hunt people to extinction." Her face is hidden in the darkness, but I can sense a sadness in her hunched shoulders and quiet voice. I grab onto the tiny string of hope she's just given me. Maybe there are more people that feel the same way that I do about this coming war. Maybe the rebels can still be saved from themselves.

"Tomorrow's another long day," Officer Mills states. "The boat might come. We should get some rest." She gets to her feet and we stomp out the rest of the fire. I hope we get moving soon because the sooner we get there, the sooner we get back and I can figure out what to do next.

Chapter 52

Dawn

"Hey Nolan, wait up!" Lucas yells as he jogs towards me. I stop my search for usable firewood and turn. "Mills wants us to stay together today," he explains. "We need to be ready if the boat comes." I sigh and follow him back.

Around midday, I start digging through our stores. It's my turn to make lunch and we were not planning on having to wait this long for a ship. Our food has to last us until it gets here. I guess it's spuds again. I set them to boil and lean against my pack on the ground. The sun streams through the leafy overgrowth and I close my eyes as the rays warm my face.

"Everyone, get down," Officer Mills yells suddenly. My eyes pop open and I see a flash in the bushes nearby. I hear the shot before I see anyone else. Suddenly, my surroundings erupt in chaos. I don't have time to think before I engage and realize that I'm unarmed, having set my rifle down to cook. Shite!

Everyone is shouting as more and more attackers show up. I throw the boiling pot at the first one who runs at me and he screams in agony.

I jab another attacker in the ribs as he brings his fist down to meet my jaw. I stumble backward as he smashes his elbow into my chest. I scream in pain and kick him in the shins. He falls to the ground and then King is there. He shoots my attacker in the head and then moves along without so much as a glance at me. I look at the bare chested dead man. The eagle tattooed across his chest. Freedom fighters. I fall back as I remember the man who tried to kill me when I first got to the colonies. Drew saved me. Images of the ruins and the bones in the dirt flash through my mind.

"King, Brent, Hipps!" Officer Mills yells. "Help Schmidt! Nolan, Lucas to me!" I look around and Schmidt has fallen to the ground with a leg wound. He still has his gun in his hands, but he can't get up. Officer Mills is fighting more than one attacker. I jump into the mix and claw at the face of a large woman. She pulls out a knife and I back away. She slashes through the air, trying to catch me. I duck and she barely misses. The move makes her momentarily lose her balance and I see my opening. I run. I'm not proud of it, but I've never claimed to be brave. I weave in and out of the fight until I reach the place where I left my gun laying on the ground. As soon as I pick it up, the woman stops chasing me. She cocks her head and stares while still holding the knife, ready to plunge it into my flesh.

"Breathe in. Breathe out," Jeremy's voice says in my mind. My finger shakes as I pull the trigger. The bullet flies wide. I try again, but I can't still my hands enough to aim. She starts at me again, but before she can come any closer, King shoots her twice in the chest. I try to stand as the fight dies down around me, but I'm grabbed from behind and thrown back down. I hit my head as I fall and am too dizzy to get back up. I use my arms to roll onto my back and am confronted with the barrel of a rebel issued rifle. My eyes shift upwards to where Soldier King still stands.

"Get up," he orders.

I do as I'm told. "What are you doing?" My voice shakes.

"I'm following orders," he responds. "Turn around."

"Please, don't do this."

"Shut up and turn around!" he screams. I close my eyes and turn.

"King," Officer Mills yells, running towards us. I hear a scuffle right before a bullet tears into my skin.

Chapter 53

Dawn

The pain shooting up my arm wakes me. I groan as my eyes pop open and the light pouring through the open window almost blinds me. There's a wooden roof overhead and I'm suddenly very aware that I don't know where I am. I try to roll out of bed. but fail.

"Don't tax yourself," Officer Mills says as she steps into the room.

"Officer Mills?" I say tentatively.

"I told you to call me Grace," she says.

"Where am I?"

"On a ship."

"What happened?"

"You were shot," she answers bluntly, looking towards the door as Brent and Lucas walk in.

"Glad to see you awake." Lucas smiles.

"How long have I been out?" I ask.

"Two days," Grace responds. "The captain has some medic training, but he had never treated a gunshot wound. He removed the bullet and sewed you up. It isn't the prettiest stitch job, but it'll keep you alive. We'll have an American doc look at it when we get there."

"It would have been worse," Lucas explains, "if Grace hadn't gotten to you in time."

"Or if this boat hadn't shown up when it did," Officer Mills says.

"What about the fight?" I ask, suddenly remembering all of the freedom fighters coming at us. The three of them look to each other, reluctant to speak.

"We took care of them," Lucas says. "But no one else made it."

A lump forms in my throat as I think of the team. I barely knew most of them. I didn't like any of them. I didn't want them dead.

"I still don't get why the freedom fighters were there," Officer Mills says pensively. "They usually stay clear of rebel territory. It's sort of an unspoken rule."

"We found signs of them," I say, suddenly remembering what Corey said. "On our way from Texas to the rebel compound."

"They're growing bolder," Lucas says absently.

"Why did they attack us?" I ask.

"Probably for any food and supplies that we had." Officer Mills begins to pace. "Freedom fighters only live from one day to the next. They don't farm. They don't settle. They take what they need. Our patrols have been having increasing problems with them, but not usually that close to the river. They have an irrational fear of water."

The door bangs open and the captain walks in.

"How's the patient?" he asks. I recognize his voice.

"Captain Collins?" I ask weakly.

"It would seem, Miss Nolan, that you're my precious cargo yet again." He flashes me a crooked smile.

"Shouldn't you be in jail?"

"Oh, that." He scratches his beard. "That fellow, the soldier, wasn't very insistent upon it. He even told me that I didn't have to go back to Vicksburg if I didn't want to. A few of my men had taken it upon themselves to change his mind, you see. Of course, they have quite slippery hands and that man was a bit too heavy to be dangling over the side of a boat."

"I get the picture." I stop him before he paints a more graphic image.

"No need to get testy," the captain says. "If I was in jail, who would have come to pick you all up? There are only two other boats coming through here this month. I would think you'd rather ride north with me than old Baker. Sobriety is a rarity among his men and you ladies might not like the drunken sailors too much. Captain Slater will be coming through with a big load, but he doesn't care much for your lot."

"Our lot?" Officer Mills says through clenched teeth.

"You know," the captain begins, "rebels, fighters, ruffians. I've been helping you folk for years and let's be honest, you're all the same. Peace bores you, which works because, in your minds, you're superior to everyone else. You want control in the colonies and will stomp out those who resist as quickly as possible. The Texans and British slavers are the same. Don't get me wrong, I'm okay with that. I tend to play all sides equally so I never lose. I don't really care who owns what land or resources so long as I always have a hot meal and a solid boat." He finishes changing my bandage in silence.

Officer Mills looks furious. Lucas has a hand on her shoulder, trying to calm her down, or maybe he's holding her back. I don't know.

"I think you'd better leave," I whisper to the captain.

"Good idea." He winks at me and then disappears through the door.

"How could he say those things?" Officer Mills breathes.

"Because they're true." I didn't think I had spoken loud enough to be heard, but the three of them turn to me.

"Soldier Nolan, what did you just say?" Officer Mills' formality towards me warns me to shut up. Maybe the pain is clouding my judgment because I answer her.

"I said that it's true," I reiterate. "Officer Mills, you yourself told me that you were worried about how many people were going to die. We shouldn't be killing each other; the land does enough of that for us. We should be standing together to survive."

"You've only been here for a short time. You don't know anything about the rebels." Mills paces the room and Lucas and Brent are suspiciously quiet.

"I know enough for them to want to kill me."

"What are you talking about?" Mills snaps. I take a minute to gather my thoughts because I'm not sure I should be telling them this.

"King was ordered to kill me," I say slowly.

"That's ridiculous," Officer Mills snaps.

"That's right. It's rubbish," I concur. "King told me he was only following orders."

"Who would ever order your death?" Lucas speaks up.

"Jonathan," I say quickly. "Or Miranda. I don't know."

Mills is shaking her head furiously. "Think about it," Lucas says to
her. "Why was she put on our patrol right out of her trials? She's certainly not the first person from the compound to disappear. This time,
they just decided to make it seem legit."

"No." Brent is shaking as he gets to his feet. He gives each of us a
long look and then stalks from the room.

"Shit," Lucas says.

"What just happened?" I ask. Officer Mills leans against the wall,
closes her eyes, and sighs before answering.

"Damn, I forgot about Kim."

"Kim was Brent's girl," Lucas explains to me. "She was a defector
from Floridaland. After being in the British military, she came here
with big ideas and was very vocal when she disagreed with something," he pauses. "She was sent out on a repair mission to one of the
windmills. It was routine and should have been safe. She never came
back. People have different theories as to what happened."

"No one ever bothered to find out?" I demand.

"How?" Officer Mills asks. "Jonathan had just come and he was already a bit crazy. People were scared of him. Plus, we're soldiers. We
do as we're told."

Chapter 54

Gabby

As soon as I get the hang of it, I can hit almost anything at a distance. We train all day, every day. It's nice to be outdoors, but it's been getting really cold. We've all been issued uniform jackets, but they only provide minimal protection from the chill of the winds.

Today I'm grateful when we're told to head inside for a nosh. My hands are cramped and hurting and my face is burnt from the wind.

I walk into the cafeteria with Shay and scan the room for Jeremy. He's sitting with a nerdy looking guy. They look up when we walk over and Jeremy's companion stops talking abruptly and shifts his eyes away nervously.

"Are you okay?" Jeremy asks me.

"Why wouldn't I be?" I snap.

"Your face is all red."

"We've just come inside," I explain as I take a seat.

"Oh." He doesn't say anything more; instead, we sit in awkward silence. Things have been like this between us for a while now. He says that I'm not the same person that he met in the camps and I think he's being an unfair git. The silence continues until Lee and Drew sit down.

"Hey guys," Drew says while Lee turns to the frazzled kid in glasses. "Conner, what's brewing in the labs these days?" Jeremy gives Conner a curiously sharp look before Lee explains what he means. "There's a rumor floating around that you guys are cooking up something good that might affect the farming output."

Conner nervously scratches his arms and doesn't take his eyes off the table as he stammers, "I'm not working on it personally. They have me on," he pauses, "something else."

"So it's true then?" Lee badgers.

"Well, yes. It's almost done."

"That's awesome!" Lee slaps the table in excitement.

"I don't understand what's so great about all of this," I say.

"We'll be able to grow certain foods that don't traditionally do well in this climate," Lee explains excitedly." I still don't see why he's so excited, it's not like it's some great weapon. I don't remember ever seeing Lee this excited. I guess this is Lee's job though. He was assigned to the resources division that keeps this place running. He is still a soldier, not a scientist, but now he has done so well that he has a seat at the table whenever there is an important meeting called in command. It's amazing how quickly people can rise through the ranks here. They reward good work. I watch as Lee talks to Conner. He uses his hands and his facial expressions are priceless.

Lee is a rare breed in this compound. He is not a radical supporter like me or unaware of what's truly going on like Drew. He's practical, a pragmatist. He knows what we're planning for Texas, but he also believes that we have no other choice if we are to survive. His entire job here is making sure that this compound is able to keep going. I, on the other hand, believe that the people in Texas deserve what's coming to them. I saw some awful things and I want revenge. I don't want the rebels to coexist with these people; I want our rebel group to exist instead of them.

I walk back to the dormitories with Drew. I haven't been around him much lately because, frankly, I've been avoiding him. He is worried about Dawn. He's not only worried because her patrol has yet to return, but also because she is against everything we're trying to accomplish here. Drew is afraid that the rebel leaders won't let her stay here for much longer. I've thought about that too, but I think it may be best if she leaves. She is my sister and I still love her, but this is not her fight. I need to be a part of this, but she doesn't.

"Do you think she's okay?" Drew asks for the millionth time in the last week.

"I'm sure she is." I sigh.

"I hope so."

I can't take this any longer. "What the hell happened to you, Drew?"

"Huh?" he says, barely listening to me.

"What happened to the guy I used to date who didn't care about anything; the guy who dated multiple women and got away with it; the guy who was smooth and dangerous?"

"We've all changed, Gab," he responds stubbornly.

"Not for the worse. You've become a right prat."

"Who says it's for the worse?" he says dangerously. "You? The girl who now hates her own sister; the very same sister that is only in this godforsaken place because she came for you?"

I feel his words as if he's just slapped them across my face. My jaw clenches. "She made the decision to come here. I didn't ask her to."

"You didn't have to." He turns into our room, but I don't follow him. I lean my back against the wall and slide to the floor. I wish everything could just be simple again. The only thing I had to worry about in London was keeping myself and Dawn alive. It wasn't so complicated. Food. Shelter. Done.

I look up to find Jeremy leaning in the doorway. "You okay?" he asks.

"Why do you care?" I say, my tone warning him to leave me alone.

"I care Gabby. I always care." He sighs. I look at him and our eyes meet. I don't recognize the look on his face. It's not love, but it's not anger either. There's pity in his eyes. A sudden rage breaks free.

"Go away," I yell.

"No." He shrugs and takes a seat next to me.

"I don't want your pity."

"Who says you have it?" he responds. "I don't agree with what you believe or what you're going to do. Maybe I don't think you deserve my pity." Anger turns to confusion and back again.

"What's that supposed to mean?"

"It means that Dawn is right," he answers.

"About what?" I ask.

"You can still be saved from yourself." I choose not to respond to his idiocy immediately. "When she gets back, you should listen to what she has to say."

"Not everything is about her." I get to my feet and leave him sitting there as I enter the room and shut the door, feeling as if I'm also shutting the door on us.

Chapter 55

Dawn

I'm just following orders.

Those words roll through my head on repeat as I open my eyes. Whose orders was he following?

My mother?

Could she have ordered her own daughter's death? Or was it Jonathan?

I'm not some brain-dead rebel. I'm not loyal to the cause. I will not follow orders blindly. That doesn't sit well with rebel command.

Everyone has been wondering how I got assigned to a patrol right out of the trials. That's it. I was put here to die.

The boat rocks back and forth. I feel sick and the pain in my shoulder is almost too much to bear.

"How're you feeling?" Lucas asks as he comes in and sets a bowl of food beside my bed. Just the smell of it is too much. There is no way I could eat anything right now anyway.

"Like I was shot," I answer finally. He laughs at that before digging into the food he brought for me. He leaves me the stale bread to nibble on.

"Captain says we'll be there soon," he tells me. I struggle to sit up and get out of bed. "No, you don't." Lucas pauses to take another bite.

"We're supposed to stay out of sight until the captain can get permission for us to enter Cincinnati." He helps me lay back once more.

"That sounds sketchy." I hesitate.

"It'll be fine. The Americans keep a strict watch on any strangers in their territory." He shrugs. "Cincinnati is the only American town that has survived longer than a few decades, so they must be doing something right. Every other time the Americans have tried to unite and settle, it hasn't ended well."

Brent and Officer Mills come in to wait with us. It's hours before Captain Collins tells us that we have been cleared to enter the town. He sent for a medic to transfer me to the clinic. A young woman shows up with two men in tow. Pain sears through me as I'm slowly lifted onto the stretcher. I clench my teeth to keep from screaming.

I'm carried up onto the deck where a uniformed man waits for us. He does not speak as he pats us down in a thorough security check. He removes any knives or guns he finds and places them in a bucket. Lucas tries to protest but one look from the security guard and he shuts up.

"Let him have all your weapons," Captain Collins says. "He'll leave them on the boat. Strangers can't carry weapons once they leave the docks."

The guard finishes his weapons search and escorts us off the boat. After seeing the docks in Texas, I expected much more from this port. Ours is the only boat here and it's a good thing because there's only two slips and a few small fishing vessels anchored nearby.

I fade in and out of consciousness as we move through town and the next thing I know I'm waking up inside a large tent filled with cots. There are a few other patients nearby and the nurses hurry between them. I shield my eyes as the tent flap is pushed aside and sunlight pours in behind the doctor.

The first thing I see is Doctor Darren Cole. Panic turns my veins to ice and I squeeze my eyes shut. When I open them seconds later, Doctor Cole is nowhere in sight. I breathe a sigh of relief as the doctor steps closer. He's young and his expression serious as he looks at me.

Good," he says, "you're awake. How are you feeling?" I try to speak, but only gibberish comes out. "I'll take that as good news." He chuckles and his resulting smile lights up his face. "I gave you a strong pain killer." Now that he says that, I realize that the pain of the last few days in gone. A question forms in my mind but then dissipates before I can get it out. My head is swimming.

"I had to reopen the wound to clean it properly," the doc explains. "Whoever fixed it did a hack job on the stitches, but he saved your life." I'm able to manage a nod.

"What are you doing Ryan?" The voice comes from behind him and his face reddens as he turns.

"We were only chatting," he explains.

"After what I gave her, I doubt she's up for much conversation. Why don't you go get her some water?" He turns to me, excusing Ryan. "I'm sorry about that. My assistant likes to play doctor." I try to smile, but my face feels numb. "I assume he told you everything you need to know. I'm Doctor Murray if you have any questions." He leaves and I doze off again.

Chapter 56

Dawn

I wake with a much clearer head. It must be late because only a few candles illuminate the darkness. Two beds away from me, a man starts screaming in pain. Two nurses hold him down as a third tries to dress a wound. I'm so focused on that man that I don't notice Ryan until he sits on the end of my bed.

"He was part of a force that was keeping the freedom fighters from our borders," he explains. "They were attacked last night."

"So, you're not a doctor," I accuse.

"I'm training to be one, but, yeah, right now I'm just a medic's assistant." He pauses. "So, Dawn, how'd you get shot." He leans forward eagerly.

"How do you know my name?" He grabs a folder that is clipped onto the end of my bed and opens it.

"Dawn. Last name not known." He reads. "Nationality, British. Affiliation, rebel."

"I get it," I snap. "You can stop now." He shrugs and sets it down.

"So, you think you can get up?"

"I don't know, why?"

"I'm supposed to bring you to Chief Smith. Your friends are already there."

"Let's go then," I say quickly, trying to sit up.

"Do you want meds first?"

"Definitely not," I say. "I want a clear head."

"Okay then." A nurse brings over a wheelchair and Ryan lifts me into it. I hold on as he pushes me away from the tent. The moon is nowhere to be seen tonight so we're in complete darkness. With every bump, the wheelchair jostles me and I groan.

We pass by wooden houses with lanterns in the windows, but I can't see much else. Lucas is waiting outside of a small cottage.

"Thank you for bringing her," he says to Ryan, expecting him to turn around and leave. Instead, he walks straight through the front door without knocking. Lucas and I share a look before following him in.

Officer Mills and Brent are already warming themselves by the fire. Ryan is in the kitchen with a pair of women; one older and one very young who are eying us suspiciously. The older woman serves us tea but doesn't say a word. After a while of intense silence, a tall man ducks through the doorway. The imposing figure walks straight towards us and collapses into a nearby chair. His long, gray hair is tied back and his beard is braided, but it's his eyes that set him apart. They're piercing as he focuses on each of us in turn.

Ryan sits on the arm of my wheelchair and chews loudly on a piece of bread. "Hey dad," he says cheerfully. He shuts up when his father's gaze lands on him.

"My horse is tied up outside. He needs rubbed down, taken to the stables, and fed," the grim-faced man says.

"Yes, sir." Ryan hurries away and I suddenly feel less comfortable.

"I'm Chief Smith," the big man states. "You are rebels and I know why you're here."

"We brought you a letter from Jonathan Clarke." Officer Mills hands him an envelope.

"I know what it says." He throws the letter into the fire, unopened. "The answer is no."

"Chief Smith-" Officer Mills pleads, but he holds up a hand to stop her.

"The rebels will attack Texas soon. That is inevitable. This I know." He pauses, "I also know that the ranks of the freedom fighters are surging. They're attacking my borders and I'm losing men in droves. I also know that my rule here is tenuous. I have power hungry neighbors breathing down my neck. I was put into this role. I did not take it and most think that I did not earn it. Foreign powers are not trusted here so I can't help you."

"Chief Smith," Lucas says, "if the Texan troops are able to be pulled from the Mexican front and our forces attack Texas alone, it could be disastrous."

"Young man that is not my problem. You forget that we rely on Texas for trade."

"You rely on smugglers," I say under my breath. They all heard me.

"You forget yourself girl," the chief says dangerously. "Our trade is completely legitimate. No smuggler would be allowed in our ports."

"With all due respect, sir, that's bullshite." His eyes narrow in response to my tone. The throbbing pain in my arm is making me angry. "We came here on a smuggler's ship."

"I will have him arrested."

"Another will just show up." I meet his gaze. "I spent months in Texas. Their greatest flaw is that they believe they're the master race. The point is, they don't believe in trade, they believe in taking. They want land, resources, and to bend everyone to their way of thinking. I know, I was there, and they are willing to kill everyone that gets in the way of their new order. If they defeat us, you may be next." The chief leans back and scratches his head. I have just challenged something that he feels strongly about.

"It's late," he says finally. "You may leave."

Lucas pushes me outside with Officer Mills and Brent in tow. The crisp air feels good after that stuffy cabin.

"You did good in there, Nolan," Officer Mills says as they help me into my bed back at the clinic.

"Thanks." I manage a small smile. I don't know what exactly I ac-complished. Things could get even worse if the Americans did choose to come to the rebel's aid. How many in Texas would die then?

Chapter 57

Dawn

We're leaving tomorrow whether we've convinced the chief to help us or not. Captain Collins sent us a message that he can't wait any longer. He needs to get back to St. Louis, the smugglers' port in Texas.

Lucas is wheeling me through the village even though I woke up this morning feeling weaker. I'm supposed to be on the mend. I'm grumpy and didn't even want to leave my bed, but Lucas made me. He thinks the fresh air will do me some good. The nurse didn't agree, but Lucas ignored her objections.

We move through the market watching goods change hands. I keep an eye out for Corey. He told me that he was headed here when he left the compound, but I've seen no sign of him or Matty. I asked Ryan about them. He said that they probably never made it here or else he would have heard about two Texans in town. I'm scared for them. Where are they if not here?

Americans glare at us as they rush about. Everyone seems to be in a hurry. It is a busy place. Lucas weaves us around stalls and through the crowd of people until our path takes us away from the bustle. We end up at a stream that has branched off from the river. Fishermen cast nets and some wade into the glassy water.

"Dawn." I look around to find the source of my name and see Ryan on the opposite bank, waving furiously. He jumps into the water with a small splash and wades towards us. The other fishermen give him disgusted looks. I assume he's just scared away a lot of the fish.

"Shouldn't you be at the clinic or something?" I ask.

"Probably." He shrugs. "But then I couldn't fish." He wrings out the bottom of his shirt and grins. "You guys up for some grub? I'm starving."

"Always," Lucas jokes as he turns my chair to follow Ryan. I, on the other hand, would like nothing more than to return to my bed in the clinic. The boys won't hear of it.

"Get those muddy boots off!" Ryan's mom barks at him as soon as we step inside. She doesn't even look at us.

The smell in here is enough to turn my already queasy stomach. There's meat on the cooker and the boys go to it eagerly. I decline a plate as I'm sure I wouldn't be able to keep it down.

"Sorry about my mom," Ryan says in between mouthfuls. I shrug and look away. I'm used to people not wanting to speak with me. Being an orphan in old clothing with a loner disposition didn't exactly make me popular in London.

"You've got to understand something," Ryan continues, "the rebels aren't trusted here. No outsider really is. Most of the people here have lived in fear of strangers their entire lives. This town has not been around long enough to forget what it was like before. Many of them were hunted and had to scavenge to survive. Even if my father were to commit our people to your cause, very few of them would actually show up." He tears off a piece of bread as he considers us.

"Can I tell you guys a secret?" he whispers. When Lucas nods, he continues, "Cincinnati would not exist if it wasn't for an outsider." He leans in closer to us. "A man named General Nolan and his people helped my father become chief and restore peace to this region." He lowers his voice even more. "General Nolan is British." I don't know what he expects from us as he looks for signs of astonishment. I wish I could say I was surprised. My father seems to have a hand in everything that goes on in the colonies.

"General Nolan-" Lucas stops suddenly when I kick him. He rubs his shin and glares at me.

"What's going on?" Ryan asks. I'm about to reply when the room begins to spin around me. My arms shoot out to grip my chair tightly. A cold sweat starts and I only vaguely hear Ryan and Lucas talking to me. I try to say something, but only garbled sounds come out. Images seem to float across my field of vision, but I can't focus my eyes on any one thing. Someone has their hand on my forehead while someone else is checking my wound. I don't know who. Who was I talking to a minute ago?

I don't feel anything as I'm lifted and positioned flat on the ground. The last thing I remember is the wonderful feeling of the cold floor on my hot skin.

Chapter 58

Dawn

My shoulder is infected. That much I understand. The rest is just noise. Doctors and nurses use all this medical jargon to talk to each other about me. It's as if I'm not even here.

All I want to do is sleep. I feel horrid and want everyone to leave me alone. I accept their antibiotics but refuse the pain meds. I don't like what they do to me and we're supposed to be leaving today. I can't have a foggy head. As soon as Officer Mills finishes her final meeting with Chief Smith, we can head back to the compound.

The nurses finally leave me be and I drift away. My kip doesn't last long as Officer Mills, Lucas, and Brent walk in, their faces grim.

"Dawn," Officer Mills says, "the chief has given us permission to let you recover here."

"What?" I snap. "No, I need to come with you."

"You may not survive the trip in your state," she pauses, "I'm sorry."

"I won't stay."

"Yes, you will," she responds. "This is an order, soldier."

"How am I supposed to get back to base then?"

"I'm sure Jonathan and Miranda will send a patrol for you in a few weeks."

"Really?" I scream suddenly. "Dammit, how can you be so daft? They would rather leave me here to rot."

"She's right, Grace, and you know it," Lucas states. "If Jonathan knows she's alive, he's more likely to send a kill squad." Officer Mills starts pacing.

"We'll figure it out once we get back." She sighs. "I'm sorry, Dawn, but you're going to have to wait here until then."

"Fine." I give in, recognizing a losing fight. "But you need to let everyone believe that I'm dead."

"Are you sure that's what you want?" Brent asks. "I know firsthand what death does to people. Your sister-"

"My sister will be fine," I interrupt angrily. "Just do it, please." They share a look and then nod in agreement. Gabby thinks the rebels can do no wrong. I don't know what this will do to her. It'll probably just drive her further into the cause. There's nothing I can do about that.

"One more thing," I say, "do any of you know Jeremy? He's an American in the compound."

"I fought him in his trials," Lucas answers.

"He needs to know what happened," I say. "He needs to know he isn't safe. Tell him I'm alive." I want to tell them that Drew needs to know as well, but I don't. I don't know if he'd believe Lucas. He has become a loyal rebel. No, Jeremy is the only person that needs to know. He needs to be careful. I only hope that I can make it back in time to help him.

We say our goodbyes and then they're gone. In an instant, I'm the lone stranger in a sea of hatred and fear.

Chapter 59

Miranda

I'm called to the garage as soon as they arrive; the patrol that was sent to Cincinnati looking for allies. I hurry to meet them, hoping they bring good news. Jonathan and I leave our offices in a rush and walk quickly down the long hallway that dead ends into the car park. There are three of them; only three. I scan their faces, but Dawn is not among them. Where is she? What happened? I recognize Grace Mills and Lucas, but the third name eludes me. They stop and salute as they get close.

"At ease, soldiers," Jonathan cheerfully says before looking around. He seems to be happy about something. I know he's a little nuts, but does he have something to do with whatever happened to the rest of this patrol? "Lucas, Brent you two are relieved of your duties for a couple of days. You may leave." They do as they're told. "Officer Mills, please come with us to make your report."

"Yes, sir," she says as we turn towards the door. We lead her back the way we'd come and go into Jonathan's office in command.

"Have a seat," Jonathan says to us both. Officer Mills collapses into the chair with a big sigh. When I look closely at her, I see how knackered she is. The bags under her eyes are dark and her movements are stiff. Her skin is burnt from the sun and the wind and her uniform is stained with dirt and something that looks a lot like blood.

"Welcome home soldier," I say. "We were expecting you back last week."

"We ran into some trouble that delayed us," she explains.

"Yes," Jonathan begins. "The rivers can be perilous. First things first, what news do you bring us from Cincinnati?"

"The chief does not have the power or the desire to get involved," the officer explains.

"What does that mean?" Jonathan starts pacing. "Dammit!" he repeats over and over. I watch him move about like a madman, but I don't speak. I don't know what to say. He did not plan for this even though I warned him that it was a long shot. I look at Officer Mills.

"Tell us everything that happened since you left." I sigh. Right now might not be the right time for this, but it's protocol. The report must be made before anything can be forgotten or corrupted. She clears her throat and then begins.

"We made it to the river with no problems, but then we had to set up camp and wait for days. That's where we were attacked by a band of freedom fighters." She stops and her eyes shift away.

"Freedom fighters? Around here? Are you sure?" Jonathan asks hurriedly.

"Yes, sir," the officer responds.

"We may have to do something about that. What happened next?" Jonathan finally calms down and sits on the corner of his desk.

"We fought, but we were outnumbered." She lowers her voice. "Soldiers Lucas, Brent, and I were the only survivors." She doesn't meet my eyes as this information sinks in. Dawn was killed and she doesn't know how I'll react to that information. I see the smugness flicker across Jonathan's face. Something isn't right. Did he do this?

"What happened next?" Jonathan prods, but I barely hear them as she gives the rest of her report. Jonathan thinks he did what is best for me. Maybe he did. I don't know. Dawn was a huge liability. She didn't believe in what we're doing and she is not the first person to be killed for that same reason. I tell myself these things, but they don't make me feel any better.

"Officer, can you do what I ask?" Jonathan says. She indicates that she can. "The official story will be that you were set upon by a Texan scouting group. Do you understand?"

"Yes," she squeaks.

"Make sure your men know this as well." I vaguely see Officer Mills leave the room and then Jonathan turns to me.

"You should have consulted me." My voice is low, dangerous. "There were other ways to deal with her. I was handling it."

"No, you were using the shrink to try and change her. I've watched her. It wouldn't have worked. This was the only way," he says rather harshly. "It had to be done and now it's over. You need to move past this right now because we have more important things to talk about."

He's right, of course. To be a rebel leader, one needs to be able to compartmentalize. My entire life has consisted of me doing things that hurt me but helped the rebels. I've learned to shut off certain emotions and not let them cloud my judgment. Why can't I do that now? I think back to the dispatch I sent out weeks ago. I have yet to hear back and I don't even know if it will do any good.

"I've had word from London," Jonathan changes the subject. This wakes me up.

"What about?" I say quickly. It's not often that we can communicate with our counterparts in England so, when we do, it's important.

"The rebels have turned things around over there."

"How?" I ask, surprised. When I left, we were losing rebels in droves.

"For decades the government has been lying about their environmental research. They've kept people believing that the climate change is on the edge of a reversal."

"But it's not?" I ask.

"They're not the only ones doing research."

"So, what's the truth?

"I don't know all the details, but it sure isn't what the government has been spewing for the last twenty years. I'm waiting for the report to reach us."

"And when the report got out, our countrymen finally joined us and turned on the government." I'm beginning to understand. "Has the military taken a stance?"

"They're divided and fighting amongst themselves," he explains. "As soon as Texas is no longer a problem, your father is going to start evacuating people to the colonies."

"What about the soldiers in Floridaland?" I ask.

"General Nolan's last message said that most of his troops stand united, but it's only a matter of time. The majority is still very loyal to British leadership, but there is also a faction that has started to dissent." He pauses. "The important thing is that they will not be getting reinforcements since London is in shambles. Once we deal with Texas, we can turn east and take out those bastards."

"I would think it should be a higher priority."

"No," he almost yells. "If we do not defeat Texas, we will never get out of these mines. They already know we're coming and have delivered a message." He hands me the message.

New Texas will drive you back into the sea.

We both stare for a moment in stunned silence. Our people face extinction if we lose this fight.

"So," I say, "what do we do? We don't have the numbers."

"Well, that's where we take a page out of the London playbook that I'm sure you know very well. We will rely on the bombs and our greatest advantage will be the element of surprise. We can't lose that. They won't be ready for us. We have to go after all three cities at once. We were hoping to have help from the Americans in the North, but we know how that turned out."

"Do you really think we can pull this off?" I ask.

"We have to."

I nod as Jonathan spreads out a map of the capitol. "Even if we fail in Baton Rouge and St. Louis, we must defeat the capitol," he explains. "The wall is nearly impenetrable."

"Can't we just blow it?" That seems like the obvious choice to me.

"Not unless we want to alert them to our presence right off the bat. Before any of the explosions, our snipers need to be in place in these sectors." He points to three areas on the map where we need to cause the most damage.

"Then how do we get in?" I know next to nothing about Texas.

"There is a door in the southern wall, here." He shows me on the map. "Our people on the inside will get us into the city through the door. Snipers first. We send in the runners next. Finally, once the explosions have started, we send in our ground troops to keep stirring things up. We blast the wall to get out."

"It's a good plan."

"Yes." There's that wicked grin again. I don't know if I should see this man as a genius or a nutter. I don't admit this to him, but this plan scares me. On paper, it looks good, really good. In reality, I think both Texas and the Rebels are in for some tough losses.

"How are you doing coordinating the boats?" he asks me.

"They're reluctant," I admit.

"They're smugglers; they help anyone who can pay them."

"Not this time, sir. They may be criminals, but they don't want to commit treason. That's what they see this as. Texas is their home." This has been the one frustrating part of this plan. "Sir, if we can't get them on board, we may have to abort the mission."

"No!" he screams. He breathes deeply to regain his cool. "Let me take care of it." Something in the way he says this has me frightened. What is he going to do?

Chapter 60

The General

"Sir." Soldier Hane enters my office. Every time someone knocks on my door, I'm hoping it's Locke. I was expecting him back weeks ago. I don't even know if he was able to get to Allison with my message. The Republic is a dangerous place right now. I finally look up at Hane. He stands in salute until I speak.

"At ease soldier." He relaxes and hands me an opened envelope.

"We intercepted this from a rebel messenger," he explains. "It had to be opened to check for safety." I unfold the letter slowly. The rebels never contact me here. They've passed right by all the protocols and now I'm not the only person to see this letter.

"You may go now," I say rather harshly. He quickly leaves as I begin to read.

David,

It's time for you to join us. There is something not right with Jonathan Clarke and I fear he will get us all killed. In just a few weeks' time, we're moving on the Republic of Texas. We don't have the numbers and he is hoping our explosives will make up for that. His plan is brilliant, but it won't work.

There is something else you need to know. Gabby and Dawn are here. One of our operatives got them out of Texas. Look past your feelings about

me because I know you care about these girls. I can't be a mother to them, not now. But I know you, David, you can be their father.
  -Miranda

I immediately pen a message back to tell her that I'm on my way and I dispatch a trusted messenger to get there as quick as she can. Miranda has left me with no other choice. If I don't leave now, I'll be arrested. A higher up will have been shown the letter. Dammit, Miranda. She blew my cover.

I hurriedly collect up some of the papers on my desk and throw them into a rucksack. The only stop I make once I leave my office is the kitchen. Next, I head to the stables. Once my horse and I are far enough from the plantation, I let out a sigh of relief and then start the long trek to rebel headquarters.

Chapter 61

Gabby

I'm collapsed in bed after a long day of sniper training when there is a rap at the door. Drew answers it and Lucas walks in. I haven't seen him since he was beating me senseless during my trials.

"Hello." He smiles tightly before turning to Jeremy. "Can I talk to you in the hall?"

"Sure," Jeremy responds, confusion shaping his features. They walk out into the hall, returning a few minutes later. Jeremy's face looks ashen. "I need to tell you all something before you hear it another way." Upon seeing the seriousness of his expression, I stand.

"What is it?" I ask. "What's wrong?"

"Dawn," he says quietly. "She didn't make it back from our assignment."

"What do you mean?" I say as the panic invades my voice.

"She's dead." I stumble backward, but Jeremy is there to catch me. He wraps me in his arms and he holds me tight. I see Drew nearby as his knees buckle and he falls to the floor. "I'm so sorry," Lucas says before he leaves.

This can't be right. I have to be imagining things. My sister will come walking in the door any minute to tell us about the adventure she's just been on. My beautiful little sister who has always been so much better than the rest of us. As Drew says, she was only here because of me. Does that mean I'm responsible for her death? A sob ripples through my chest and I push Jeremy away. Drew is still in shambles on the ground and Jeremy's eyes bore into me. They're caring and kind. He wants to comfort me. I don't deserve any of it.

I leg it out of the room and down the hall, looking for that familiar door that will lead me into my sanctuary. I find it and enter the shooting range. This is the only place I could think of to go. It's my church; my safe haven. I pick up a hand gun and start shooting the target rapidly. By the time I hear the click, signaling the need for more ammo, tears are running down my face. I reload the gun and can barely see the target through watery eyes as I squeeze the trigger once more.

The last thing I said to my sister was that I didn't want to see her face anymore. I pull the trigger.

For months now, we have done nothing but fight. I pull the trigger.

My sister must have thought that I hated her. I pull the trigger.

She thought I had become a horrible person. Maybe I have. I pull the trigger.

I will never get the chance to apologize and tell her everything is going to be okay. I reload.

"I couldn't protect her," I say aloud. I couldn't save her. I failed my baby sister. I pull the trigger again and again until all I hear are clicks and my own sobs. I cradle the gun and sink to my knees, rocking back and forth. I'm so sorry, Dawn.

Chapter 62

Gabby

The next morning, Jeremy finds me in the range and wakes me up.

"Hey," he says softly as he shakes my shoulders. "You okay?"

"My sister is dead," I answer. "So, no I'm not okay." I sit up and my body is stiff from sleeping on the hard ground. I stretch out my limbs and stand up.

"They've called a breakfast meeting that we're all required to attend," he says, glancing behind me at the target I destroyed last night. He sighs and tries to hug me. I duck away from his open arms and head to the cafeteria. I look around at our table. Drew's uniform is wrinkled, his hair is a mess, and his eyes are bloodshot. Lee and Conner have hopelessly sad expressions and there is even sympathy in Shay's eyes. Jeremy takes his seat, but I walk right past all of them to sit by myself. I can't take all of their sadness and pity.

Jonathan and Miranda walk to the microphone at the front of the room. I stand along with everyone else to give my salute because this is all I have left.

"At ease," Jonathan says and we all sit back down. "Thank you all for being here."

"Today is a sad day," Miranda chimes in and I could almost swear that she looks directly at me. I watch as my mother talks about her own daughter's death. "One of our patrols was attacked by the Texans." The entire room sucks in a collective breath. "We lost eight good soldiers. It will not be forgotten."

"In the aftermath of this atrocity," Jonathan begins, "we have set a date for our assault on Texas. Three weeks from today, they will pay. We leave in four days. Your commanding officers will have your assignments. We will be going after three cities at once. Everyone will have a job to do because we will not be able to rely on numbers. I will now let you all in on something that we have kept secret." He pauses, "our brilliant technicians have developed bombs." No one seems surprised as I look around. "Our success is going to rely on stealth and cunning. We're going to destroy their cities before they even see us coming. To anyone still questioning our fight, I say this, destroying the Texans will allow England to relocate its people here. A natural tragedy is befalling our beloved island nation. Within 50 years it will be nearly unlivable. The survival of our culture depends on your bravery. We need to succeed here in vanquishing those who would deny our people their future. Texas must be crushed."

"You all need to be ready," Miranda says. "We may ask you to do things that are not easy. Train like you never have before. We may not have the biggest force, but we will have the best. In London, we had a phrase to describe these game-changing events. It will be a Day of Reckoning!"

I join in as a round of shouting makes its way across the room.

"Rebels!" I yell along with everyone else.

Miranda and Jonathan watch the scene with smiles on their faces.

"You are dismissed," Jonathan says. People rise, but they don't leave the room as the roaring grows louder. Someone starts a chant and soon everyone has joined in.

I need to yell; to let everything out. It doesn't feel good. It just feels right. I will go on with grim determination. This is personal now. I want to make them pay. I will make them pay.

Chapter 63

Dawn

My strength is returning quickly, but my shoulder still throbs whenever I lift my arm. The dizzy spells are coming less frequently, but I'm still in the clinic because they have nowhere else to put me. Ryan is usually with me when he's not fishing, chopping wood, training horses, or performing one of the million other jobs around here. I've asked him about that a few times and he says that no one here is simply labeled as one thing. He is training to be a medic, but he will never be just a medic. His days are filled with whatever his father wants done. His favorite job is working in the stables and that's where I find him on this cloudy day.

When I see him, he is walking a large, black horse in circles around the yard. He beams as I walk up. I can't help but draw parallels between this boy and Sam. They're the only people I've ever known to smile this much; to make you feel like they're always happy to see you. When I think of Sam like this, his smile and his joy, I can finally do so without the overwhelming grief that used to accompany any reminder of him.

Ryan walks the horse towards me and I step back. I've never been around horses and I'm suddenly nervous.

"Duke won't hurt you," Ryan laughs. "Come meet him." When my feet stay in one place, Ryan comes closer. The big animal blows air into my face and then nudges me with his nose. I'm frozen on the spot. Ryan's laughter becomes hysterical.

"I don't see what's so funny," I say through clenched teeth. Duke's big eyes bore into me.

"He wants you to pet him." I glare at Ryan. "Come on," he encourages me. When I don't move, he takes my hand and puts it on Duke's nose. After a few uncomfortable moments, I run my hand along the length of his nose. He is surprisingly soft. Suddenly, he takes a step forward and I jump back.

"Let's put Duke away," Ryan says, much to my relief. "I should probably be getting to the clinic anyway." He leads Duke into the stable and hands him off to someone else.

"So," I start, "I've been feeling a lot better."

"That's good," he says cautiously, knowing where this conversation is going. I've been bugging him all week about getting back to the rebel compound.

"I need to get back before the rebels march on Texas."

"You know what I don't get?" He pauses. "You're only one girl. What makes you think the rebels need you so bad?"

"They don't." I stop. If I need to trust someone, I guess it might as well be this American boy who will probably never be farther south than this town. "The rebels are planning to kill a lot of innocent people."

"I've heard the stories about that place. Texas doesn't seem all that innocent to me."

"No, but many of the people are." I look towards the gray sky. I need to make him understand. "The rebels are going to destroy a lot of valuable food sources and then they're going to bomb the cities."

"So, you aren't a rebel then?"

"Well, technically I am."

"You're a traitor rebel then?"

"I wouldn't put it that way."

"You're actively planning on betraying them?"

"I guess." I stop walking and look at him. "A lot of people are going to die."

"Sometimes people have to die so that others can live. It's the reality of our world."

"That's it," I say quietly, an idea coming to me. "What do you think would happen to Texas if they no longer had their prophet?"

"A civilization cannot run without a strong ruler. They'd surrender to whoever spared their lives."

"I need to see your father," I state, changing direction.

"He won't see you," Ryan warns, catching up to me. "He's refused you all week. He can't be seen speaking to foreigners again. He's barely holding on to his power as it is right now."

"I'll have to make him see me," I say confidently.

"Why would he agree to that? Why now?"

I don't have time to explain everything to him as I barge into the Smith house. Ryan's mother looks up from her sewing in surprise and is about to say something until Ryan walks in behind me.

"Where's dad?" he asks. His mother looks from him to me and then back to him.

"He went to the north fields to check on the planting." Ryan and I hurry out of the house.

"You really want to see him?" he asks.

"Yeah, I do."

"It would take all day to walk there. Come with me." We end up at the stables and my eyes widen as Ryan takes a saddle off a hook and walks in. He returns with Duke. "It's the only way," he explains. He gets himself situated in the saddle before offering me a hand. It takes a few tries, but he's able to help me into the saddle behind him. I can feel the horse's every movement beneath me and we start out at a slow walk. I wrap my arms around Ryan and clamp my hands together in front of his chest. There is no way I'm going to fall.

"Hold on!" Ryan yells as he gives Duke a light kick and we pick up speed. People stay out of our way as we pass the edge of town. It takes us quite a while to reach the north fields where people are spread out working the ground.

Chief Smith sits atop his horse, surveying the field. Ryan slows Duke as we get closer. The chief sees us and shakes his head.

"What are you doing out here son?" he demands. "You're scheduled to work on the new construction this afternoon. We need to get that finished before the storms come."

"Dawn said it was important." He shrugs.

"I'm sorry, Dawn, but I can't help you." The chief keeps his eyes focused on his son as he speaks to me.

"You don't even know what she's going to say," Ryan protests.

"Son, look around. This is not the place." The workers nearby have stopped their work and are openly staring at us. "Have Dawn tell you what it is and we can talk tonight. Right now, you have to leave. Don't bring her here again." The chief turns his horse to walk away.

"Wait!" I yell. He stops but doesn't face us. "General Nolan is my father." I don't know what I was expecting, but the chief digs his heels into his horse and gallops away. I'm left dumbfounded. Giving up, we ride back to town.

"Dawn Nolan," Ryan says under his breath.

"Do you have something you'd like to say to me?" I snap, suddenly angry at both the chief and his son.

"No," he says quietly.

"Yes you do," I respond. "Go on then. Spit it out."

"You should have told us sooner."

"Why would I have done that?"

"You really don't understand, do you?" he says. "General Nolan collects debts. He does something for you so that he can count on you for a favor at some point in the future. My father owes him a lot for his chiefdom. General Nolan took it by force and by the time he gave it to my father, that power was tarnished. My father has to look over his shoulder at every turn, waiting for someone to take everything away. Loyalty is hard to achieve when you're seen as a foreign puppet. Our family is the largest in town, but if the other families were to band together, they would destroy us."

We've reached the stables and as I'm helped down off of Duke, I ask, "Is that why your father won't speak to me?"

"No," he answers, hanging up the saddle. "People watch everything he does and he can't appear to sympathize with a foreigner. Ever since the great collapse and the Eastern war, us Americans don't trust any power, any government, and certainly not anyone called 'General'. You see, my father seems to think that your father is a friend to him. A friend that he owes big time. He doesn't see what I do. Your father ruined him. The chiefdom is a curse more than anything else."

"That is not my father's doing," I state defensively.

"You're right, of course. If you see things as my father does. But you're also dead wrong."

We put Duke away and Ryan heads off to work as I make my way back to the clinic.

Chapter 64

Dawn

I'm awakened in the middle of the night by someone holding a lantern by my head and saying my name. I open my eyes and am shocked to find Chief Smith bent over me. He puts a finger to his lips and motions for me to follow him. We go outside to where the moon's silver light dances across the town. In a groggy haze, I almost trip over my own two feet. The chief doesn't say a word as we walk through the marketplace that will be teeming with people in a few hours. Right now, though, it's deserted.

We hear footsteps echo off the stones and the chief pulls me into an alleyway that is pitch black. I try to ask what's going on, but he covers my mouth with his hand. Once all is quiet again, we step back out onto the road. He starts to run. I keep pace with him until we reach the stables. The side door opens and we stand frozen until Ryan pops his head out and we can breathe again.

"Took you long enough," Ryan whispers, waving us inside.

"What's going on?" I'm finally able to ask.

"They know who you are," Ryan explains.

"Who does?"

"The other families," the chief explains. "They're coming for you and I can't stop them. Most of our men are out dealing with the freedom fighters. We're defenseless."

"I don't understand," I whisper.

"They want to lock you up and probably execute you publicly as a sign that foreigners are not welcome here."

"Why are you helping me?" I ask. "Won't they just go after you now?"

"Your father is a good man and I owe him everything," he says before turning to Ryan. "You ready?"

"Almost," he answers. "We just have to wait for mom to bring Emily." As if on cue, the two women walk through the door. Ryan's young sister looks terrified.

"Wait, you guys are coming with me?" I won't lie, I'm a bit relieved that I won't be on my own.

"It isn't safe here for them anymore," the chief says sadly. "My enemies will use them to get to me." He then stares at his wife. "I wish you would go too."

"Not without you," she says simply.

"I can't. Our family, along with the smaller families, need me here to protect them. I have to stay."

"Then I have to stay as well." She hands Ryan a saddle bag full of food and he attaches it to Duke's saddle. She then takes Emily into her arms. I watch her cling to her mother and realize she can't be more than ten.

"I don't want to go," she mutters over and over with tears streaming from her large eyes. Ryan kisses his mother and hugs his dad before leading the horses from the stable. Chief Smith manages to pry Emily from her mother and help her up into the saddle of her horse. Ryan climbs onto Duke and once again helps me up.

"Take care of my Emily," Ryan's mother sobs.

"I will," he chokes out his response. I feel his body shake in front of me as the tears come freely.

"You must go now," the chief says. "You only have a few more hours of darkness." Ryan and Emily look at their parents one last time before kicking their horses into a run. I grip Ryan even tighter. I glance over at Emily and her long, black curls are blowing out behind her. She doesn't look back at me.

Chapter 65

Dawn

We ride on for hours before we stop. "We need to water the horses," Ryan tells me. I slide down with stiff legs that ache as I walk to the stream that we have found. I bend down immediately and cup my hands to bring water to my parched lips.

Here I am again, running for my life. Does it ever end?

Emily and Ryan sit near me as the horses drink gratefully. Brother and sister both look like they could fall to pieces at any time. I don't blame them. Gabby was younger than Emily when we became parentless, but she still remembers what if felt like to be part of a family. I only remember bits and pieces of my family and I think it's better that way.

"I'm so sorry," I say, knowing how little those words actually mean. I feel like a prat because I don't know what else to say.

"You should be," Emily snaps. "If you hadn't shown up, none of this would have happened."

Is she right? Am I to blame for ruining her life?

"That's bullshit, Emily," Ryan says. "That's just mom talking. This has been coming for a long time. If I didn't have to get you out, I would have stayed to fight." Emily jumps to her feet.

"Fine," she screams, "if you want to go back, don't let me stop you. Go ahead and get yourself killed. Me and Jasmine will be just fine." She tries to make as much noise as possible as she stomps away.

"Who's Jasmine?" I ask.

"Her horse." He glances back to where the horses were just a moment ago. Only Duke is there. "Shit, Emily," he yells as he shoots to his feet. He climbs onto Duke without a saddle. "Don't you dare jump that stream bed. It's too far," he yells after her as he takes off, but then pulls up short of the water as Emily and Jasmine fly through the air and land safely on the other side. "Stay right there!" Ryan commands.

"Fine!" she gives in. Ryan slides down and saddles Duke. He gets on and I hand Jasmine's saddle to him before I climb up. We wade carefully through the stream and then Ryan thrusts the saddle at his sister.

"Jasmine doesn't like saddles," she says as she rubs the horse's nose. Jasmine lowers her head so that Emily can plant a kiss on her.

"Put the saddle on her," Ryan demands. She gives in again and before we know it, we're on the move.

Chapter 66

Gabby

I'm so ready for this. I've been assigned to Vicksburg, the Texan capitol, along with Jeremy. Lee and Drew are both going to be headed for St. Louis. They say that we have to use different tactics for each city and ours will be the hardest to defeat. I'm up for the challenge. I check every inch of my sniper rifle before packing it away. The next time I will shoot this gun will be from atop a building, aiming at real live targets.

I'm not looking forward to another boat ride. I know this one will be shorter and we won't have to hide away in some cramped room, but still, this sucks. None of us know the entire plan because Jonathan is very secretive. I'm not even sure Miranda knows it all. We have each been told our part.

People are saying that Jonathan has gone mad. He isn't sleeping or eating. He's not even marching with us. Everyone around here is a bit scared because we don't know what we'll be walking into. Some of the officers have even taken it upon themselves to create contingency plans. If Jonathan finds out, we're all buggered.

"You ready?" Jeremy asks as he walks up behind me and hoists his pack onto his shoulders. He has been assigned to what we're calling the bomb squad or the runners. They will place the bombs at their designated targets and then the explosives will be detonated remotely.

"Can't wait." I grin. He doesn't return my smile, but he also doesn't lecture me on being too eager for the fight. Ever since my sister's death, he has been walking on eggshells around me. He's been trying harder to be my friend, but that's it, my "friend". He's made that perfectly clear.

The ramp opens and everyone shields their eyes at once. Most of the soldiers have not been outside in a very long time and the sun is blinding. I'm one of the lucky few who have spent an enormous amount of time out here lately.

We move as an elite force, as one. Having left our uniforms at base, we wear plain clothes that will be less noticeable. Of course, before entering the Texan cities, we will have to change again to blend in with them.

We march down an old road, littered with broken pieces of concrete. It takes us all the way to the river and, by then, the atmosphere is buzzing with excitement. By dusk, there are three boats moored nearby. We're all surprised to find Jonathan standing on the deck of the nearest one. He was missing when we left base, but Miranda had taken charge.

The man up ahead is not the same man I met at the compound. He is unshaven and unkempt. As I get closer, I can see that the wild look in his eyes has only gotten stronger.

"Welcome," he booms. We salute and he continues. "Come aboard, soldiers. If you have been assigned to the capitol you're with me. In the second boat, Captain Collins will take those headed for St. Louis. Everyone else is in the third boat. Hurry up, we need to get moving."

"I hate sailing at night." Captain Collins steps forward but shuts up immediately with one look from Jonathan. Fear flashes across his face before he limps away.

"You will sail tonight," Jonathan calls after him. Something has happened to the captain, but I doubt I'll ever get to find out.

We're told that all three boats will stay together for a couple days. I walk past Jonathan and almost run into Jeremy who has stopped suddenly in front of me. I'm about to push him along when I see what he is staring at. There is a smear of blood on the railing and another one on the deck. Shite.

"Jonathan," I hear Miranda behind me, "where is the captain? I must speak with him."

"I'm the captain now, Miranda," he says harshly. "That old man was useless. What was his name? Slater?" I don't hear anything else because Jeremy pulls me through a door.

"You don't think Jonathan…" My voice trails off.

"He probably killed the captain," Jeremy states. "He's clearly gone off the deep end." I feel light headed so I take a seat.

"At least Captain Collins is still alive to take troops to St. Louis. I wish we were on his boat because I trust him a hell of a lot more than Jonathan."

"Who's Captain Collins?"

"He got us out of Texas before," I explain. "What do we do now?"

"Nothing, Jonathan is dangerous." I stand, unable to take this any longer.

"Jonathan is only one man," I say. "He is not the rebels." This is more to comfort me than anything else. As more soldiers pile into the room, Jeremy sits down and leans back, lost in his own thoughts.

Around dusk, we drop anchor and take a small boat to shore before sending it back to pick up more people. Further inland we come upon a set of ruins in the middle of a patch of wild forest.

"This is where we spend the night. I hate sleeping on a boat," Jonathan says as loudly as he can. "Let's get some fires started and some food cooking. Get to it."

I join the group looking for firewood because it gives me a chance to explore. I've never seen any of the ruins in the colonies, but from what Dawn told me, they're usually not this well preserved. I walk around the outside to look at the walls. Enough of them are standing to be able to imagine what this place was like. It's a massive structure that once had many rooms. Large scorch marks mar much of the surface. Something happened here. A shiver runs down my spine.

"Gabby." I jump as Lee walks up, his arm loaded down with brush to fuel the fires.

"You scared me," I say.

"Sorry." He smiles before saying, "this place has always been kind of creepy."

"Yeah," I respond, "but also brilliant."

"These are the most well-preserved ruins in the colonies. No one can explain why."

"So you've heard about them?" I ask.

"I've actually been here before, a long time ago." He looks away.

"Really?"

"I was raised near here." His voice grows quiet, solemn. "My sisters and I used to run through these rooms all the times. I was usually chasing them." He laughs softly.

"I didn't know you had sisters."

"I had three. All younger than me."

"Where are they now?" I ask, regretting it instantly. Dawn was always telling me I'm too nosey and I know she was right.

"The youngest two succumbed to illness," he explains, his voice hoarse as he tries to control it. "The third was taken by the British along with my mother and another girl that I knew." He shakes his head as if to clear it of those thoughts. "Let me drop this stuff off and then I want to show you something." I follow him to one of the fires that is being started and he drops the brush on the ground. When I first met Lee in the camp, I thought he was just some brainless American prat who had nothing better to do than follow Dawn to Floridaland. I was wrong. In reality, he's just like me. His family was taken from him and he's a survivor.

"We call this place The Mall," he tells me. "This is why." He points to the wall in front of us where the word mall is etched into the stone. It looks like something else used to precede it, but that is gone now.

"That's really cool," I say. Lee stares at that word until Miranda's voice calls out, announcing meal time.

Chapter 67

Gabby

I wake before sunrise to screaming. I quickly get up and run outside. Something is burning in the distance as fires stretch across the horizon. Miranda pushes past me cursing.

"Where is Jonathan?" she yells. We also seem to be missing quite a few soldiers. "Shite. What is that arse thinking? Everyone, prepare to move out." We hurry as we pack up camp and get into formation. We march straight towards the burning fields.

Jonathan and his troop walk straight towards us and then stand across from us as if this is a battlefield. Jonathan leaves his men and comes close to us.

"What the hell do you think you're doing?" Miranda screams at him.

"It needed to be done." He shrugs. "This way, whatever Texan troops aren't fighting in Mexico will be called out to the fields." He seems pleased with himself.

"We can't afford to be burning crops." Miranda is angry. "Whoever planted them. Have you forgotten that we're going to be inundated with new mouths to feed from England? Don't even get me started on the fact that we just warned Texas that someone is coming for them. Let's just hope we get there before their reinforcements do. The next time you get one of these brilliant ideas, try sharing it with your second in command."

I'm stunned that Jonathan doesn't seem bothered by what Miranda said, even if it's the truth. He just turns around and starts issuing orders.

"Back to the ships," he commands. Half the soldiers stay put, unsure if they should follow Jonathan. I'm among them.

"Just go," Miranda barks at us.

When we disembark next, we'll be in Texas, so it's time to say our goodbyes and good lucks to those not going to Vicksburg with us.

Lee wraps his arms around me first. "Stay safe," he says. I hug Drew next.

"For Dawn," he whispers.

"For Dawn," I respond, quickly wiping away the tears that come to my eyes. They shake hands with Jeremy and then they're gone.

"You good?" Jeremy asks.

"Yes," I grunt. "Let's go." I sling my bag over my shoulder and step onto the boat.

Things are quiet on board as people are frightened and confused. The unit that set fire to the fields also destroyed the farming village, but they don't speak about it. There seems to be a clear divide between the soldiers that are completely loyal to Jonathan and those of us that have started to question him. Anyone can see that our leader has cracked and we could be screwed if we follow him.

The next day, we come upon a Texan checkpoint, but there is no one in the tower. All we see are the bodies along the riverbank. Jonathan sent people on ahead to make things easier down the road. This is what that meant. Day after day, each checkpoint, it's the same. We pass the last one and pull up along a makeshift dock. We're given orders to disembark and the dock sways beneath my feet. I've never been happier to be on solid ground.

Jonathan is ahead, calling out orders. Most of us, though, rely more on the orders from our officers. I stand behind Officer Lincoln with the rest of the snipers, waiting for his order to move.

After a day of hard marching, we come over a hill and see them. The walls of Vicksburg seem even more massive and impenetrable than I remember.

"Miss it?" Allison asks as she walks up beside me, the sarcasm dripping from her voice.

"Like I miss hot pokers in my eyes," I snort. She laughs before yelling.

"Pick it up, everyone! The quicker we move, the sooner we can tear those damn walls down!"

"Yeah!" I roar along with everyone else.

Chapter 68

Drew

"Unlike our counterparts in the other cities, we'll be sailing right into the city," the officer informs us. Her name is Officer Mills and she's been put in charge of the attack on St. Louis. I can't look at her as she speaks because she was there when Dawn died and it hurts too damn much to think about it. She must sense it because she never meets my eyes and has never spoken directly to me.

Lee drops into the seat beside me and Lucas sits across from us. When I look at him, all I see is another person who let Dawn die. He treats me like I'm wounded and that only fuels my anger. I stand up from the table in one brisk movement and push my stool back. Lee looks as if he's going to say something so I hurry up the stairs for some much-needed air. I grip the railing tightly and lean over the side to stare into the dark water. I hear a door open and turn to see Captain Collins limping from his quarters. I follow him aft.

"Why are you following me?" He stops walking but doesn't turn.

"Are you okay?" I ask.

"Why wouldn't I be?" His voice sounds tired. He turns and leans on the railing for support. His every movement is slow and strenuous. He scans my face before saying, "I know you."

"You saved my life," I say gratefully.

"Oh yes, I remember. Glad to see you're alive, boy. Now, leave me be." He tries to walk past me, but his hand slips on the railing, sending him sprawling onto the deck. I run forward and help him to his feet. He doesn't protest as I let him lean on me to get to his door. I get the big man in bed, but not before seeing a bruise along his shirt line.

"Who did that to you?" I demand.

"Get me some rum, boy." He points to a small table in the corner. "And close the door." I do as he asks. He sips his rum and sighs. "Go on then, I see there's no getting rid of you so you might as well pour yourself a glass and sit." It's not a suggestion, but I don't listen, instead, I walk straight towards him and lift his shirt. He tries to push me away, but he is too weak. His torso is covered in dark purple bruises. I remember his limp and roll up his right pant leg, revealing a festering knife wound.

"Like your irony, boy?" he asks with a harsh laugh. "The only person on this ship that could fix that is me." His laugh turns into a cough. He downs the rest of his rum and holds out his glass for more.

"What happened?" I ask again, this time holding his rum just out of reach. I want answers. He sighs.

"So that's how it's going to be? You're stubborn, boy. I guess this is what I get for helping rebels." He pauses. "The name itself should be enough to warn people from getting involved. It wasn't."

"What are you talking about?"

"Can I trust you boy?" He stares into my eyes and laughs when I shift them away. "You have secrets."

"Everyone keeps something to themselves."

"Don't worry, boy, I don't trust a man that has nothing to hide. Men experienced in secrets are better at protecting them." I nod and let him continue. "I was like you once. Young and idealistic. Making choices that you think are right. Eventually, you grow up. Eventually, you realize that you never really had a choice at all. Doing right for one group means doing wrong for another. Over the years you learn to cope with failure until the one time when it's all too much. I couldn't protect them." He turns his head away as a tear runs down his cheek.

"Who couldn't you protect?"

"Dana," he says quietly. "Henry. Tony."

"Are they your family?" I ask softly. "What happened?"

"They're the only reason I'm doing this. I'm a Texan. I do not want the rebels to win, but I can't abandon my family."

"What if we could save them?" I don't know why or how, but I get this feeling that this is something we need to do.

"Who do you think you are?" the Captain growls and I'm thrown off by his sudden change in tone. "You come in here and offer false hope? You're just rebel scum. You say what you think I want to hear. You don't really care about my family. Get out" I don't move until he yells, "Get out! Get out! Leave me alone!" I leave without another word.

My mind is elsewhere as I walk around the deck. I hadn't even noticed the people out here until I run directly into Officer Mills.

This snaps me out of my stupor and I see that I have spilled rum on her. I must have taken my glass with me when I left the captain.

"Soldier." Officer Mills looks at the glass in my hand. "Where did you get that?" She doesn't even seem to notice her wet jacket.

"Oh." I think for a second. "The captain." She looks deep into my eyes, probably trying to obtain my level of drunkenness. In truth, I've had no more than a sip. She must accept my soberness because her voice softens. "Are you okay, soldier?"

"Sir," I begin, but I can't finish that sentence. I really don't know how to answer her. This is the first time I'm talking to my superior and I'm acting like a proper toss pot. She probably thinks it's because of Dawn because she guides me down the stairs to an empty table in the corner. She takes the glass from me and sets it aside as she sits across from me.

"I like to know what's going on with my soldiers," she begins.

"I don't think I can tell you," I say quietly.

"Do you trust me, soldier?"

"I don't really know you, sir."

"Fair enough. Can you tell me if something is wrong that will affect our mission?"

"Something is wrong with the mission," I blurt before realizing what I just said. I prepare myself for a reprimand, but it never comes.

"Soldier," she begins, "command is not on this ship with us. In fact, now that we're a separate force, I think I have some information that will make you trust me. Not all of us believe every word that Jonathan Clarke spits out. Your friend Dawn helped me see who he really is." I look away to hide the grief that comes every time I think about her.

"I'm starting to think Dawn was right," I mutter.

"I know she is," Officer Mills states. I focus on the grains of the table until her words sink in. I look up slowly.

"You mean was?"

"No. I mean that she still is right because she's alive." Officer Mills looks as though a huge weight has been lifted from her as I try to process her words.

"Dawn," I say and Officer Mills nods. My heart pounds faster with each passing minute and the sadness of the past few weeks is washed away with one phrase. "Dawn is alive."

Officer Mills explains to me everything that happened on their mission and I instantly know what I have to do. The thinking that was tethering me to Jonathan Clarke is replaced by a need to do the right thing. The need to do what Dawn would do. I tell the officer everything and then we go barging into the captain's quarters so she can look at his leg and get more information about my new mission.

Chapter 69

Dawn

We cover a lot of ground during the day, but I can't wait to be out of this saddle. My arse and my legs are killing me. My back doesn't feel so good either. We go out of our way to stay out of sight of any of the farming villages. I made the mistake of suggesting we ride at night to keep from being seen and Emily bit my head off.

"Do you want to get our horses injured?" she yells. Ryan tells me to ignore her and then explains that we can't risk running our horses over the rough terrain in the dark. I suddenly feel daft. Emily tends to make me feel like that a lot. I think she takes pleasure in it. Her horse is quite a bit faster than Duke since she only has one rider and Emily uses that to her advantage. She runs ahead of us and comes back with scouting reports. Ryan tries to stop her every time, but she doesn't listen to him. Emily is only ten, but when she is on a horse you would assume she is older.

We stop for the night on the outskirts of a town - if you can call it that. There are about fifteen shacks huddled together on the edge of a spud farm.

"We're getting close," Ryan states. I stare at him in surprise. I've been hoping for those words for days.

"How do you know?" I ask, but it's Emily that answers.

"Because we've been riding hard for almost a week and any brain-dead fool should know how far Texas is."

"Em," Ryan chastises.

"What?" she demands. "I was just being honest." She walks off to mope.

"Sorry." Ryan sighs.

"It's okay," I say. "She's been through a lot."

"So have you," he says. "All of us have."

"She's just a kid." I don't know why I'm defending her.

"Aren't we all?" His question surprises me. I haven't considered myself a kid for a very long time.

"I don't know if I've ever really been a kid," I say honestly. "My sister and I had to grow up in a hurry over in London."

"What's it like over there?"

"That depends on where you live," I explain. "Gabby and I lived in the east end. That's the dodgy part. We thought our father was dead and our mother abandoned us. She just walked away." My voice trails off.

"So, who took care of you?"

"My sister. I was the one who was going to get a placement in Uni after grade school so she let me focus on my lessons while she always made sure I had a roof over my head and food in my stomach." I pause. "When she was arrested, I knew that it was my turn. I knew I had to be there for her." I grow quiet as I think about my sister. She's probably preparing for the assault on Texas. What will they make her do? I turn as Emily walks towards us.

"You shouldn't eavesdrop, sis," Ryan says softly. She ignores him as she looks at me.

"Were you always this brave?" Her voice is small and full of fear. Through all her bratty behavior, I'd failed to see the scared kid who was just taken from her parents.

"I'm not brave," I say plainly. It's the truth. "I don't know how I got here; how I became this person that would risk her life. It's like bravery or cowardice doesn't mean so much when someone you love is in danger." She sits next to her brother and leans into him.

"She's not in danger anymore though," Ryan says. "You could have walked away from this."

"No, I couldn't. Gabby is the danger now. I have to keep trying to save her even when she doesn't want me to. She's my sister. I can't ever give up on her, or else what would that make me? Sometimes, it's like banging your head against a wall, but we fight through the pain. We keep pushing."

"So, you're like a hero," Emily says. "Trying to save everyone and all that."

"No, definitely not a hero." I think for a moment. "I'm a sister."

"Oh, well Ryan better not expect me to go after him if he does something stupid," Emily says. Ryan tickles her and she giggles.

"What about you?" I ask Ryan. "Why are you helping me?"

"Well," he smiles, "I am a hero." That sets us all off laughing.

Chapter 70

Dawn

Emily trots towards us with the hint of a smile playing on her lips. She's decided to hate me just a little less after our conversation last night, but she still spent the day roaming out in front of us.

"Jasmine wants to run," she told us hours ago before setting off to explore the hills before us.

"Nice of you to join us," Ryan says. We've all been trying really hard to keep things light this morning. The more we smile and pretend at fearlessness, the less we think about what's coming. Every river that we've crossed and every stretch of land that is now behind us has brought us closer to this. Emily pulls up beside us.

"I didn't know they were so big," Emily says as we stare at the walls stretching out in the distance. Silence looms between us as we slide from our mounts. Ryan unties his pack and begins searching through it. He pulls out an assortment of knives and begins tucking them away. I watch him in awe as he gears up. He pulls out two handguns and offers one to me. I take it slowly and he shows me where to conceal it.

"What about me?" Emily squeaks.

"You're not coming." He doesn't look her in the eye as he prepares for the oncoming screaming.

"Yes I am," she states calmly.

"Someone needs to stay with the horses," he explains, although, I know that's not the real reason.

"So you're gonna leave me out here all alone?"

"It's safer than in there surrounded by Texans." He stares at her until her shoulders sag and her resolve dissipates.

"Fine." She sits cross legged on the ground. Ryan opens his mouth to say something else then clamps it shut.

We've arrived in perfect timing. The sun went down about half an hour ago and the remaining light is fading. We've had plenty of time to talk over our plan. Our main priority is to get to Darren and Tia Cole before the entire city is destroyed and then we need to find my sister.

As we move closer to the wall, we see a group of people waiting next to the open gate that trucks are driving through. There's a small door next to the gate where two Texans in full protective gear are standing. They scan a device over each person's forehead before allowing them to enter the city. Almost every time, we hear them yell "clean". There are a few people, however, who get the designation "impure". Soldiers then rush to take those people away.

"What are they doing?" I ask.

"I've heard about this," he starts. "The farmers that work the land close to here live in the city. Every time anyone is let past the wall, they're scanned for any sign of disease. Even a cold is enough to be taken away. They're also checking for foreigners that are trying to get in. Unlike St. Louis, only pure Texans are allowed within Vicksburg limits."

"Then how did Gabby and I end up there?"

"You already know they wanted something from you. I'll bet that having you in custody was leverage against your father." He quiets and I force myself to turn away and focus on how we will get in.

Every day, a number of supply trucks enter and exit the city. The last few always arrive just after dark. There's always a truck with a red ribbon near the tire. I learned from the rebels that this is how they get in and out to deliver messages. You wouldn't even see the sign if you weren't looking for it.

This time of year, the trucks are full of food crates from the nearby farms. We leave Emily sulking in a thicket of trees and leg it towards the trucks. They're stopped as they enter the gate to be inspected and a line of them sit unmoving on the road. I look for the truck that will take us in. The ribbon is small, but I can see just enough of it.

"This one," I whisper to Ryan.

Every inch of each truck is inspected as they pass into the city. Well, almost every inch. When the rebels helped us flee from Texas, Allison showed us a compartment behind the cab that is never checked because the guards are in too big of a hurry. They call it the smuggler's den because smugglers use the space to move their goods.

Ryan and I use the darkness as our cover and pull ourselves into the back of the truck. We move on silent feet to push the crates out of our way. We're not finished when we feel the truck lurch forward. I trip over a box in back of me and Ryan grabs my arm to keep me on my feet. The truck stops once more and I finish uncovering the trap door.

Ryan pulls on the small metal ring and the small door swings upwards. We pull the door shut behind us and wait. The truck moves forward again and when it stops we can hear muffled voices.

"Papers?"

"Of course."

"All clear back here!"

"Papers are in order. You may go."

"Thank you."

The truck bumps along the Texan roads and comes to one final stop. After a few minutes, there are footsteps in the back of the truck. I don't know how long Ryan and I are huddled together in silence before a truck rumbles by and all the voices fade away except for one.

The door to our hiding space is open and a man offers his hand to help me out.

"It's all clear out here," he says. "You must be part of the attack, right?"

I let out a sigh of relief. I was right about the red ribbon. This man is a rebel. "Yeah," I lie. "They sent us in early to get into position."

"Well good luck," he says as he walks away.

"I can't believe that worked," I whisper as I step down and stretch my legs. It seems like a lifetime ago that I was escaping from Texas using this same car park. Now I'm breaking back in. I must be a right fool.

"What now?" Ryan asks, looking to me for direction. We'd come to the conclusion that we can't do anything without help. I don't know when the rebel assault will take place, but it should be any day now. We can't wait for that.

"Come on." I lead us out onto the street. Curfew was at sundown, but there are still a few stragglers lurking about. I use the shadows and alleyways to our advantage. To most of these people, we might look like just a couple of curfew breakers, but if they get a closer look, they'll be able to tell just by our clothes that we don't belong here.

"Move along," a soldier yells down the street. "Get inside before I have to arrest all of you." We duck into a doorway and wait for him to pass. We try to stay quiet, but every step seems to echo off the brick. We hurry up our pace and I hope we're going the right way. I have only been in this part of the city once before and it was not my best night. The one and only time I've been drunk was at Landon's illegal party, but I remember enough to get back to his place.

We reach his building and go to the third floor. His party was in the basement, but I remember him mentioning his flat. I count the doors and stop before we reach the fifth one in from the stairwell. We fling the door open and Ryan stops me before entering. There are voices coming from inside and none of them are Landon. I look around the corner and his flat is a wreck; his belongings strewn everywhere.

I run back to the end of the hall and down the stairs. What happened to Landon? Where could he be? I don't stop running until we reach the basement. I open the door at the bottom without even thinking.

"Landon," I call out desperately in a hushed voice. There's no response. "Landon," I try one more time. A man steps out of the shadows and at first, I think it's him. It's not.

Adrian.

My breath catches in my throat as I try to speak. We're done for. I just know it. Adrian killed his own mother because she was a rebel. Gabby saw it first hand. What will he do to us?

Adrian squints as he tries to recognize me in the dim basement light. "Dawn?" he asks, confused. I pull out my gun and aim it high on his chest.

"Don't come any closer," I bark. Behind me, Ryan stands at the ready.

Adrian looks me straight in the eye as he pulls his own gun from a holster at his waist.

"Drop it," I command. He raises his arm in surrender and lets his gun clatter to the floor. "Where's Landon?"

"So, it's true," he says calmly.

"What the hell are you talking about?" I try to control my voice, but it betrays me.

"Landon was arrested on suspicion of being a rebel," he explains. "He got you out, didn't he? And that boy of yours?"

"Shut up," I scream. I run my free hand through my hair. I'm not meant for all of this. I need help. Landon would've known what to do. Ryan puts a hand on my shoulder to lower my gun as he raises his own.

"What are you doing here?" Ryan asks.

Adrian glares at him. "Who the hell are you?"

"That doesn't matter, does it? I have the gun," Ryan responds. "Now, answer the question."

"I tried to get here before the police, but I was too late," Adrian answers before turning to me. "Why did you come back? You were supposed to be safe."

"What do you mean?" I ask, my voice low and quiet. "Why do you care?"

"I helped you." He tries to take a step towards me, but Ryan gets in his way.

"Is that why you killed your mother? To help us? She was the one who was on our side,"

Adrian looks away from me and stares at the ground. "I had to," he whispers. "My mother and I had a deal that we wouldn't let each other be confined in those labs and tortured."

"We don't have time for this." I turn away.

"You have no clue what would have happened to her if I hadn't shot her." I stop and turn, considering his words.

"That doesn't mean you wouldn't turn us in," I growl.

"Are you here with the rebels?"

"No." I figure there's no point in lying. "The rebels are here to kill a lot of people. We're only here to kill two."

"Tia and Darren?" he asks. When I don't respond, he continues. "Let me help you." He pauses. "For my mom." I look at Ryan and he shrugs. He doesn't know Adrian like I do. There was a time when I trusted him. Do I have to trust him to use him now? "My father died in those labs," Adrian explains. "He died at the hands of Darren Cole. Let me help you."

"Ryan, take his gun," I say. Ryan grabs it from the floor and tucks it away. "One wrong move, Adrian, and I will shoot you myself."

Adrian tells us that there is a meeting for government officials to-morrow night. That's when we'll make our move. What that move is, I don't really know. Adrian agrees to hide us in his flat until then. I notice that Ryan keeps his weapons handy and I'm secretly glad for that. We can't trust Adrian, but I don't know if we can do this without him.

Chapter 71

Gabby

"Weaponry and stealth," Officer Lincoln is saying. "We can't rely on numbers, but we can rely on our training and of course, our fire power. We can't force our way; we can't create a war with the Texan people. Create chaos. The runners will set things off with their explosions. Remember, only use buildings on the edges of town to set up because the runners will be targeting those in the center of everything." He looks away before delivering his final instruction, "Jonathan has requested that you target civilians. Make them believe their own soldiers have turned on them. I know there are casualties in every war, but it's different when you're asked to create civilian casualties. I'm sorry." He bows his head. "May God go with you now and forgive you later."

I don't believe in God, but Linc's prayer sent me off with a feeling of comfort. No matter what you believe, when someone prays for you, it's a profound thing. They believe it will keep you safe. They care if you come back.

The snipers are sent in first. Jonathan's voice issues commands over our wrist coms, but I tune him out. Officers can give as many orders as they want, but most of them fly out the window when the real work starts. We skirt the city at a distance, moving through the woods until we can see the back gate. "That's where we enter," Linc informs us. I pull the sleeve of my Texan military uniform down to hide my com and leave the safety of the trees with the rest of my unit.

"Remember," Jonathan's voice comes over our coms, "our goal is not to beat these people. Our goal is to help them beat themselves. Mayhem. Not war." Shay rolls her eyes at me and I can't help but laugh a little. Jonathan has said that line to us probably a hundred times by now.

Officer Lincoln reaches the wall first and I see a small door that I didn't notice before. It looks almost as if it's part of the wall itself. He raps his knuckles on the door three times and then twice and then three times again. When it doesn't open right away, he looks around nervously. After a few minutes, he knocks again.

The door swings open on rusty hinges and I cringe at the sound it makes. I recognize Clay and Jack as they wave us through. Jack is grinning broadly, but Clay has a scowl on his face.

"Welcome to Texas," Jack whispers as he hurries us along. He leaves the door partially open for the next wave of rebels. "Good to see you're alive, Gabby." He claps me on the back. Clay is silent as we meander around the unconscious guards on the ground.

"Each building has stairs on the outside going to the roof," Clay informs us gruffly. "They serve as fire escapes. Do not enter the buildings because you may not get back out. Use the fire escapes to get into position." I don't linger as Shay pulls me into a run. As the two best snipers, we have been assigned to the government building. I only hope I get a clear shot at Adrian.

We slow down and lock step as we pass a group of Texan soldiers. The officer leading the unit salutes us and we almost pass each other without a word. I said almost. At the last minute, he motions for us to stop. A lump forms in my throat.

"Where are you headed, soldiers?" he asks, eying our uniforms up and down.

"We were just relieved of our post along the wall," Shay speaks up. I stay quiet because my accent would give us away.

"You wouldn't be heading to your bunks now, would you?" He stares us down and I suddenly don't know what the right answer is.

"No, sir," Shay says tentatively.

"Good answer," he says. "Then I'm sure you got the orders to go to the government sector. The meeting tonight requires extra security. Anyone whose shift has ended is to report for extra duty. The orders went wide and I'm sure you were just heading there."

"Yes, sir," Shay says with confidence this time.

"You might as well join us then," he says before issuing the command to move out. Shay and I bring up the rear and try to match their marching.

"Shite," I whisper. "What now?"

"We don't have time for this," Shay says a bit too loudly. The soldier in from of us turns to glare. Marching is an incredibly slow way to get anywhere. We walk straight down the center of each road. I would prefer the shadows. The bag that is slung across my back seems to weigh more and more the closer we get. The government building is surrounded by soldiers milling about. Officers yell out orders and I briefly see government officials stepping through the front door amidst their own security. How are we supposed to do this with all these armed Texans around?

As soon as our marching unit is engulfed in the sea of Texans, we're able to slip away.

"Snipers in position?" Jonathan's voice surprises me. I had almost forgotten about the com on my wrist. How stupid can I be? A few minutes ago, that would have gotten me killed.

"Snipers 1 and 2 not quite ready," I reply.

"Get ready," the response is harsh. We're running way behind by the time Shay and I find the fire escape at the back of the building. For now, most of the Texans are in the front receiving their orders so we immediately jump into action. Linc told us that the snipers are to remain hidden at all costs. If chaos erupts before the runners are in position, we will fail.

I run up the metal stairs with my rifle bag flapping against my back. I cringe as each step echoes off the brick building. By the time we climbed all seven stories to get to the roof, I'm panting and wheezing, unable to catch my breath. We have no time.

"Snipers at the ready." The fact that it's Officer Lincoln's voice and not Jonathan's only registers for a second before I start assembling my rifle. Shay is already set up on the other side of the humming generator and the solar panels that power it. I stand next to her and look over the edge of the roof. The security forces would be overkill on any other night. Tonight, it will play perfectly into our plan.

I hear a voice I don't recognize giving directions to the runners. By now they've entered the city, Jeremy among them. Focusing my scope, I watch the street below. We aren't using self-guiding ammunition and I have never hit a moving target before. I pick out soldiers to track. Curious civilians have come out to watch the scene unfold. No one cares about curfew when the government officials are out late on important business. They all want a glimpse of their prophet.

I kneel and rest my rifle on the roof's edge and wait for the first explosion.

"Sniper positions check in," Linc commands.

"Government building, check," Shay reports. We hear every position check in and then Shay gives me a wicked grin. "You ready for this?"

"Hell yes."

Chapter 72

Drew

Officer Mills is convinced that Captain Collins' family is in even more danger than we thought. She knows Jonathan on a level that I never want to. The captain's family is not being held by just any rebels. They're hostages of Jonathan's people. There's a difference. Most of us never knew about the secret group within the rebels that are completely loyal to Jonathan. They've done things that none of us ever want to think about. I saw what they did to the farms we came across and the guards at the Texan checkpoints. They weren't just killed. Whoever did that took pleasure in it.

The captain seems to think his family is in danger from more than just that faction of rebels. He won't tell us why, but the Mexicans are after them as well. Unlike Vicksburg, Mexicans are allowed in St. Louis and even control a part of the city. The prophet and her people tried to keep them out of every city in Texas, but that was impossible for a city with docks full of smugglers. That's why the captain had been moving his family from village to village. But now, Jonathan has moved them to the city.

We arrived in port yesterday, but we're waiting. I don't know why. Every soldier has had to stay below deck for twenty-four hours and it's getting rank. In this city, if enough money changes hands, a boat can escape inspection. People here will do pretty much anything for a good bribe. That's what will bring them down.

"I need all my snipers," Officer Mills calls out. They huddle together in the corner and after a while, they disperse. Officer Mills motions me over. "You're going with the snipers," she informs me. "Who here can you trust?" I look around the room and then back to her.

"Lee," I say. "I can trust Lee."

"No," she says. "I need Lee with me."

"What for?"

"I have a mission too," she says evasively. "He has certain skills that I need. I'll send Lucas with you." I start to protest, but she cuts me off. "You can trust him." She looks around to make sure we're not overheard. "Start the search near the water. The kind of people who spend time at the docks, are the people who may be able to help you. Stay safe."

"You too."

The snipers are dressed in the traditional Texan outfits. Unlike in the capital, the people here don't trust the military. They obey them and support them with taxes, but they won't talk to them. Lucas and I leave before anyone else and the darkness is our friend. There are quite a few ships in port and that will work to our advantage. With this many people around, someone has to know something.

Dawn would be proud of me. I don't know if I'm defying the rebels so much or just Jonathan, but she'd be proud either way. If I ever get the chance, I will take Jonathan down for everything he's done.

People here are dodgy and distrustful and I have to force myself to be calm or I'll never get the information I need. Lucas and I head for a place called the Watering Hole. They serve home-brewed beer to the smugglers that come into town. Alcohol is illegal in all of Texas unless you find an official to bribe. The heavy door is shut, but the sounds from inside drift out towards us. Lucas raps his knuckles on the door and we wait. A small window is opened near eye level.

"Who's there?" a gruff female voice barks. Her eyes shift from Lucas to me and then narrow. We don't look like we've spent our lives on boats. We don't look like we belong here.

"We need to speak with Fitz," I say.

"Never heard of him."

"That's a shame," Lucas pipes in, "being as this is his place."

"Who is it, Lara?" a man calls out.

"Tell him that Captain Collins sent us," I say impatiently. We don't have time for this. The door groans as it moves on its hinges and reveals a short woman with sun damaged hair and a wrinkled face. Her teeth are yellow and her voice is hoarse from years of hard living.

"Well, get in here," she barks before slamming the door behind us. The room we enter is full of people. I can't make out many of the faces in the dim light, but I feel their eyes on us. The woman, Lara, tries to force a couple beers on us, but we decline. "Don't just stand there," she says as she lights a cigarette. "Fitz is in the back." She ushers us through another wooden door into a room very much like the other. Five men sit around a table playing cards.

"Collins sent you?" one of the men asks, not bothering to look up from the game. "Where has he disappeared to?"

"I heard he got mixed up in some trouble," the man to his right says as he places a bet.

"His ship's in port," a third chimes in.

"You just going to stand there, boys?" the man at the head of the table demands.

"Captain Collins is in trouble," I explain.

"I knew it," one of the men says as he puts his cards face up on the table. "Full house." He rakes in his winnings as the other men throw down their cards in annoyance.

"I need the room," the fifth man says. The others file out quickly.

"Are you Fitz?" Lucas asks. The man just grunts.

"We need your help," I say simply.

"I know," he says. "I've had my ear to the ground for the past couple weeks for news of Collins' wife and children."

"You already know about the kidnapping?"

"I know everything that happens in my city."

"What can you tell us?" I ask.

"There's a warehouse not far from here, number seven. They were there last week. They're long gone now, but that's where I'd start." We immediately say our thanks and get out of there.

We walk the dock to find anyone that will tell us which way to go. Finally, an old gaffer recognizes our desperation and points us in the right direction. The warehouse is located at the far end of the port. We come upon it from an alleyway and look through the large industrial windows. I only see two men. No woman. No children. My heart sinks.

"They aren't here." I turn my back on the building before us, but Lucas uses his weight to bull through the door.

"What the hell?" The shouts come from inside. I swear as I pull out my gun and follow Lucas in. Lucas keeps his arm steady as he puts one of the men in his sights. The second man begins to reach behind him.

"Hands where I can see them," I yell. Lucas grabs one of the men and shoves the nose of his weapon into his back before speaking in a low voice.

"Get down," he says. Both men comply. They don't ask us why we're here. That usually means they already know. Guilty. We disarm both men quickly.

"Where are they?" I growl.

"Where are who?" I use my foot to press his cheek into the cold concrete floor.

"No games." I remove my foot and crouch down. I grab the man by the shirt and yank him up so that we're face to face. "There was a woman here. And two kids. It's best if you just tell me where they are. Trust me, you don't want to do this the hard way."

"Snipers are set," the voice comes over my com. "Runners ready."

"You guys are rebels?" The man Lucas is all but sitting on says with a hopeful look towards my com. "So are we. We should be fighting together."

"We are not the same," I yell. "Where the hell are the captain's family?" Before either of them can answer, the door bursts open and bullets fly by. I scramble to my feet and duck behind the metal beam in the center of the floor. I return fire as Lucas uses one of the men as a shield. His body jerks with each bullet that pierces his flesh. Lucas drops him to the ground as he reaches me. He puts up a hand for me to stop firing. There's a pause in the action as our attackers reload.

Lucas and I run into the open and fire rapidly. There are three men plus the one that I had been restraining. We each drop a man as we run towards them. We reach them before they have managed to reload. Lucas tackles a large Texan with long stringy hair and I deliver a knee to the gut of another. He doubles over and I use my knee again. This time, his face takes the blow. A third raises his newly loaded weapon and I look up just in time to see him point it at me. The sound of a bullet exploding fills my ears. As if in slow motion, I wait for the impact, but it never comes. The man's head snaps back and his gun collides with the concrete floor seconds before his body does the same.

I don't have time to think as the man beneath me struggles to get free. I knock him unconscious using the butt of my gun and look around. Lucas has killed the remaining intruder and the man we had been questioning faces us, gun still held out in front of his chest. He saved my life.

"Drop it," Lucas commands. He doesn't budge.

"You can't take us out at the same time," I say. "You'll just end up with a bullet between your eyes."

"Isn't that what you're going to do anyway?" he says.

"You shot your own man there." I look behind me at the dead guy. "Why?"

"He was not one of us," he spits. "Filthy cartel." He lowers his gun. Lucas walks up to him and takes it.

"What business does a cartel have with you?" I ask suspiciously.

"You want to know about that smuggler's whore?" he asks. Lucas hauls off and punches him. I grab his arm when he winds up again.

"Wait," I tell him. The man looks at me as he wipes blood from his lip.

"We had her," he says. "It was on Jonathan's orders."

"That means nothing to us," Lucas barks.

"It did to us." He takes a step back to create more space between him and the imposing Lucas. "We had orders."

"Orders to hurt a woman and her children?" Lucas' temper boils and his face reddens. "That's sick."

"Lucas," I say calmly. "Let him talk."

"Thank you," Jonathan's man says.

"It isn't for you," I snap. "Where are they now?"

"The cartel took them. One of the boys isn't Captain Collins' spawn." He pauses. "He's Mexican."

"Why would the Captain be protecting a Mexican boy?"

"Do you guys know anything?" he retorts. "The boy's a Moreno. You know – the Moreno cartel. His mother smuggled him out of Mexico and Captain Collins has been taking care of him ever since while the boy's mother is a prisoner of her own brother. It's kind of been a big deal around here. Everyone knows." He pauses. "One last thing, the cartel will have no problem killing a child."

I turn to Lucas. "Let's go!"

Chapter 73

Drew

As soon as we're back on the street, a nearby explosion shakes the ground beneath our feet. People pour out of the buildings closest to us and off of boats to see what is going on. All of a sudden, we're engulfed in a throng of people. There's another explosion in the distance.

"It's started," I yell as Lucas and I push past people at a run. "We're running out of time."

"Go for explosion 3," the order comes.

"That's not Mills giving the orders." Lucas grabs my shoulder so that I stop and turn to him. "Where is she?"

"I don't know, but we need to keep going." I speed up my pace and he's right behind me. We left the man at the warehouse to take care of the unconscious cartel member after he gave us a possible address. The cartel controls a sector not far from the docs.

"I thought the cartel couldn't get into Texas," I yell above the noise that now surrounds us.

"They can't get into Vicksburg. But then, no one can," Lucas explains between short breaths. "St. Louis is anyone's city. The cartel won't lift a finger to help the Texans hold us back. Destruction leads to easy pickings for them. They would love to seize power once the city is in chaos. We can't let that happen."

"Our only mission right now is to save that family," I remind him.

"I know."

We follow our directions carefully as well placed bombs go off not far from the alleyways we run through. I turn the corner of our destination and immediately go back into the shadowy alley.

"Five men in black," I say to Lucas.

"We can take them," he says quickly.

"No, I have another idea." I lead him around to the back of the tall apartment building. There are no back doors, only a small window near the ground. "If you were holding hostages, where would you put them?"

Lucas grins as the answer comes to him. "The basement."

"You stay up here to help us get out." He nods in agreement. The glass shatters with one swift kick. I look around to make sure it went unheard and then use the sleeve of my shirt to brush away the remaining shards and slide through. My feet dangle as I hang from the window sill by my fingertips and then slam into the concrete floor as I drop to the ground.

Looking around, this place is almost identical to the basement I remember so well from the capitol. A woman shields two children in the corner of the room. I put one finger to my mouth to keep them quiet.

"I'm a friend," I whisper. Her eyes shift to the door, but she doesn't say anything. "Dana, Captain Collins sent me." She stares at me and then her shoulders sag as a silent sob escapes her. She moves into the dim light and I let out a small gasp. Her face is swollen and the dark circles under her eyes make her look gaunt. Every movement is an effort for her. There's a hand print on her neck and left arm. She reaches back and pulls the two boys forward.

"Henry," I say softly. "Tony. I'm going to get you out."

"My name is Antonio," the young dark haired kid corrects me. I smile at him, but he does not return the gesture.

"There are guards," Dana whispers.

"Runners keep it going." I cover the speaker on my com with my hand to quiet it and Dana looks towards the door sharply. No one comes.

"Come on." I pull the boys to the window. "Lucas," I call in a hushed voice.

"I'm here," he says, sticking his arms through the window. I lift Antonio first and Lucas pulls him out. Henry goes just as easily. As I turn to Dana, there are voices at the door.

"Whose turn do you reckon it is?" a man asks. "With the whore I mean."

"You can always make it your turn," someone else laughs.

Dana grabs my arm and points to the window. "Go," she whispers urgently. I'm about to say no when the door opens. Dana launches herself at the man. I have no other choice. I look back at her one more time as she scratches and tears at the man with her nails. I grip the edges of the window sill and pull myself up. When I'm halfway through, Lucas grabs my hand to help me out. I hear yelling behind me and then a gunshot. Lucas looks at me, but I just shake my head.

"We have to get out of here," I state. "We need to get back to the boat." As soon as the words leave my mouth, a large man rounds the corner and barrels towards us. I'm out of ammo so Lucas and I shield the boys behind us. The man is almost on us when he suddenly collapses in a heap. I look to the rooftop where a sniper is positioned. I throw her a salute before taking off.

"Runners cease the explosions," Officer Mill's voice commands. "We have reached an agreement and St. Louis has surrendered." An explosion nearby shakes me to the core.

"Grace," Lucas speaks into his com, "where have you been?"

"Switch to beta frequency," she responds. I can no longer hear them on my own com, but Lucas is loud enough for me to pick up a few things.

"Report," Officer Mills says.

"We have the boys, but the woman is lost to us," he replies.

"Get back to the boat as soon as you can. I want to get us away from the docks as a precaution."

"What happened?" Lucas asks.

"Lee and I negotiated a deal with the ruling family here in St. Louis. That's all I can tell you right now. There are people who will be angry we didn't completely destroy the city. I decided it was more important to save as many people as I can."

"What about your orders?" Lucas says to her. "You don't have the authority to do this. Think about this, Grace. When Jonathan gets his hands on you…" Lucas' voice cracks with fear.

"Everything is going to be okay," she says before her voice is on my com as well. She orders all rebels to return to the ship.

We start moving through the streets quickly, but Henry doesn't follow. He stands stalk still with big eyes and pale skin. We don't have time for this so Lucas sweeps him up and carries him. Antonio, on the other hand, has a steely look in his eyes as his little legs try to keep pace with us.

People are frantic. They fight and kill around the ruins of broken buildings. The city is on fire. I leap over a body on the ground, but my foot catches and I land on top of the corpse. I scramble to my feet just in time to go flying through the air as the structure next to us explodes into flames. I hit the ground and small rocks imbed themselves in my knee as it twists under me. I cry out in pain and cover my head to protect it against the fallen debris. My ears are ringing. My heart is pounding. My head is throbbing.

Antonio tugs on my arm. "Get up," he yells. I wince as I stand and put pressure on my feet.

"Where are Henry and Lucas?" I ask the frightened child. He points towards a pile of debris. "Shite."

"Halt the explosions," Officer Mill's plea to her soldiers is frantic. She expected every rebel to quit when she negotiated a surrender. I could have told her that wouldn't happen. There's a lot of hate here.

A group of Texans has started to look through the rubble for survivors. A man with tears running down his face digs frantically. I look up and see Henry standing a few paces away. I run to him and grab his shoulders. "Where's Lucas?" I yell.

"I'm here," Lucas's voice is weak. He's trapped underneath a metal beam.

I ignore the pain as I kneel. "Are you okay?"

"I think I'm stuck," he says with the hint of a laugh. I turn around and around until I see people that might be able to help me.

"Please," I yell. "I need help." No one moves. "Please!" I look back at Lucas, who is struggling to breathe.

"Hang on," I yell to him. "I'm going to get you out. Somebody help me." I try to lift the beam by myself, but it doesn't budge. I don't quit. The veins pop on my arms as I use every ounce of strength. The beam is too much for me.

The smuggler from the tavern, Fitz, steps forward and braces himself to help me lift. The beam shifts and we hear Lucas groan as it presses down on him. Following Fitz, a few more men step forward to help. "We've got you, son," Fitz reassures Lucas. Red faced and sweaty, they're able to lift the beam just enough for me to slide Lucas out. They set it down and disperse. Only Fitz stays. Feeling something hot and sticky, I pull my hand away from Lucas. It's covered in blood. The big man has a large wooden splinter sticking out of his side.

"We need to get him to Collins," Fitz says. "He can help him."

It takes every bit of strength we have to get Lucas to his feet, one arm draped across each of our backs. He's conscious, but only just barely. People run into us and jostle us, making me come close to dropping him, but I maintain my grip. His blood has now soaked through my shirt. He's losing too much. I don't have to be a doctor to know that.

Henry and Antonio stick close to us and when we get to the ship, a couple of Captain Collins men take Lucas from us and carry him below deck.

"Thanks," I say to Fitz before he goes.

"Young man," he begins, "you saved those boys today." He pauses. "You always have a friend in St. Louis." He holds out his hand and I shake it before ushering the boys forward.

Below deck, Captain Collins has Lucas on a table and is cleaning the wound.

"He's unconscious," Lee tells me. Officer Mills is sitting by the table holding his hand with defeated eyes and slumped shoulders.

"Captain," I say, unsure if I should be interrupting. He turns towards me, probably to tell me to shut up. His face softens as he sees the two children standing next to me. He puts down the tweezers he was using to pick out the rocks and wipes his bloody hands on a rag.

"Dad!" Henry runs towards him. The captain bends down to wrap his arms around his son and kisses his head. As each second passes, father and son only cling to each other tighter. Captain Collins looks over his son's shoulder and mouths one word to me "Dana?" I shake my head and he buries his face in the sobbing Henry's neck. I step forward when the captain seems to have trouble standing because of his leg. He uses my arm to straighten himself.

"Antonio." He holds out his arms and the child steps into them.

"We're losing him," Lee yells as Lucas convulses on the table. The captain starts working furiously to stem the bleeding that has started again. I can't take my eyes off of my friend. My ally.

"Get Henry and Antonio out of here," Captain Collins yells. Lee and I take the boys into a separate room where they can lay down. It doesn't take long for them to fall asleep and then we leave to check out the situation on the dock.

The port has been sealed off to unauthorized visitors so it has calmed quite a bit. I look at the line of boats just in time to see the farthest one go up in flames. Three fellow rebels come sprinting towards us. "They're torching boats," one of them yells as she tries to catch her breath. I immediately turn and pound down the stairs. I barge into the room.

"Captain, there are ships on fire out there." He looks at me as the realization dawns on him. He once again sets his medical instruments aside.

"What about Lucas," Officer Mills pleads.

"He's stable for now," the captain responds. "There's nothing more I can do. I won't let them have my ship. She's all me and my boy have left." He turns to me. "Tell the crew we're shoving off." I do as he says.

The rooms below deck have become more crowded with rebel soldiers, but I know we're still missing quite a few.

We're off in no time. It won't be long now until I can see Dawn again. As soon as we get back to the compound I'm leaving to search for her. I'm consumed by thoughts of her when Lee tells me that the captain would like to see me. I head to the bridge.

Captain Collins opens the door as soon as I knock. He offers me a drink, but I decline this time so he sets the bottle aside. I'm surprised to see tears in this tough man's eyes as he looks at me. "I can never repay the debt I now owe you," he says.

"There is no debt," I reply. He shocks me by pulling me into a rough hug.

"You brought me my boy. I can never thank you enough."

"You don't have to thank me," I say. "Just protect him."

"He's never leaving my ship again," the captain says in all seriousness before launching into a more solemn tone. "Did Dana have a good death?"

"She saved us all," I say honestly. He smiles and I can see how much he loved her. "Can I ask you a question?"

"At this point boy, you can ask me anything you want."

"Antonio?" I ask.

He sighs. "Ah, that. His uncle is a drug lord." The captain stops to close the door and lowers his voice. "I'm told that a few years back he saw something that he wasn't supposed to. His parents sent him from Mexico. When I found him, he was an orphan in one of the farming villages. The No one there would care for him because he was Mexican. I decided to raise him with my own boy. It took him a year or so to tell me what had happened and I still don't know what he saw in Mexico. I don't want to know. They're still after him. I've been hiding him in different villages for a few months at a time." He pauses, "to tell you the truth, if I had known everything on the day I found him, I might have left him to starve. By the time I found out about the Mexicans, I already loved him like a son. I had to protect him." He chokes up as he opens the door, effectively ending the conversation. I put a hand on his shoulder before I leave.

Back downstairs, I relieve Officer Mills of her watch over Lucas, but she doesn't willingly.

"You need sleep," I tell her.

"Why?" It's not really a question so I let her continue. "Because I just fought a battle and negotiated a surrender?" She laughs. "Sleep is overrated."

"Until you don't have enough of it."

"By your reasoning, you need sleep just as much as me and since we aren't leaving Lucas alone and neither of us is going to get some shut eye, let me see that knee of yours."

I look down at the spot where the skin has been all but turned to shreds. "I'd almost forgotten about that." I sigh as I collapse into a chair.

"It doesn't hurt?"

"After a while, I stopped thinking about it. There were more emergent things to keep me busy." I watch her pick the rocks out of my flesh and then clench my teeth as she pours alcohol over my knee. We don't speak until my wound is bandaged. "What's going to happen now?" I ask her. "With St. Louis, I mean."

"I left some people in place to make sure the surrender is honored by both sides, but our work isn't done here."

"Will Jonathan be okay with this?"

"No," she states. "I'm counting on him losing his power."

"Do you know something?"

"You'll know soon enough. It's better that you're in the dark for now." She pauses. "There are going to be a lot of changes coming. I had orders to make sure that not every city is destroyed."

"Orders from who?" my voice comes out louder than I had planned. Officer Mills looks around nervously to see if we've been overheard.

She then leans forward and whispers, "someone who is much better suited to lead the rebels than Jonathan Clarke."

Chapter 74

Dawn

We move through the frantic city of Vicksburg with Adrian out in front of us. Both Ryan and I have our guns readily available if he chooses to betray us. Down the street, someone darts out of the shadows and crosses in front of us. Stealthy. Fast. The rebels are here. I'm knocked to the ground as a woman barrels out of the building to my right. I hit the pavement as the building explodes. Ryan and Adrian are thrown back. I cover my head as debris rains down around me. The girl that knocked me down only a moment ago now lays motionless beside me.

Ryan runs over and pulls me to my feet and I stare into the flames. I jump back away from the wreckage, my mind in a daze. Adrian is yelling to us, but I can't hear him over the ringing in my ears as another explosion sounds somewhere in the distance.

"Come on!" Ryan grabs my arm and the three of us take off running. We stop in front of the church to catch our breaths. My lungs burn every time I inhale and my side aches where it slammed into the ground.

We're about to start running again when Jeremy comes sprinting out of the church with a huge grin on his face.

"Jeremy," I yell and his grin broadens when he sees me.

"That's one bomb that won't be going off," he says with pride. "It's not the only one either."

"Conner?" I ask.

"Yep," he responds, bending over to catch his breath. "Genius found a way to disable the bombs. Well, the ones he worked on at least." Jeremy looks curiously at Ryan and Adrian, but this is no time for introductions. "Damn, it's good to see you, Dawn."

"Want to defy the rest of the rebel plans?" I ask, already knowing what his answer will be. He smiles again. It feels strange because I should be a part of the rebels. I was commissioned into their army. Drew is a rebel. My own sister is one. Sometimes I feel like I'm betraying them and not just Jonathan. Jonathan tried to have me killed and now he wants to kill hundreds of people. I don't think he cares about destroying the Texan labs or their precious prophet. No, he wants to control Texas. He is drunk on power and something has to be done.

We run the rest of the way to the government building and before the final turn, we hear voices. Lots of voices. Some are barking orders. Others are receiving them. Everything is chaotic. I flatten myself against the building and crane my neck around the corner to get a better look.

"They're leaving," I report, confused.

"Attack protocol," Adrian mutters and we all turn to look at him.

"Explain," I say.

"There's a plan for when the city is attacked. It's never had to be used, but all new cadets have to memorize the plan."

"Mind telling us what it is?" Ryan asks impatiently.

"Protect the walls. Texans have long believed that no one can defeat us as long as the walls stand strong. The protocol was created long ago and has never been used, so they just never changed it even though they probably should have."

"So, they're moving to the walls?" Jeremy says gleefully. "What a bunch of dumbasses. They'll leave the center of the city completely unprotected."

The last of the troops disperse and the four of us descend on the government building. I reach the steps as the door opens and come face to face with a Texan soldier. I slam the door back in his face and run down the steps.

"Give me my gun," Adrian yells as the guards start piling out of the building followed by scared government officials. Ryan tosses the gun to Adrian and the two start firing as Jeremy and I duck around the corner. I cover Jeremy as he walks into the open to get a better shot. The government officials have reentered the building to hide from the fight.

"Shite," I rasp when I stop feeling the force of bullets breaking free. I didn't bring more ammo. "I'm out." This doesn't seem to be a problem because Ryan has already disarmed a few of the guards. He battles two men at once with a knife in each hand. He slashes through the air as he spins and both men go down. He finishes a third by burying a blade in his throat.

By the time I join the fight, there are five bodies crumpled on the ground. I throw a punch at an attackers' jaw, but he's too strong for me. He catches my fist and twists my arm behind my back. I kick him in the shin. When his grip loosens, I spin around and break free.

I see the gleam of a metal blade as the big Texan comes towards me once again and I duck his first slicing attempt. I kick my leg out and catch him in the groin. He trips, but stays on his feet. As he rights himself he cuts through the air with his knife and it's only inches from my chest when he suddenly collapses with a bullet between his eyes. As Ryan, Adrian, and Jeremy finish off the last guards, I look towards the roof and there is a girl standing at the top, watching us through the scope of her rifle.

I say a silent thank you to her as I run up the steps two at a time and enter the building.

Chapter 75

Gabby

From atop the government building, I watch over Vicksburg, the Texan capitol, until the first explosion reverberates through my body and the city sirens come on loud and incessant. Down below, the Texan soldiers don't seem to know what to do. A few officers start issuing instructions and they start to disperse. Scared civilians pour out of the buildings, afraid that their homes will be next. It's happening just like we thought it would. People are panicking as more bombs rock their seemingly safe world. I watch with a surprising amount of horror as the screaming and sobbing continues down on the street.

"Snipers begin," the command comes through.

Shay has already started tracking targets and taking them out. We've been ordered to shoot ordinary civilians. It's one thing to be given that order weeks ago when this all seemed so far away. Now that we're here though, it's an altogether different directive. Shay hoots and hollers as she hits her targets. She seems to have no problem with our mission.

"What are you waiting for?" she yells to me. She's right. I have orders. I tell myself that these people deserve it and put an eye to my scope. I find a man walking slowly among the chaotic crowd. I think he's alone. I pull the trigger and watch as he drops, a victim of my good aim. I love to shoot. I do. This is different. These people aren't paper targets in a sound proof room. To my dismay, a woman runs out of the crowd with a kid in tow and immediately kneels to cradle the head of the man I've just killed. The frenzy is in full swing, but I suddenly realize that I haven't heard or felt an explosion in a few minutes.

"What do you think is going on?" I yell to Shay.

"I don't know. Some malfunction with the bombs?"

In that instant, I know exactly what has happened. Jeremy and Conner, what have they done? Jonathan is going to kill them for this, actually kill them. Shite. There's nothing I can do about it now. I look down and a fight has broken out on the steps of the building. At first, it's a firefight, but then it turns into more. It's the Texan guards against a smaller group. I don't think they're rebels because this wasn't part of the plan. I press my eye to my scope to get a better look.

A boy I don't recognize is holding his own against two large Texans. Next to him, I see Jeremy. Wait, Jeremy? What is he doing? To his right, a Texan has gotten the upper hand on another man and sliced him across the back. I recognize him. Adrian. My anger flares up inside of me as I point my gun at him. I'm about to shoot when someone else comes into view. A girl is being beaten by a man three times her size, but she doesn't quit. I get a glimpse of her brown hair and skinny frame. I must be dreaming. I shake my head and rub my eyes before looking again. The girl is a crap fighter, but she's persistent. My breath catches in my throat.

She's also dead.

My sister, Dawn, is dead. That can't be her. It just can't. I aim my rifle at the man standing above her and fire one quick shot. I hit him squarely in the head. I drop my gun and run to the edge of the roof. The fighting has ended and the girl looks up at me briefly before she runs through the front door.

I grab the handgun from my bag and leave my rifle in place before taking off sprinting towards the stairs.

"Where are you going?" Shay yells after me, but I don't turn around. I pound down the fire escape as if my life depended on it. I need to see for myself. Is my sister alive? It gets louder as I near the street, but

I only have one thought on my mind as I push my way through the rioting crowds.

When I enter the building, the sounds from the street outside immediately die off, but I'm confronted with an altogether different scene. "Everyone move," the boy that I didn't recognize barks. The entire government must be in this one hallway. The people I saw out on the street follow them with guns at the ready towards a conference room. Adrian enters a code at the door and we all pass through. No one has noticed me at the back and I haven't seen the girl yet.

"Sit down," Adrian commands.

"You don't know what you're doing nephew," Tia Cole says.

Adrian looks her in the eyes, but she doesn't back down from him. "You told me once that I have to choose a side," he says. "I did." He straightens up and walks straight through a door at the opposite end of the room without a backward glance.

A nearby explosion rocks the building and I use the wall to steady myself. When I've regained my balance, I step further into the room. The officials are now seated around a table, defeated.

"Who are you?" some git asks me. I raise my sidearm until it's aimed high on his chest.

"If I counted correctly, you're out of ammo and that means that I get to do the questioning." He looks around nervously. I lower my gun. "I saw a girl with you out on the street. Where is she?"

"I don't know who you're talking about," he responds.

"Bullshite," I snap. His eyes shift towards the door that I'd seen Adrian disappear through.

I walk quickly to the door and push through it. Adrian and Jeremy are there, but my eyes land on the girl they're talking to. I'm face to face with my dead sister.

Chapter 76

Dawn

"What now?" I ask Jeremy. We're in a room next to the conference area. On the other side of the wall are all the leaders of Vicksburg. Ryan is guarding them. We came here on a mission and now that we've made it, I don't know what to do. Can we just kill them in cold blood? Do we have to kill everyone in that room or can we just deal with Tia and Darren?

Adrian stands beside me and I'm suddenly uncomfortable. That's his family in there. Whether they're good or bad, for him, they're blood. When I look at him, his eyes are blank. He catches me staring and quietly speaks, "it has to be done." I continue to look at him and realize I don't think I could ever really trust him. His loyalty changes faster than the weather. Adrian moves aside as the door opens.

Gabby.

She glances briefly at the boys and then her eyes lock onto mine.

"Gabby," Jeremy starts, "what are you doing here?" She puts up a hand to silence him. She takes one step forward and then another, her eyes never leaving me. I prepare for her to yell at me for making her believe that I was dead and then working against the rebels. She doesn't say a word. She reaches her arms out tentatively and grabs my shoulders. Very slowly, she looks me up and down. She closes her eyes and when she opens them again, a single tear rolls down her cheek. I smile at her and she suddenly pulls me into a hug. She holds on tight as if she'll never let go again.

"Gab, it's okay, I'm here." I pat her back. She releases me and wipes the tear away quickly.

"Dawn," she says quietly. "I thought you were dead."

I smile tentatively. "You're not getting rid of me without a fight, sis."

"This is all very touching girls, but we have to do something about the people in that room," Adrian states. Gabby glares at him and then turns back to me.

"What's the plan?" she asks finally.

"Gabby." Jeremy touches her arm. "You need to know that this isn't a rebel mission."

"Well, yeah," she says. "The rebels would never work with scum like him." She points to Adrian who scowls in response. "What's the plan?"

"Tia and Darren run things around here," Adrian explains. "The rest of them hold empty positions."

"Then we have to do something about the two of them." Without coming up with a real plan, Jeremy heads through the door. We follow him.

"What are you going to do with us?" Tia asks harshly. I narrow my eyes at her, but it's Adrian who answers.

"Whatever the hell we want."

"After everything we have done for you nephew," Darren Cole spits, "this is how you repay us."

Adrian moves around the table until he's near Darren. He bends down and looks into his eyes. "What you've done for me?" he growls. "I've been nothing but a prisoner to you, always having to follow orders. I had to kill my own mother to protect her from you."

"Your mother was nothing but a traitorous whore," Darren retorts before spitting in Adrian's face. Adrian calmly wipes his face and stands up straight. He flattens the front of his jacket and then quickly pulls out his gun and fires three bullets into his uncle's chest. Blood spatters onto his uniform as the people around the table begin to scream.

"My mother was a better Texan than you ever were." Adrian drops his gun to the floor and walks from the room. I look from the door to the dead former doctor in disbelief. Jeremy lets out a low whistle.

"What about Tia?" Gabby asks, recovering before the rest of us.

Before I can respond, I hear Jonathan's voice. "All troops retreat. Meet at the rendezvous. We are moving out."

I look around for the source of the voice until I see Gabby speak into something on her wrist.

"We need to go now," she says. I glance around at the frightened people in the room and my gaze lands on Tia.

"Get up," I say. "You're coming with us."

"What?" Gabby argues. "Why don't we just kill her now?"

"Because we're not killers," I respond.

"Maybe you're not." Gabby aims her weapon. I grab Tia by the arm and yank her out of her chair. She doesn't resist.

"You're not a killer, Gabs. Maybe you don't know that, but I do." I shove the nose of my gun into Tia's back. "Move," I command.

"You don't know what you're doing," Tia screams. "I'm a prophet from God. He will punish you!" I don't pay any attention to her as we escort her from the building to where Adrian is waiting for us outside.

"Why is she still alive?" he asks wearily.

"Because we take prisoners apparently," Gabby answers before raising her weapon. "That's good news for you because otherwise, I'd kill you on the spot. You're coming with us as well, Adrian."

"Gabby, don't." I try to push her gun away, but she doesn't budge.

"You didn't see what he did Dawn."

"No, I didn't, but I know why he did it." I try to meet her eyes, but they shift away. She puts a hand on my arm and guides me away from the others.

"He knew what was happening to Drew," she whispers. "He knew the whole time, Dawn. He's no better than his family."

The sudden anger is all I can think about. He knew. He was spending time with us while I was mourning Drew. My mind goes back to the boy that I was reunited with upon our escape. His body survived, but I don't know if his mind will ever be the same. Texas broke him. Adrian and his family broke him. I walk back to the others. Still holding my gun, I smack it across Adrian's face.

"Move," I say. I won't kill him, but that doesn't mean I won't hand him over to the rebels. He can rot in a cell for all I care. Gabby no longer argues with me as we pick up the pace. Around us is chaos. Buildings burn while people fight in the street. Texan soldiers try to calm the riots, but they're beaten back. I keep a gun pointed at Adrian as we move through the city and Ryan and Gabby both have theirs trained on Tia. Jeremy leads us through the streets, but I don't recognize where we're headed. We're moving towards the South end of the city when we hear an explosion up ahead.

"They must have blown the wall," Gabby says, speeding up. She's right, of course. Smoke and debris fill the air as we near our exit point. Only moments before, a tall, impenetrable barrier stood here, keeping Texas from the outside world. Most of the wall still stands, but one section has been blown away. There are Texans in the area looking towards the wall with apprehension. They don't get close. Most of the rebels are running by now. I step through the hole and over fallen stones.

As we run faster, a part of me wants to avoid those trees at all costs. I don't know what the reaction will be when I show up. I haven't had the chance to ask where Drew is, but I'm more worried about my supposed mother. What will she do when she learns that her attempt on my life has failed?

I would consider not going back at all if it wasn't for my family; Gabby, Jeremy, Lee, and Drew are all I have. By the time we reach the woods, most of the troops have already returned. I scan the crowd for Drew, but he isn't here.

"We need to find Emily," Ryan whispers to me. Guilt stabs at my heart as I realize I'd almost forgotten about her. She's out here alone.

"Who's Emily?" Gabby interrupts.

"My sister," Ryan explains. "She's waiting for us near the gate where we entered the city."

"We'll find her." I make the promise, unsure if I can fulfill it. As if every emotion I've been feeling for weeks comes back to me, I reach out and hug Ryan. He stiffens in surprise.

"Thank you," I say honestly, "for everything." He kisses the top of my head and I freeze, looking behind him.

"You okay?" he asks, turning to see what I'm looking at. "Oh my God." The rebels don't have horses. What are Duke and Jasmine doing here? The horses that got us here from Cincinnati stare right at us as if accusing me of leaving a young girl out here by herself. Emily. Where are you?

"We found them wandering around the night before we went into the city," Jeremy explains.

"Did they have a rider?" Ryan asks urgently. "A young girl?"

"No. I was there when we found them. We thought it was kind of strange to find them on their own." Ryan leaves us to check on the horses and see if Emily left any clues on them. I'm still watching him when Gabby loops her arm through mine.

"Where are Adrian and Tia?" I ask.

"Tia wouldn't shut her mouth so they knocked her out and took her away. Don't worry, sis, I don't think they're going to kill her, yet."

I don't respond as Jonathan rushes forward with a group of soldiers. They form up around us.

"Take them into custody," Jonathan commands.

Chapter 77

Gabby

"What's going on?" I demand as I watch my sister pushed to the ground. They make her lay on her stomach as they tie her hands behind her back. The soldiers then restrain Jeremy and Ryan in the same fashion. I don't understand.

"Dawn and Jeremy have committed grave crimes against the rebels," Jonathan explains. The corners of his mouth turn up into a smug smile. He wanted this. There's nothing I can do as the soldiers haul the prisoners to their feet and push further into the woods. Dawn is yelling obscenities at Jonathan. Jeremy is quiet as he keeps his eyes trained on the ground. What have they done? I'm too stunned to speak, but I hurry after them. I only just got my sister back hours ago and I still can't quite grasp that. I'm not going to let anything happen to her now.

"Well," Jonathan begins as he hurries after us, "if it isn't our little traitor." I'm shocked when he walks right by Dawn and directs this to Jeremy. He steps closer and studies his face. "You've cost us a great deal." Jonathan tries to keep his voice calm, even. He fails. I see the anger flare up in his eyes before I hear it in his voice. After a few moments, he can't control it any longer. He tackles Jeremy to the ground and proceeds to beat him.

"Do you have any idea what you have cost us?" he screams. Two nearby rebel soldiers move to pull him off of Jeremy, but Miranda stops them as Jonathan yells, "You're going to pay for this! We lost this fight because of you." He finally stands and stalks off, leaving Jeremy barely moving on the ground. Dawn tries to push her way to him, but she's restrained. I rush to his side and crouch down.

"Jeremy, open your eyes," I say as I grab him by the shoulders and lightly shake him. One eyelid opens slowly, but the other is swollen shut. After a couple minutes, he tries to sit up. Every movement seems laced with pain. I help him, but it's difficult because his hands are still tied together. I give him some water and try to get him to talk.

"What did he mean, Jeremy?" I whisper. "What did you do?"

"Conner," he starts, barely audible, "he disabled many of the bombs he worked on. About half of the ones meant for the capitol. I helped him." Shay comes to us and we get Jeremy to his feet. "I had to." The words barely make it past his lips.

"What?" I ask softly.

"The rebels can't win without bombs," he clarifies. "I had to save people." I don't get a chance to ask him anything else before he's taken away. My head is a mess right now. My sister is alive and arrested. Jeremy is a traitor. What's next?

"You left me on that roof." I'd forgotten Shay was standing next to me.

"What?"

"You ran off and abandoned your post and your partner." Irritation floods her voice. She's right, of course. I'm surprised I haven't been arrested after disobeying my orders. I was supposed to stay on that roof with my partner and, instead, I ran off without her.

"I'm sorry," I say. There's not a chance to say anything else as we get the command to move out. Shay stomps off without another word.

Many people are injured and all of us are knackered so we travel slowly. We left the city burning so there's the feeling that we don't have to worry about anyone coming after us. They have enough to deal with and I doubt they even know we've taken their prophet yet. They probably think Tia is dead, just like her husband. She is still unconscious so they've got her strapped onto Duke's saddle. Adrian walks next to it with his hands bound.

Not everyone made it back and the mood is somber. You can train as much as you want, but no one is ever ready for war. You can steel your heart against the inevitable losses, but they still break it right open.

We didn't win. I don't know if anyone ever really wins a battle like this, but the feeling is that we're heading back to the compound with our tails between our legs. Jonathan is narked. I hope they fared better in the other two cities, but it was the capitol that mattered the most. That's why Jonathan almost killed Jeremy. Vicksburg is still standing. One of the leaders is dead and another is in our custody, but it's still standing strong. I was slightly surprised that Miranda and Jonathan didn't kill Tia on the spot, but they want to make a spectacle of the whole thing. They're going to hold a trial and an execution. It's going to be a circus.

It seems to take us twice as long to get back to the ship and three times as long to sail up the river to rebel territory. We don't make any stops because the whole of Texas is volatile right now; even the farming villages.

When we are finally back safely in the compound, I go looking for Miranda. Dawn has been hauled off to a cell, but I'm confident we can get her out. She says she's not our mom, but words don't mean a thing. I'm sure she won't let her own daughter rot in a prison.

When I find her, she is overseeing the cleaning of the weapons.

"Gabby," she says as her way of greeting.

"What are you going to do about Dawn?" I ask bluntly.

"Why would I do anything about her?" she responds. "Your sister is a traitor."

"Your daughter you mean?"

"Gabby." She closes her eyes and sighs. "Don't worry about Dawn."

"Of course, I'm going to worry. She's the only family I've got."

Miranda leans in close to me and lowers her voice, "she won't be there for long."

"What's that supposed to mean?" I ask. She looks nervously at a camera on the wall behind us.

"Just that things are changing. Be prepared."

Chapter 78

Dawn

Ryan, Jeremy, and I are led down a hallway by a single pair of soldiers. They must think that there is no way we could escape from this compound. They're probably right. Jeremy is having trouble just walking right now so it's not like he'd be any help. My wrists have been tied behind my back and I stare at my feet as we pass groups of people that were once my peers. They now see me as a traitor. I guess I am. Their narrowed eyes follow us as we go.

There were no signs of Emily on our journey back and Ryan thinks it's his fault. He looks defeated. He looks lost.

"We'll take it from here soldiers." I look up when I hear the familiar voice. Officer Mills and Lee are relieving the soldier of his duty. Lee winks at me.

"We have orders, sir," the soldier stammers.

"I know you do," Officer Mills states. "Now, leave us." Even Gabby probably wouldn't defy her when she uses that tone. The soldiers salute and then leave us. Lee hugs me in that strong way of his. He doesn't seem to care that I can't hug him back.

"It sure is good to see you," he says.

"I missed you," I respond. He smiles.

"This is touching and all, but we have to go." Officer Mills brings us back to the reality, but I catch a glimpse of a small smile playing on her lips.

"I missed you too," I tell her. She leads us down another hallway and I don't recognize it. "I don't think this is the way."

"We're taking a little detour," Lee says smugly. They're up to something. They lead us around the corner and I see what that is.

Drew steps out from a doorway up ahead. When he sees me, he stops. After a moment of uncomfortable staring, he runs towards us and almost collides into me. He wraps his arms around me and squeezes as if his life depends on it.

"Get my hands free," I yell to Officer Mills. As soon as they're loose, I wrap my arms around Drew, not caring that the others are watching us. He runs his hands along my arms and my back as if he's making sure that every inch of me is real.

"I'm here," I assure him quietly. He kisses me then. It's tentative and shy at first, but then it intensifies as if he's pouring every emotion from the past weeks into that single act. The loss. The anger. The joy. All wrapped up in a moment.

I break free and my breath is ragged. "Whoa," I whisper, still looking into his eyes. I cup his cheek in my hand and look at this boy. I never saw him coming, but I can't imagine my life without him. He is everything.

"We have to go," I say, more to myself than anyone else. I look at him one last time and then offer my wrists to let Lee bind then again. I don't look back as we walk away.

"Don't worry," Officer Mills reassures me. "You won't be held for long."

"What?"

"There are changes coming," she says.

"What's going to happen?" I whisper as we walk back out into the main hall that is lined with cameras. She smiles but doesn't answer me. Officer Mills takes on a much more formal stance as we're sure we're on camera right now.

We're handed over to the guards near the jail. The jail only consists of two rooms. I'm assuming Tia and Adrian are in the first one because we're escorted into the second one and the door is locked behind us.

Conner is already here. He looks up as we come in and he seems even more disheveled than usual, if that's possible. His hair is sticking every which way and he is not wearing his glasses. He says they were broken during his arrest. I'm shocked to see Corey and Matty are here as well. Matty runs to me as soon as he sees me and I lock eyes with Corey.

"What are you guys doing here?" I ask.

"You know that day we were supposed to set out?" Corey answers. "They wouldn't let us leave."

"You've been here since then?" I gasp, sitting down next to Matty and folding him into my arms.

"Yeah, but I wanna know how the attack on Texas went. Were you able to foil any dumbass rebel plans?" It seems like Corey has been talking to Conner. I fill them in on everything from the capitol, including how Conner ruined the rebel plans brilliantly.

Jeremy doesn't say anything or even take pride in what we've accomplished. This worries me. After the beating that he took from Jonathan, this past week has been really hard on him. He hasn't been given the medical attention he needs. He is slumped along the wall and doesn't move much because every time he does, he is wracked with pain. I try to help him as much as possible, but it's hard for him to even eat. I cradle his head in my lap as he tries in vain to sleep. His hair is soaked in sweat. I don't know how much longer he can last. Jonathan must have broken something or ruptured something. I don't know. I'm not a doctor.

After days of imprisonment, Jonathan comes to see us. His smile is smug and his eyes show more than a hint of crazy.

"Hello," he croons as he unlocks the door and pushes it open. "Today is a good day! Well, not for you."

"What do you want?" I spit.

"Your trial has finally finished," he says cheerily.

"What trial? Don't we get to be there?"

"Not when you're being tried as a traitor my dear," he says with a sneer. "My rules around here. I have no tolerance for traitors and I just don't like any of you. Your executions are scheduled for next week."

"Executions," I gulp.

"Yes, Miss Nolan. That's what we do to people who can't seem to follow the rules. You're supposed to be dead by now anyway."

"But you failed, didn't you?" I scream. He leaves the room, but I don't stop. "You failed."

Execution. That's how it ends. What did Officer Mills mean when she said we won't be here long? I hope that she hurries with whatever plan she has. I lean my head back and start to cry. Everything I've been holding in suddenly bubbles to the surface and I can't contain it any longer. Ryan takes my hand in his. He doesn't say anything because there's nothing to say.

Jeremy wheezes beside me. How did it come to this? If Officer Mills can't get us out, what will it do to Gabby and Drew to lose me again? A million questions race through my head.

Gabby and Drew will move on as all mourners eventually do. Life goes on whether you're there or not. My chest heaves as I struggle to breathe through my constant sobs. I almost wish I'd died in the fight like I was supposed to. That would've been a better end.

Drew once told me that death is not the end. He believes that his God has prepared an afterlife. I've never believed in God, but I wish I did in this moment. It's a selfish reason, but I can't bring myself to believe that I will just cease to be; that the last thing I will ever see is the firing squad.

Time seems endless in this cell. We receive one meal a day. I've counted five. At first, we talked. Conner told me that Lucas is in the hospital and I told him stories from the fight. After a while, nothing we said seemed important so we just stopped talking.

Jeremy's breathing is labored and he doesn't open his eyes most of the time. It reminds me of how we found him in Floridaland. The difference now is that I can't get him out. I can't save him this time. I can't even save myself.

My tears have long since dried by the time we hear footsteps on the fifth day.

"Which cell are they in?" a man's voice echoes down the hall.

"Right here." I recognize Officer Mills. I shake Jeremy to wake him, but he doesn't open his eyes. Frantically, I feel for a pulse and find it as the door opens. A bright light pours in as a flashlight illuminates the darkness.

"Get that boy to medical," the man orders. Two others rush in and lift Jeremy carefully. The man to whom the voice belongs steps into the room and moves the light so that it's out of my eyes. "Dawn," he says, "are you okay?"

It takes me a moment of disbelief before I can respond. Only one word escapes me.

"Dad."

Dear reader,

We hope you enjoyed reading *Day of Reckoning*. Please take a moment to leave a review, even if it's a short one. Your opinion is important to us.

Discover more books by Michelle Lynn at
https://www.nextchapter.pub/authors/young-adult-fiction-author-michelle-lynn

Want to know when one of our books is free or discounted? Join the newsletter at http://eepurl.com/bqqB3H

Best regards,
Michelle Lynn and the Next Chapter Team

The story continues in:

Eve of Tomorrow

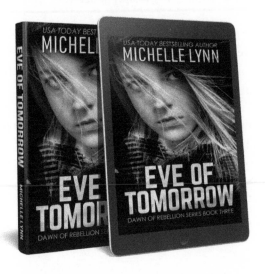

To read the first chapter for free, please head to:
https://www.nextchapter.pub/books/eve-of-tomorrow

Acknowledgments

Life doesn't always turn out the way we planned, but it's the people in our lives that make it all worthwhile. This book is about love and trust. It's about the strangers that turn into family. It's about people doing extraordinary things for one another. I have been blessed with an amazing family. Thank you, mom, for continuously supporting me in everything I do. Thank you, dad for the countless hours you spent talking through ideas, taking part in the editing process and the cover design. None of this would have been possible without you both.

I'd like to thank everyone else who contributed to this book. Linda and your proofreading skills; my network of authors who have spent their time offering feedback as well as reviews; my friends that keep me moving forward with their ongoing encouragement. We were strangers once but now you're family.

Last, but not least, I would never have become a writer if God had not put me in a position to do so. Everything happens for a reason and sometimes we need to find the good in a bad situation. This book is my silver lining.

Books by Michelle Lynn

Legends of the Tri-Gard (Written as M. Lynn)
Prophecy of Darkness
Legacy of Light
Mastery of Earth (2018)

Dawn of Rebellion Trilogy
Dawn of Rebellion
Day of Reckoning
Eve of Tomorrow

The New Beginnings series
Choices
Promises
Dreams

The Invincible series
We Thought We Were Invincible
We Thought We Knew it All

Standalone
Lesson Plan

About Michelle

M. Lynn has a brain that won't seem to quiet down, forcing her into many different genres to suit her various sides. Under the name Michelle Lynn, she writes romance and dystopian as well as upcoming fantasies. Running on Diet Coke and toddler hugs, she sleeps little - not due to overworking or important tasks - but only because she refuses to come back from the worlds in the books she reads. Reading, writing, aunting … repeat.

See more from M. Lynn
www.michellelynnauthor.com

Day of Reckoning
ISBN: 978-4-86752-190-8

Published by
Next Chapter
1-60-20 Minami-Otsuka
170-0005 Toshima-Ku, Tokyo
+818035793528
28th July 2021